Mountain Woman Rides Again

A Kate McAlaster Adventure

Johnny Fowler

Mountain Woman Rides Again © 2011
by John R. Fowler

ISBN-13: 978-1466206205
ISBN-10: 1466206209

This novel is a work of fiction. All of the events, characters, names and locales depicted in this novel are entirely fictitious, or are used fictitiously, though reference may be made to actual historical events or existing locations.

DEDICATION

My love and thanks goes to my daughter, Vanessa, for being my mentor, sounding board, and faithful supporter. Without her expertise, I feel my novels would never have appeared in print. She took my manuscripts, and with unwavering dedication, turned them into published novels.

I'm eternally grateful to her for devoting her time, effort, and utilizing her knowledge and know-how in these endeavors.

Other Books by Johnny Fowler

Mountain Woman
Panhandle Blizzard
Eclipse of the Heart
Treason at White Sands
Hidden Agenda
Kill Without Remorse
Love Walked In
Explosions of Fire
The Mercenary's Daughter
DEA Conspiracy
Diplomatic Immunity
Spanish Fly
Vengeance is Mine
Murder in the Loop
Right Place, Wrong Time
Sarah

Kate McAlaster Adventures:
Mountain Woman
Mountain Woman Rides Again

Mary Hardy Series:

Hardy, Texas Ranger: The First Female Texas Ranger
Hardy, Texas Ranger: In Oklahoma Territory
Hardy, Texas Ranger: In the Davis Mountains
Hardy, Texas Ranger: In the Big Thicket

MOUNTAIN WOMAN RIDES AGAIN

Chapter 1

Kate McAlaster and Homer Manchester rode toward the Oregon coast after leaving The Fort. Kate was astride Redbird and Man was seated on the prancing Arabian. It had been several days since the horse had any exercise; he was frisky, and wanted to run. But Man kept him in check as he was leading two pack mules carrying their supplies.

The magnificent gray and white horse with a dark-gray mane and tail with a perfectly shaped neck and head quickly settled into a ground-eating pace.

Kate and Man were three days from The Fort, when the happy couple topped a rise and saw a setter's cabin below. As they looked, a frown crossed her face. "Something's wrong," she said.

Man sat his horse trying to see what caused Kate to make that statement. He shook his head from side to side. "Not that I see, there's nobody in sight. Chickens are around the barn, a cow is in the lot, and a calf outside."

"It's mid morning, and a cold wind is blowing," she said. "Why isn't there smoke coming from the chimney? The cow's in the lot as you said, but she wasn't milked this morning. From the way the calf is bawling almost every breath, he's hungry for his breakfast."

Man tied the pack mules to a limb, pulled his new Winchester Model 1873 from the scabbard, and levered a bullet into the firing chamber. "I'll take the barn; you circle the house and go in from the opposite side."

She jerked her rifle, held it at the port position, and jacked a bullet into the firing chamber as Man had done. She touched her spurs to the gelding's side and turned

9

Redbird's head to the right as they eased their way down the gentle slope. Man urged Arabian to the left as they made their way down to the homestead.

Kate dismounted behind trees not far from the cabin, watched until Man tied up, and he slipped inside the barn. A few seconds later, he appeared at the big door and gestured toward the cabin. She hurried to the side of the log cabin. There were no windows, so she moved to the front and stopped at the corner.

Man was waiting at the other corner. "Hello the cabin," he shouted in a loud voice. They waited, but there was no response.

He moved cautiously to the door and pushed it open with his foot, his rifle in the ready position. Kate moved quickly and was behind him when he entered.

He moaned at the sight.

"A woman and a boy about twelve are dead," he said. She moved to his side to see inside the cabin. The woman lay on the bed with her hands tied to the bedpost. Her throat had been slashed. The boy was on the dirt floor with a bullet hole between his eyes.

"Damn them," he growled. "They had no call to do this."

Kate moved to the body of the woman, touched her hand, and lifted the arm. "Cold and stiff," she said. "Sometime yesterday would be my guess. I wonder where the man of the cabin is," she said as she looked around.

"There was nothing in the barn," he said. "No horse or saddle. He was either away from home, or was killed somewhere else. I doubt she and the boy lived here alone. I saw a field with corn stalks from last summer, and another cleared for spring planting."

She walked outside and began to circle the front of the cabin looking for tracks. He saw what she was doing and made a wider circle. "I found them," he shouted. He was standing beside a grove of trees about a hundred yards from the cabin. Five horses were tied here. From the droppings, I would think over night."

She hurried to his side and studied the tracks and the area around them. "If it's them, where are the tracks from the wagons?" she said.

Without speaking, they went for their horses and started a wide circle around the cabin. She was about a half mile from the cabin when she saw signs and reined Redbird to a small clearing and sat looking before stepping down to examine the dirt. It took only a few moments. She went to Redbird and urged him into a gallop toward where Man was waiting.

"Four wagons were there," she said, as she pointed. "They had horses tied behind. It's them, no doubt."

Man nodded agreement and turned Arabian back toward the cabin. Redbird moved to his side and the pair walked back toward the cabin. "I'll dig the graves," he said.

"I'll milk the cow and turn the calf in for his breakfast," she said. "Then I'll cook something for us to eat. I know you'll be hungry after digging two graves."

She went to where they tied the pack mules, brought them to the cabin, and found Man busy digging a grave. He found a shovel in the barn.

"Help me wrap the two bodies in blankets and we can carry them to the grave site before I start cooking," she said. "Using the woman's home and fireplace with her dead on the bed isn't right."

***

Kate McAlaster was lucky, and survived an attack by Indians on their wagon train bound for Oregon on the Oregon Trail. The wagon train of settlers was anxious for a new and better life, but they were overrun by Indians in a battle that lasted only minutes. The huge number of warriors swooping down on the hapless settlers was overwhelming. The men were farmers and businessmen, instead of trained soldiers.

The night before the expected attack, Jake, the Wagon Master, and his scout, Slats, along with Kate's father hid her in a cave, knowing there was no chance for the train to survive an Indian attack. They were so outnumbered; the result was a foregone conclusion. The train was on a trail where there were only two ways to move, forward or backward, and the Indians had both blocked. Their only option was fight.

Thankfully, after the vicious battle, Jake survived long enough to give Kate advice on how to survive in the mountains. She would be alone with winter approaching and without help, her chances of survival was slim to none. Her food supply would last only a couple of days.

Jake told her to take everything that could be useful from the burned out wagons and find a cabin owned by Homer Manchester, but called, Man. He was a friend of his and Slats and made a few trips on the Oregon Train with them.

Kate found the cabin and moved everything salvageable from the train to the cabin using one of the burned wagons, but the axles and wheels were intact. She improvised a bed by salvaging wood from other wagons and stretching hides over the boards.

***

Kate located the cabin nestled in a grove of trees with the back against a sheer rock mountain wall. A small spring ran water from a fisher in the stone face of the mountain, and supplied water for the cabin and animals.

Homer Manchester hadn't arrived for the winter, and it gave Kate time to work on the cabin and forage hay for her horse. She had to hunt for food for the winter.

A few days later, Kate was hunting and found a wounded man on the trail. He was near death due to a gunshot wound and exposure to the elements. He was ambushed for his winter supplies and left for dead.

Kate managed to get him back to the cabin where she discovered he was Homer Manchester, the owner of the cabin. Following his instructions, Kate nursed him back to health, and was pleasantly surprised when she had him cleaned from the ordeal on the trail. He was handsome without an unsightly beard and dirty clothing.

12

She was happy Man was with her. Jake warned her of the dangers living in this desolate and volatile land. There was almost no law enforcement in the wilderness, and her only protection would be her wits and weapons.

While Man was recuperating, Kate devised a warning system around the cabin by stringing the lines from the wagons in the train to a cowbell she found in one of the burned wagons. She was worried about men approaching the cabin and waiting in ambush when they walked out of the cabin. Her concern was well founded.

The men that ambushed Homer discovered the wagons and followed Kate's wagon tracks to the cabin. They were hoping that whoever took the valuables brought them to the cabin.

With vengeance, Kate and Man fought off an attack by the ambushers. Instead of waiting for another ambush, Kate and Man tracked them into the mountains for a kill, or be killed battle. It was a desperate move, but they needed the supplies stolen from Man to survive the winter.

The couple tracked the outlaws for several days before the showdown. The killers were waiting to waylay them, but Kate devised a method of turning the ambush into a surprise attack, and the bushwhackers were killed.

Kate and Man retrieved the stolen supplies, weapons and horses, and turned back toward their home for the winter.

Blue Hawk, an Indian friend of Man, approached them and offered to make them clothes in exchange for the horses they took from the slain killers. A deal was made as Kate and Man needed the fur-lined skins to withstand the winter winds and snow high in the mountains.

When spring was nearing, Blue Hawk came to Kate and Man for help. His daughters and wife were taken by slave dealers. With the aid of Kate and Man, the kidnapers were tracked and killed and the Indian women were returned to their homes. This experience, working with the friendly Indians taught Man and Kate a lot about survival in the mountains.

***

After a long hard winter, when the snow melted, and the ground turned green, Kate and Man headed their wagon toward the west and Oregon.

During the winter in the cabin, a romance bloomed and Man asked Kate to marry him when they reached The Fort. She happily agreed they would be married as soon as possible.

Kate had never seen The Fort, as it was called. They halted on a high ridge and surveyed The Fort below. Kate expected a real Fort, similar to the Forts she had seen on the way west with the wagon train. This wasn't a Fort with soldiers; instead, it was a trading post for the early settlers of Oregon. The Fort had evolved into a place for trappers to trade their furs for merchandise, and a marketplace for the farmers to sell their grain and livestock.

***

George Bowman, a merchant from St. Louis, built the first cabin in the middle of a huge valley with a mountain stream circling through it. He was cautious about raids from thieves and Indians, and built a log fence around the building with a gate that could be closed at night. The settlement resembled a real fort, thus it was referred to as The Fort by the trappers and settlers.

As the trading post grew with added stores and cabins, the fences were moved farther and farther back until the enclosure circled several acres.

Kate drove the wagon through the gate with Man riding his prancing Arabian gelding in front her. He took the lead, guided the wagon to the rear of the settlement, and stopped beside the livery stable. A man dressed in a leather apron for shoeing horses came out to greet them. He was wiping his hands on a dirty towel as he peered at the couple.

As soon as Man stepped down from the horse, the hostler recognized him and shouted. "Man, it's you, really you. We heard you was dead."

14

"Not me," Man said. "I was ambushed, but this lady saved me." He gestured toward the wagon with a big smile. "I would have been dead if she hadn't come along. She was on the train with Jake and Slats. I guess you heard it was wiped out by Indians and everybody was killed?"

"Yea, we heard. How did she get away?"

"Jake, Slats and her pap hid her out the night before. They knew what would happen to her if she lived through the attack."

"That was smart," the old man said. "I had a look in an Indian camp once. White women captives were treated worse than dogs."

Man went to the wagon, reached for her hand, and helped her down. He made the introductions. "This is Kate McAlaster, soon to be Manchester, I hope. Kate, meet my friend, Buck."

Man turned to Buck. "I never heard your last name."

"I've had so many; I don't rightly recall what I started out as. Williams, I think it was, but now, I'm using Smith."

"It's nice to meet you," Kate said, "Mr. Buck, uh Smith."

Buck was looking at the pair. "From the way you two are armed, you must have run into some trouble. I notice you both got two Walker Colts on your hips. Kate has her rife on the seat beside her, and yours is kept handy in that scabbard on the saddle."

"We had some problems getting here. We had a battle with a band of slave traders stealing Indian women for sale on the coast. We also met up with renegade Indians and trash that had rather steal than work for a living. That's how we got the Walkers and that Arabian horse I'm riding."

"But getting back to more enjoyable things," Man said. "I'm looking for a preacher to make it legal with Kate. We were married, but it wasn't a proper, in a church wedding. Is there a bible-thumper here now? I heard there was the last time I was here."

15

Buck pointed toward a building. "That's a church. The preacher's a regular sort of guy, but not what most expect from a man of God. He goes by the name of Quinn. From the talk, he rode the other side of the law before getting religion."

"Buck, would you see to the horses and mules? Give them a good feed of oats and hay. They earned it. We'll be back later for the wagon. Park it out back somewhere. It's loaded with my furs and our supplies."

"Sure will, Man. I can see that look in your eyes; it's easy to see you're in a hurry. Your wagon will be parked in back where I can keep an eye on it." He took the reins and led Arabian inside the barn with the mules pulling the wagon. Redbird was tied to the rear of the wagon.

Man reached for Kate's hand and led her toward the building Buck pointed out as a church.

"If we're going to be married, I need a dress," Kate said. "These skins aren't what I would call a wedding gown. Every dress I had on the train burned."

Man didn't slow his pace, anxious to find the preacher. "We'll find the preacher first, arrange for a wedding, and then we can shop to see what dresses ol' man George Bowman has for sale. I don't expect much more than everyday dresses. There's not much call for formal gowns out here where women dress for practicality and survival, not show."

She squeezed his hand. "I suspected that, but a pretty print dress would beat what I'm wearing. A woman shouldn't be married in pants made of deerskin."

Man opened the door to the church and stepped back for her to enter first. They saw a large man dressed in black pants with a white shirt. He had on boots with spurs. A string tie was around his neck. "Are you Quinn, the preacher?" Man asked.

The man came to meet them with a smile. "Yep, I'm Martin Quinn. I serve the lord in this small, but growing church. What can I do for you?"

"We want to get married. I'm known as Man, but my

16

legal handle is Homer Manchester. This lady is Kate McAlaster."

"I've heard of you Man. I believe you worked with Jake and Slats bringing in settlers. But, I heard they were killed by Indians."

Man nodded with a grimace at the reminder. "Kate was the only survivor on that train."

"I'm glad you lived through it young lady," Quinn said. "I can marry you tomorrow morning, say around ten. I have a funeral today and immediately after, I'm riding out to be with the grieving family of settlers. The grandpa is on his death bed."

"We'll be here tomorrow morning," Man said. "We're going over to George's store and see if they have anything more appropriate for her to wear as a wedding dress. She doesn't think what she has on now is appropriate. All of her dresses burned in their wagon."

They hurried out a side door when people began to file in for the funeral. Man led her down the alley until they came to the side of a huge building constructed of logs. He took her arm and they climbed the steps to the porch and went inside.

An old man with a bush of white whiskers was standing behind a counter. He looked once, then shielded his eyes, and stared. "Man, you're a sight for sore eyes. We heard you were dead."

"So Buck said, but as you can see, I'm alive and looking at the green side of the grass."

Man led Kate to the counter and made the introductions. "We're going to be married tomorrow morning, and Kate needs a dress. She doesn't think a woman should be married in pants made from skins."

George came from behind the counter and led her toward a section where several dresses hung from a rod. This is the dresses I have in stock. There's not much call for dresses out here. Most of the women make their own, as they can't afford store-bought dresses. Look through them and if you find something, my wife can do alterations

17

if needed."

Kate went to the dress section and began to thumb through the selections.

Man walked to a cabinet filled with rifles. George hurried to him and pulled out a rifle and handed it to Man. "I got in a shipment of the new Winchester Model 1873. They have the deluxe lever action that uses center fire bullets, the same caliber as those twin Walkers on your hips. This is the rifle that earned the name of one in a thousand. I ain't saying these are in that category, but they're the smoothest action rifles on the market today. I've had men tell me they keep on firing after being dropped in mud and dirt. I was lucky to get any at all. I was in San Francisco when they arrived, and I bought a dozen. I have four left."

Man picked up one of the rifles and worked the leaver and sighted out the front door. "What you asking?"

"Sixty dollars, I know it's steep, but they're worth it. A man can't put a price on a weapon he can depend on in a serious fight."

"I'll take all four," Man said. "I hope you have a supply of cartridges?"

"Of course, no point stocking rifles without ammunition. How many boxes do you want?"

"I'll take a case if you have them. Since the bullets fit our pistols, we won't have to worry about two kinds. We won't be back until fall, and no telling what we'll run into this summer. We're going to the coast and work our way north until it's time to start back before winter."

George lifted a wooden box from under the counter and placed it beside the four rifles. He took a box from the shelf and began loading one of the rifles. Man did the same with another.

"A rifle is worthless if it ain't loaded," George said. "A piece of wood would be just as effective, but why pay sixty dollars for a club."

Kate walked toward them carrying three dresses. "Mr. Bowman, do you have a place I can try these on to see how they look and fit?"

He led her to an opening and shouted, "Ma, we have a young woman wanting to try on dresses."

A woman came hurrying from the back. She appeared to be about the same age as George with her gray hair tied back making her eyes appear squinted. "This is my wife," George said, proudly. "Maude, meet Kate McAlaster as of today. But from what I'm hearing, tomorrow, it'll be Kate Manchester."

"This summer me and Maude will celebrate our fiftieth wedding anniversary."

"Congratulations," Kate said. "That's special, being married for fifty years."

"I wish we had a better selection," Maude said. "But there ain't much call for dresses here. We live in the rear of the store, and I have a sewing room with a mirror." She reached for the dresses and led Kate toward the back. "You can try them, and if you like any, I can make alterations as needed."

George watched the two women leave. "You've got yourself a fine looking woman. That red hair of hers and those eyes are either green or blue, I can't decide in this light."

"Mostly blue," Man said, but with a hint of green."

Handsome woman," George said. "If she's going to spruce up for a wedding, you need some new duds as well. As she said about skins and a wedding, a man shouldn't get hitched in deer hide clothes. I have pants and shirts that will make her proud to stand beside you. Those boots you're wearing have seen too much hard wearing."

He ushered Man to the men's section and soon had him outfitted in new clothes, including a black coat, white shirt, a black string tie, and new boots.

Kate came from the back wearing a green dress. Man immediately saw her and gave out a sharp whistle in admiration. She seemed radiant wearing women's clothing; it had been such a long time. Her eyes were sparking with happiness.

19

She gasped when she saw him. He was handsome in his skins, but dressed in town clothes, he was a sight to behold. Tall and straight, his brown hair with darker eyes caused her heart began to flutter. This man would soon be her husband.

George saw her look and smiled. He knew he would make more sales. She would have him dressed properly before they left.

"What do you think about this dress?" she asked.

"I love it; it makes your hair shine."

"I have two more dresses to try on," she said. "I'll go change and come back to show you."

They watched her walk away, admiring her wearing a dress. Her long lean body was swaying as she walked.

Man brought George back to the present after watching Kate disappear in the back. "George, my wagon is parked at Buck's Livery. I have furs for you to look at."

"Bring them over and drive to the warehouse behind this building. Pound on the back door and I'll come out and look at them. I'm glad you came in when you did, because I'm ready to ship this winters harvest to Portland in a couple of days. In fact, I have the wagons loaded. I'm waiting for one of my drivers. His pa is about to die. After the furs are shipped, there would be no market, unless you took them to Portland yourself."

"I'll bring the wagon over as soon as Kate finishes shopping."

Kate came in and showed him another dress, a pretty print. Man nodded approval and she hurried to the back for another. She soon reappeared wearing the third. It was sky blue. "Which one do you like best?" she asked.

"We'll take all three," he said. "George would you have Maude show her the other things women need?"

George hurried to the back for his wife. "Man," Kate said. "Are you sure? I mean, well, three dresses."

"We have the money and you looked so pretty in the dresses. Buy everything you need, we may not visit another store before we come back here before winter."

She beamed and hurried toward the back to meet Maude.

While Kate and Maude were busy on the dresses and selecting other things, Man went for the wagon and pulled it to the warehouse behind the store.

George was waiting and went through each pelt examining it and making an offer. "Man," he said, "you learned in a hurry how to care for the hides, and I'm offering you top dollar for them. The quality is much better than most of the furs brought in for sale."

George and Man moved the pelts to a wagon, ready to transport to Portland to a wholesale buyer. "I have four wagonloads this year," George said. "The volume is increasing each year as more pioneers move into the North Country to settle and trap during the winter to support their families. However, I can see the time in the near future when the supply will dwindle to the point it isn't profitable. Maybe a couple or three more years and the fur trade will end. When that happens, Maude and me will retire, and get out of the business."

"Each year more and more settlers are coming west," Man said. "The Oregon Trail is coming as busy as Main Street in most towns. But, so far, there's nobody close to where Kate and I live, but this rich beautiful country will fill, as the land becomes more scarce back east. I'm glad I got here early enough to see it before it's overrun with farmers and cities spring up."

George nodded agreement, and the two men went back to the store to check on Kate and her purchases.

She had the things she wanted on the counter when the men came in and Man gasped in disbelief, but in a teasing manner.

"George," Man said, "make a tally and tell me how much I owe over the sale of the furs."

"With the cost of the four rifles and ammunition, I can tell you're already behind." Kate had a worried expression on her face, wondering if she would need to put back some of the things she bought.

Man dug into the money belt and paid the difference and shook hands with George and Maude. He and Kate took their purchases out to the wagon.

Man helped her on the seat and hurried around and jumped in beside her and flipped the reins at the rumps of the mules. "Do you want to camp inside or outside tonight?" he asked.

"Outside," she said. "There are too many people in here. Can you find us a good place by the creek, away from prying eyes? I have something special planned for tonight."

"I would feel better having our horses with us," Man said. "Old habits are hard to break, and just because we're near The Fort doesn't mean we're safe. The same riffraff we've encountered are here as well."

They went by the stable and paid Buck for feeding the stock, picked up Redbird and Arabian, and drove out the gate. He found a good campsite close to the creek. The snow had melted, and grass was plentiful for the livestock. Together, they made camp beside the wagon and Kate started a stew cooking.

Kate left him to finish cooking, and went into the wagon. Man was resting with his back against a tree watching the fire when she came out wearing a new dress. He jumped to his feet and gathered her into his arms and twirled her around as their lips met.

"God you're so beautiful," he said around their kiss. "How was I so lucky for you to find me on the trail that day, more dead than alive?"

"I'm the lucky one," she said. "Without you, I wouldn't have survived the winter alone. But, we both owe a debt of thanks to Jake for sending me to your cabin."

He kissed her with a meaning that she understood.

"Put me down," she said. "I see a cloud cover moving over the mountains. It'll be dark soon. We need to eat and get settled in for the night. I think I smell rain."

She went to the fire and stirred the stew.

"Do we sleep in the wagon or ground tonight?" he asked.

"In the wagon, will all the furs gone, there'll be ample room, and as I said, I smell rain. Besides, I think my husband to be will need some special attention tonight." She chuckled as she put food on plates for them.

***

The roar of gunfire woke them early in the morning. They both had their Walker Colts in their hand by the time the first volley ended. There were a few more spaced shots followed the initial bombardment.

"It came from The Fort," Man said. They both scrambled for their clothing and dressed in a hurry. They stepped outside and were met by a drizzle and blackness. However, a pink hint in the east offered just enough light to see the outline of the fence around The Fort.

The sound of wagons moving fast broke the silence, and they were coming in their direction. Without speaking, both grabbed their rifles from the scabbards on their saddles and took cover behind trees.

Four wagons raced toward them. A rider in front had a rifle in his hands. "Those are the fur wagons belonging to George," he said. "Somebody stole them."

He stepped out when the lead rider was within thirty yards of them. "Halt," he shouted.

The rider was fast, his rifle swung around, and he fired. Man was faster and was behind the tree when the bullet tore bark from the tree where he took cover. Kate tried to get a bead on the shooter, but he disappeared behind trees that lined the trail beside the creek. She brought up her rifle and fired once at the last wagon driver as he raced away. They heard a yell, but the wagon kept going. It wasn't a kill shot and the bullet probably was close enough to him to cause the shout.

"I think I know what happened," he said. "Somebody stole the fur wagons from George, but the barrage of shooting worries me. We need to go to The Fort to offer help if needed."

Kate hurried and brought the saddles while Man went for Redbird and Arabian. They had finished saddling when riders raced toward their camp. A man they had never seen before pulled up in front of them. Man walked out to meet him.

"They robbed the warehouse belonging to George Bowman," the posse leader said. "There was five of them."

"We already knew that," Man said. "We recognized the wagons. Kate got off one shot, but we don't think she drew blood on the driver of the last wagon. The man out front fired at me as they raced by."

"We're going after them," he leader of the posse said.

"Was anybody hurt?" Kate asked.

"Yes, but I don't know the number. As they were leaving the warehouse, they met a man on horseback. They shot him, and then began to shoot at houses as they stormed away."

He spurred his horse and about a dozen well armed men followed in pursuit of the outlaws. "Watch out for an ambush," Man yelled. "They may expect somebody will follow. There were horses tied behind the wagons, they could drop back and waylay you."

Kate and Man mounted and spurred their horses into a lope toward The Fort. They slowed to a walk when they entered the open gate and saw the inside was bustling with people scurrying about in excitement.

It was light enough now to see as the sun had peeked over the mountain in the east, but a fine mist was still falling. Man and Kate rode to the rear of the store and saw George lying on the ground with Maude on her knees beside him. Kate leaped from Redbird and hurried to the supine man.

Maude seemed to be in shock, and was just holding George's hand crying. Spectators were standing around watching, but nobody was doing anything to help George.

Kate dropped on her knees beside Maude to see the wound. A bullet hole was located on his left side.

Thankfully, it was away from the heart, but still damaging. It appeared to have gone in just above George's collarbone.

She saw she needed to take charge, as Maude was still confused. "Maude, we need to get him inside," she said. "Man, get help and carry George into the house where I can look at the wound."

Man and three men came to help. They gently lifted George and carried him into the back of the store. Thankfully, he wasn't conscious, as the pain would have been horrendous when the men picked him up by the arms and legs to carry him inside.

"Show them where to put him," Kate said. Maude understood and hurried to lead the way. The men placed him on the bed and stepped back for Kate to do her doctoring.

"Now get me light," Kate said. Man lit a lamp, and one of the men brought two more. Kate pulled her skinning knife and cut the shirt away from the wound. It was an angry blue with a dribble of blood seeping from the hole.

"Lift him up," she ordered. She cut the shirt away and looked at his back. "It went through," she said, "which is good. From the angle, I don't think it hit anything vital. Maude, bring me alcohol."

That brought her out of shock, and she hurried to the door into the store. She came back with a bottle. Kate poured the clear liquid into the hole on George's upper chest. He moaned in pain as the alcohol burned like liquid fire.

She waited for a few seconds and filled the wound again. This time George was silent.

"Roll him on his belly," she said. The men came to help and she repeated the process, filling the wound with alcohol. Man, bring my sulphur from my saddlebags and moss."

He hurried from the store. "Thank you for bringing George inside," she said to the three men. "Maude and I'll take over from here. I don't suppose there's a doctor here?" she asked.

Maude was the first to reply. "No, there's no doctor."

"Then we can do it. I have experience with gunshot wounds. I'll need clean white material for a bandage."

Maude again hurried to the front. Man came back and handed her the jar with the sulphur, and took the roll of moss to the stove. He knew how to prepare it. Kate packed the back wound with the yellow drug and Maude came back with bandages. She helped pull George over on his back and Kate repeated the process on his chest.

Man brought her two balls of moss and she placed one on each wound, and he helped her tie the bandage tightly around his body.

She turned to Maude. "Keep him warm and in bed. I'll come back later to check on him."

She led Man outside. "Was anybody else injured?" she asked.

"Not that I know about," a man outside the door said. "One man was killed as the thieves raced toward the gate. Martin Quinn was coming back from visiting a family and rode right into them. They shot him down in cold blood. He wasn't even armed."

Kate glanced at Man and shrugged her shoulders, but didn't speak, so much for her wedding day.

***

Man and Kate rode back to the wagon and she put breakfast on to cook. She glanced at him and understood his sorrowful expression. "Man, Martin Quinn wasn't the only preacher in Oregon. We have the summer in front of us. You said we were going to the coast, and I know there are towns there with preachers. Besides, we're already married Indian style. That's good enough for me until such time we can stand in front of a preacher and take our vows."

He only grunted. She went to sit beside him and held his hand. "Man, I'm not going to go anywhere, you're

26

stuck with me."

"Does that mean you're saying yes?" he asked.

She wanted to giggle, but suppressed it. "Homer Manchester, I knew I would marry you soon after I found you on the trail. We've been sharing a bed most of the winter. I'm already your wife in every respect, except saying, I do, in front of a preacher. Now relax and eat your breakfast."

He pulled her into his arms and kissed her deep and hard. She pushed him back. "Eat first," she said with a chuckle.

***

She was washing dishes and Man was resting on their bed in the wagon when they heard riders approaching. They both scrambled for cover with their rifles in their hands. The posse rode into their camp with three men over their horses. They noticed the leader was one of them.

One of the men pulled up in front of Man and Kate. "Jacob didn't heed your warning about an ambush. He rode right into a bullet. They got two more before we knew they were waiting beside the trail."

"What did they look like?" Man asked.

"Five men, all dressed mountain man, dirty skin clothes, bearded. I heard one of them call another Bull. Bull was the leader of the gang. After they fired, they melted back into the trees, and we heard the wagons leaving. We didn't fire a shot."

The posse continued on toward The Fort.

***

It was well into the afternoon when Kate and Man rode to The Fort to check on George. They went in the back door and found Maude seated beside his bed. She stood when they entered.

"How is he?" Kate asked.

"He seems about the same. He sleeps most of the time."

Kate walked to the bed and pulled the quilt down to

inspect the wound. She removed the bandage and rolled the soggy moss into the cloth. "Man, I need more," she said.

He turned and left. She cleaned the wounds with the alcohol and packed it with sulphur again. Man came back and motioned Maude to follow him to the stove. He showed her how to prepare it in the boiling water. "When we're gone," he said, "you'll need to do what Kate is doing."

Maude watched Kate dress the wound. "Twice a day for five days," Kate said. "I'll leave you enough sulphur and Man can show you the tree to get fresh moss every time. Boil it for about three minutes, take it out, let it cool, and squeeze all the water out, divide it into two equal balls, one for the front, and one for the back. Wrap it with a fresh clean bandage pulled tight."

Maude nodded she understood. "Why the moss?" she asked.

"It draws out the poison and infection," Kate replied. "The sulfur helps prevent infection. He's looking good. There's no sign of any infection, and his body temperature feels normal. He doesn't have a fever, which is a very good sign. With rest and care, in a week, let him move around, and he should be fit to go back to work in about three weeks. But don't let him lift more than ten pounds for a month. The wound needs to heal inside and out, straining might open it, and the healing process would have to start over."

For the first time since the shooting, George spoke. "Maude told me what you two done for me. I appreciate it. I was making coffee when I heard the wagons, walked out the back door, and a man on a horse shot me without saying a word. That's the last thing I remember until a while ago."

"You're going to be fine," Kate said. "Maude knows what to do, and you had better mind her. Follow her orders and you'll be up and going in a couple of weeks. As I told Maude, don't lift anything heavy for four weeks.

28

That could open the wound. It's already healing, but it will take time."

He relaxed back on the bed. Talking took his strength.

Maude followed them to the door. "How can I ever thank you?" she said.

"You just did," Kate said. "That's enough, we were glad we could help. Feed him thick meat broth and mashed vegetables several times a day. He'll need food to get his strength back."

***

Kate and Man walked to the cemetery with most of the people in The Fort. The four men were buried. Since nobody was taking charge, Man stepped forward and said a few words, and then, the procession walked back inside the gate of The Fort. Man and Kate went back to their camp.

"What now?" she asked.

"As soon as Maude can open the store for business tomorrow, we need to buy supplies, and point the noses of our horses toward the west."

"Will we take the wagon?" she asked.

"I don't see much point in it. Riding would be easier, and we can move a lot faster and go more places. Besides, that old wagon has about had it. I suggest we park it behind Buck's Stable and pick it up this fall, or trade it in on a better wagon."

"Could Buck repair it this summer," she said. "Maybe new wheels, axle, and bed would be cheaper than buying a new one."

"Good point," Man said. "I'll talk to Buck."

***

They found George propped up in his bed. "Welcome Kate and Man," he said. "I heard that Martin Quinn was killed and it ruined you're plans for a wedding."

"We'll find another preacher this summer," Kate said. "We're headed west to the coast. That's one of the reasons we came by, other than check on you. We need

29

supplies for the summer."

"Maude is up front; too many people needed things to stay closed. She'll be happy to fill your order."

"When did Maude change your bandage?" Kate asked.

"Early this morning," he said.

"Man, check on Maude, if she's not busy with a customer, bring her back. I would like to check George to make sure there's no infection."

Maude came back with Man a few minutes later, and he went for fresh moss. "It's doing good," Kate said after examining both wounds. "There's no redness or swelling and his body temperature is normal." She let Maude dress the wounds, and then, they walked to the front of the store as George lay back to rest.

"Continue doing what you've been doing and keep him in bed," Kate said.

"I will as long as you said, but he's already worrying about the store. With the loss of the revenue from the sale of the furs, he said times are going to be tough replacing the merchandise we need."

Man and Kate walked around the store and selected the things they would need in the weeks ahead. She put a sack of rice on the counter. "Unless you see something else we need, that's about it," she said.

"Maude," George shouted.

She hurried to the door to talk to him. "Their supplies are on the house," he said. "After what Kate did for me, it's only right."

Man and Kate heard his comment. "Maude, what we did was the neighborly thing to do, and we don't expect anything in return," Kate said.

Man was nodding his head in agreement. "Total it up," he said. He stood where he could see to make sure she didn't try to hide anything from being put on the tally. He paid her and took their supplies out to the horses.

Their next stop was the livery stable. Buck came out to greet them. "I have something to discuss with you,"

Man said. "But, can we go inside out of the wind to talk? Spring is close, but that north wind is still biting."

They found a place to sit around a potbellied stove that gave off a welcome heat. Buck poured coffee for them. "What's on your mind?" he asked.

"Kate and I are going to the coast and work north and not come back until fall. We're going to take the two mules as pack animals and leave the wagon here. It's about gone all the miles it can stand. After the Oregon Trail and being burned, well, we need to do something. What we wanted to discuss with you, would you like to repair it this summer? It'll need new wheels, axles, bed, covering, the works, or would it be better to trade it for a better wagon. I know you'll be honest with me, and I'll do what you recommend."

"Let me show you a Conestoga I'm trying to sell for a widow woman. They came out last year, and I worked it over for them. It's almost as good as new. I did all the things you mentioned yours needed. The man died a few weeks ago, and she wants to go back home."

They walked out to where the Conestoga was parked under the trees. Kate crawled inside and examined the covering. Man knelt down and examined the wheels and axle.

Buck was right; it was in near new condition.

"If you was of a mind to buy it now," Buck said. "She would like to go back as soon as possible. One of the wagon masters going after a new train has agreed to take her back."

They walked back inside and Man asked, "What does she want for it?"

"She would be happy with eight hundred, and it's a bargain at that price. It would help you and her out."

Man glanced at Kate. She nodded.

"We'll take it, but what about our wagon?

"In the current condition," Buck said, "to be honest, I don't want it. But, if I have all summer to work on it during my spare time, by fall, I expect it would net you three, maybe four hundred."

"Do it," Man said. He pulled the money from the money belt that he took from Leach, the slave trader, and paid Buck.

"Do you know anything about the five men that robbed George and stole his fur wagons?" Kate asked.

"Not much, but I saw them a few times. The boss was called Bull. I think they were all kin from what I picked up. Pure trash was my opinion of them. I had to stand up wind when they were around. I've been around hogs that smelled better."

Kate grimaced. She recalled the men that came to the cabin to rob them. That's how they smelled.

"You might talk to George. When they first rode in, they had furs for sale. Bull asked if there was a buyer here. I sent him to George. From what I put together later, they stole the furs, they were damn sure not trappers."

"Why are you asking?" Buck said.

"As we said, we're going west. It is not likely, but who knows, we may run across them, and I wanted a description just in case."

"Should you run into them, they shoot from ambush," Buck said. "I expect those two horses you and Kate are riding, and the two pack mules loaded with supplies would be enough to set them on you."

He glanced at Kate a moment. "That, and the other reason, don't let them get their hands on you."

"I don't intend to let them get close. We'll be on the lookout," Kate said. "We have experience along those lines already."

They walked back to the horses and Kate asked, "Do we visit with George again? He may not know who shot him."

"Good idea," he said.

They found George asleep, but Maude woke him, knowing Man and Kate wanted to talk.

"We talked to Buck and he saw the men that robbed and shot you. The leader of the gang was called Bull. He

32

said they had furs when they first rode in, and he sent them to you."

Maude let out a moan. "They came in the store, and I almost gagged at the stench. George told them to meet him at the warehouse."

"I bought furs from them. Fair quality, but they didn't know beans about them. I had no proof, but I was almost sure they stole them. I admit, I didn't offer them anywhere the normal price, but they were happy."

"They spent every nickel George paid them in the store," Maude said. "Mostly they bought whisky, ammunition, and some food. I had to open the front and back door after they left to air the store out."

"They got a look inside my warehouse when I bought their furs," George added. "They saw the four wagons loaded and ready for shipment. I guess they saw the opportunity and took it."

"I didn't have time to see who shot me, it was dark, and it happened so fast. But, thinking back, it was Bull."

Man pulled their wagon behind Buck's Livery and they went by to tell Maude and George goodbye before riding through the gate and turned toward the west.

Chapter 2

Their supplies for the summer were carried on the two mules, as they would be sleeping in the open. Kate was jovial and enjoyed seeing the new scenery as they left the mountains. But, she knew Man was disappointed they weren't properly married by a preacher. She rode close and reached for his hand. "At the first opportunity, we'll be married. Maude found me a dress you haven't seen. It's bad luck for a man to see his bride in her wedding dress before the wedding. Or so somebody once said, but I think that's an old wives tale."

He gave her hand a squeeze and smile. The happy couple found a place to camp early in the evening. A small stream overflowed a rock formation forming a natural pool of clear blue water.

"I know it will be cold, but I want a bath," she said as she looked down at the water.

"Kate, if you get in that water you'll turn as blue as the water. That water came from melting ice and snow."

"I know, but I want a bath. I may not get in, but I can wash my body and hair."

He knew her mind was made up and she was determined. "I'll build a warm fire and have blankets ready when I drag your frozen body back," he teased.

They made camp close to the pond as she undressed while he built the fire. The clouds had cleared during the day and the warm sun helped as she strode proudly to the pond and sat on a rock to wash. Man followed and perched on a fallen log and admired her sleek body. The sun caught her hair and the reddish highlights were bright in the evening rays.

She sat at the edge and washed her hair first and dipped her head under to wash the soap away, then used a washcloth to go over every inch of her body.

He was ready with a blanket when she finished and wrapped it around her shivering body, and carried her back to the fire. She was laughing as he put her down and watched her work on her wet hair with a towel.

"You're next," she teased. "I'm not letting a dirty old man in my bed tonight."

He began to remove his deerskins and walked to the pond. It took him half the time to bathe as it did her, and he rushed back to the fire. She was waiting with a warmed blanket. She used the towel to dry his hair, and then folded into his arms for a kiss.

She nibbled on his lips and whispered, "Your woman needs her future husband." She led him to the bed she had ready. A sigh of contentment echoed down the peaceful valley and caused the horses and mules to look up from munching on plentiful spring grass.

Two days later, they found the homestead, which ended their joyful mood.

***

Kate helped Man move the bodies to the suitable site under tall Pine trees. He found a shoved and pick in the barn and started on the unpleasant task of digging two graves.

Kate went back to the cabin and located a bucket and went to the barn to milk the cow. The calf continued to bawl, as she was anxious for Kate to finish so she could have her overdue breakfast.

Kate took half of the milk and left the rest for the calf. She watched the calf suck and though how nice it would be to have a milk cow at their cabin next winter. Chickens were around the barn, so she went inside and found nest and gathered eggs.

She had a hot meal ready when Man came in from burying the woman and boy. The look on his face caused her to hurry to wrap her arms around him to give him a badly needed hug and comfort from his awful chore. "It's a violent unsettled territory," she said. "But times are changing, someday there'll be enough settlers to warrant law enforcement, and hopefully put an end to the brutality as we saw here today."

"You're right. But I saw violence in a so-called populated, so-called civilized area as I came west. I'm afraid it's something we'll always experience as long as there's greed and unconcern for others."

To pull him away from his melancholy mood, she took his hand and led him to the table. "Fresh sweet milk, hen eggs, bacon, and biscuits are ready."

As they ate, she shared her earlier thoughts. "Man, could we buy a cow and a few chickens for next winter? Maybe we could have a hog or two for meat during the cold months."

Man smiled for the first time since coming inside. "I expect that could be arranged. That would mean turning me into a farmer. We would need grain for them."

"Would that be so bad? Look at this place; they made a home for a family. Besides, as George said, the furs will dwindle in time, and with a grain and corn field, we could manage nicely." She bore into his eyes and added, "Especially after we have children."

His head jerked up at her comment. "Are you pregnant," he asked.

"No, but after we're married, and the time is right, I want to have a family." She paused for him to comprehend what she suggested, and then added. "That will be a while in the future. We have the summer in front of us to roam and see this beautiful country."

She watched him finish the last bite and then cleaned the table. He walked to a homemade chest of drawers and picked up a bible on top. Inside the first page, he found writing.

"Oh my God," he exclaimed.

Kate hurried to him to see what caused his outburst.

"I know them. The woman's name was Rachel Knox and her husband is Melvin. Their son was named Melvin, but called Junior. They were on the first train I was on with Jake and Slats. I thought she looked familiar, but it didn't register. I think because of the condition of her face was in, that is, until I found this bible with their names and

36

dates they were married, and the birth date of their son."

He added, "If I recall correctly, there were two families traveling together. They were related, cousins or something. The other family was named." He paused in thought as he rubbed his chin, before he continued. "Lucas Musick and his wife was Richelle. They had a daughter about the same age as Junior. I think her name was Annie, but I may be wrong on that."

"I wonder if Lucas and Richelle settled near here?" she asked.

"I have no idea. After we arrived at The Fort, the settlers went in different directions to find a place to homestead. When we move out, we can keep our eyes open for another cabin close by. In fact, maybe we should make a circle to check. I hope Bull didn't find them as well."

"I wonder what happened to Melvin," Kate said.

"We may never know, or we may find his body. If he met Bull and the gang, I suspect the latter. They shoot on sight."

They slept in the barn. Somehow, it didn't seem right to sleep in the bed of Melvin and Rachel.

The next morning as they saddled Redbird and Arabian, Man said, "Circle out about two miles. I'll go out three miles and we'll meet back here. I doubt Bull and his gang are close, but be careful anyway, and keep a sharp eye out. I expect they went on west. They have furs to sell and I think they're on the way to Portland, or some other coast settlement."

Kate and Man rode out together about two miles and she turned Redbird to make a circle. He continued on for another mile before starting his circle.

He finished making his loop around the homestead and spotted her waiting on a small hill. He touched his heels to Arabian's sides and loped to where she waited. He was shaking his head from side to side.

"I didn't see any signs of a homestead or tracks either," she said.

37

They rode back to the cabin, loaded the pack mules, and again went toward the west.

It was late the next afternoon when a wagon came into sight. It was pulled by two plow mules, and they were walking slow like they learned pulling a plow.

Man was looking intently at the driver. "It's Melvin Knox," he said. "I recognize him."

"Oh my," Kate mumbled. "How do we tell him about Rachel and Junior?"

They stopped under the shade of a tree to wait for the wagon. "Hello Melvin," Man said when the wagon was close enough for conversation.

The man in the wagon was startled at a stranger calling him by name. He peered from under his hat brim at the tall man wearing deerskin clothing. He took in Kate as well, noticing she was dressed the same as the man, and wearing twin pistol on her hips.

"Who are you?" Melvin asked.

"Homer Manchester, but you should remember me as Man. I was with Jake and Slats on the wagon train with you and Rachel."

"I remember you now. You were just a green kid at the time."

Man knew he needed to get it over with and relay the awful news. "Melvin, we bring you sad news," he said.

Alarm registered on his face. "Something happened to Rachel or Junior?" he asked, quickly.

"There's no easy way to put this," Kate said. "We found their bodies at your cabin."

A scream of anguish echoed as her words registered. "What happened?" he demanded with his fist doubled and his neck strained.

"We found them in the cabin, they were murdered," Man said.

"Who did it?" he demanded as he reached for his rife laying on the seat beside him.

"We don't know, but we have good suspicions. If you want, get down we'll tell you all we know," Man said.

They dismounted and Man tied the horses to a limb and met Melvin at a clump of rocks in the shade of a tree. Man started with what happened at The Fort, and reported seeing the wagon tracks near the cabin.

"I buried them under the clump of trees near your cabin. We wondered what happened to you, and made a circle searching. We were afraid they ambushed you."

"I took a load of grain and my furs into Portland to sell, and buy supplies. Rachel and Junior stayed at home to care for the cow and our three horses."

"There was no sign of horses," Man said. "The cow was in the lot and the calf outside. We turned them out before we left so she could find feed and the calf needed milk. They apparently took the horses. What did they look like?"

"I raised a colt, a fine animal, Chestnut with a blaze face. There were two roans that my wife and son rode."

Melvin sat in silence for several moments, his head down. He finally looked up. "I think I saw the four wagons you mentioned. I turned off the main road to visit friends. As I was coming back to the road, I saw wagons from a distance."

"Would that be Lucas Musick and his wife Richelle?" Man asked.

"Yes," he said. "But how did you know?"

"I remember them from the train, and recalled you were traveling together. In fact, when we made the circle searching for you, we looked for another homestead."

"Luke found a place he liked better to settle," Melvin said. "It's off the Portland road about two miles."

"I hope Bull and his gang didn't spot it," Man said.

Melvin's face turned ashen. He hurried to the wagon and circled and whipped the mules into a run. Man and Kate mounted and raced to catch him.

Man rode to the side of the team, and pulled the mules down to a walk. Kate rode to the side of the wagon. "If they found the cabin, we're too late. We'll go with you. Bull and his gang shoot first, and don't bother to ask questions. If they are there, we'll take them, but no need committing suicide by riding hell-bent for leather into their rifle fire. As we said, they killed three men riding after them. They hid beside the road and shot them down in cold blood."

He calmed at her words as they made since to him, even though he was in a state of shock and grief.

"You're right," he said. "If they spotted their cabin, it would already be too late to help."

"Lead the way," Man said. "We'll follow."

They stopped where they could see the homestead. A sigh went up from Melvin. "I see Luke chopping wood," he said.

Man and Kate followed Melvin's wagon to the cabin. A woman with dark hair wearing a homemade long dress came out on the porch along with a young woman. The girl was dressed similarly, and had her hair tied in back with a ribbon.

Luke planted his ax in the log and walked out to meet them. "What brings you back so soon?" he asked.

Melvin stumbled and almost fell climbing down from the wagon. The anguished expression on his face caused his friends to rush to him. Richelle put her arms around Melvin's shoulder, and Annie clutched his hand. Luke waited in front of Melvin.

"Somebody murdered Rachel and Junior. They're dead." Then Melvin's emotions erupted and he began to cry. Richelle pulled him toward the cabin.

Kate gestured with her head and Man turned his horse toward her and the pair rode away. "He's with friends and family now," she said. "We're outsiders, and it would be best for us to move on to leave Melvin with them for his grieving." Man reached for her hand and gave it a squeeze, as he understood her logic.

They rode back to the Portland road and she began to look down at the tracks. "Looking for four wagons?" he asked.

"If the opportunity presents itself, I want my sights

40

on Bull's nose after what they did to Rachel and the young boy."

Man moved off to the side of the road and Kate went to the other and they searched for tracks as they rode west.

The next morning as they rode on west, Man suddenly pulled up and dismounted beside the road and knelt down. He looked up and saw Kate sitting astride Redbird watching. "Four wagons passed this way," he said.

Once they found the killers trail, the heavy wagons were easy to follow and they made good time. The next morning, the Willamette River came into sight, and buildings could be seen in the distance. "They beat us here," he said.

The couple rode into Portland and the tracks disappeared in the multitude of wagon tracks on the dirt road. As the couple rode down Clay Street, people turned to look at the man and woman dressed in deerskin clothing, with two pistols on their hips.

Kate spotted a building with a Portland Police Station sign on the front. "I suggest we report to them about George, and the murder of Rachel and Junior Knox."

A policeman was standing near the door when they dismounted. "Is the chief here?" Man asked. The lawman eyed the couple for a moment, especially the pistols.

"Come with me," he said.

He led them inside and into a big room with cells against the back wall. A small man with a magnificent handlebar mustache came to greet them with a coffee cup in his hand. "I'm Chief Kline," he said.

Man stepped forward with his hand out and introduced Kate and himself. "We rode in from The Fort, and thought we should report an incident there."

"Why here in Portland?" Chief Kline asked.

"A kind of long story if you have time?" Man said with some irritation reflected in his tone. "And it's not too much of a bother," he added.

"Go on, I got time to hear," the Chief said as he went behind a desk and put his cup down. He didn't offer them coffee.

"George Bowman owns a store and buys furs at a settlement called The Fort. He was robbed of his furs and shot. A man called Bull and four men gunned down the unarmed preacher, and killed three men in a posse that chased them. Bull and his men took four wagons loaded with furs George bought from trappers. Anyway, on our ride here, we found a homestead belonging to Melvin and Rachel Knox. Rachel and their son, Junior had been murdered. The boy was shot between the eyes and Rachel's arms were tied to the bedpost. Her throat had been cut."

The policeman made a note on a scratchpad on the desk, and then looked up for Man to continue.

"We buried Rachel and Junior and came on toward Portland and met Melvin on the trail. He was returning after selling his grain and furs here. We followed the wagon tracks, but lost them when get got on the busy streets."

"We think Bull and his gang brought George's furs here to sell. They also stole three horses from Melvin. Melvin described one as being a Chestnut with a blaze face. The other two were roans."

The other policeman was standing at the door listening.

"That's our report," Man said, and he and Kate stood and went to the door.

"We'll look into it," Chief Kline said.

Kate and Man mounted and turned their horses down Clay Street and the Willamette River.

Kate reined Redbird close to Man to talk without shouting. "Now what?" she asked.

"I suggest we find a hotel, and a place for our horses and mules."

"I've never been in a hotel," Kate said. "What do I do?"

"I stayed in a few when I had the money on my way west. We go in and to the desk and rent a room. They'll give us a key and we go to the room. Hopefully, we can locate one with a stable behind. Most of the better hotels provide them for their guest."

Kate gestured toward a two-story building with a sign on the front. "Portland Hotel," she said. Man turned Arabian toward it, and Kate followed. They tied up at the hitching rail in front and went inside.

A bald man was behind the desk watching the pair enter. His eyes opened wide at their appearance, wondering what this mountain couple was doing inside the hotel.

"We want a room," Man said. "Do you have a stable for two horses and two pack mules?"

"That will be two dollars a day," the clerk said. "The animals will be grained and hayed."

"We also want a bath for both of us. Is that extra?"

"Yep, two bits each, which includes plenty of hot water, and clean towels. A tub and water will be delivered to your room."

Man pulled a five-dollar gold piece from his pocket and paid. "We'll be here at least two days," he said. "Maybe more, we'll let you know tomorrow."

The clerk pushed a book forward for Man to sign. He wrote with a flourish, Mr. and Mrs. Homer Manchester.

The clerk glanced at the name and pushed a key toward Man. "Room twenty-six, Mr. Manchester. Turn right at the top of the stairs, it's the last room on the end."

"We'll go out and stable the animals and come back," Man said.

"Very good, there's a door from the stables into the hotel. Your tack and supplies will be safe. Brock is the holster and has a room for them. Somebody is always on duty day and night."

They met a man at the gate and he took the reins of the two horses. Man led the two mules inside the barn.

43

"Are you Brock?" Man asked.

"Yep," he replied.

"I'm Homer Manchester and this is Kate," Man said.

Brock stopped and eyed Man closely. "Are you known as Man and rode with Jake and Slats?" Brock asked.

"I made a few trips with them," Man replied.

"I wintered at The Fort once and got to know them," Brock said. "Is it true about them getting killed?"

"Yes," Man said, and that was all he offered. He was anxious to get inside and discussing his friends being killed still hurt.

Kate carried their saddlebags and the bundle containing their new clothes. As a precaution, Man brought the two extra rifles inside. They were too expensive to take the chance of them being stolen.

The clerk gasped when he saw Man carrying three rifles and Kate had hers under her arm. That coupled with the twin Walker Colts on their hips caused his concern and apprehension, but he said nothing.

Kate stood inside the hotel room looking around. "I didn't know what to expect. Maybe I anticipated something a little larger and plusher. At that price it should be fancy."

"I agree, but the hotel rooms I've seen are basically the same. We need to get our things ready; the bathtub should be here shortly."

Kate began to put their new clothing on the bed. Before she finished a knock sounded. A man brought in a tub and two young teenage boys carried buckets of water. The deliveryman pointed toward two of the buckets. "Those are hot, be careful. Two towels and soap are inside the tub. Either put the tub and empty buckets outside, or tell the clerk when you're finished and I'll come for them."

"Thank you," Man said and closed the door behind them.

"You first," he said. She began to remove the

44

deerskin clothing as he poured the hot water in the tub.

He sat on the bed and watched her bathe, and then poured water over her head to remove the soap from her hair and body. She perched on the bed cross-legged and rubbed her long reddish hair with the towel as he bathed.

"Which dress do you want me to wear?" she asked. He rubbed his chin as he looked at the three dresses she held up for him. "The print," he said.

He dried and put his new clothes on casting happy glances at Kate as she put on women's underwear. When they were both dressed and Kate had her hair combed, he stood and gave her another contented glance. "Shall we go?" he asked.

"What about our weapons?" she asked. "I don't want to leave my Walkers in the room. Will our rifles be safe here? The man that delivered the tub must have a key. He said he would come back after the tub if it wasn't outside."

Man dragged the tub out in the hall and Kate put the buckets and towels beside it. "There's no reason for him to come into our room now," he said.

But as a precaution, he put the four rifles under the mattress. "At least they won't be in plain sight," he said. Kate put her pistols in her coat pockets. "I'm not leaving them," she said.

"I'll wear mine," he said. He wore them high and the coat almost covered them. Only the tips of the holsters were visible.

They went down the steps and used the back door. He saw Brock inside the stable and turned toward him. "Where's a good place for supper?" he asked.

He eyed Kate in her pretty dress before he replied. "I recommend a place named, The River Crossing. It's about four blocks on Clay Street. They have fresh fish, salmon, or steak."

"Thanks partner," Man said.

As they walked, she was looking inside the windows of the many shops and stores. "Tomorrow, can we walk through some of them for me to look? I've never been in

45

stores like these."

"Of course, we aren't in a rush to get somewhere. We can spend as much time as you want shopping."

They saw the, River Crossing Café in the next block. "What do I do when we get there?" she asked. "I've never been in a café."

"It's easy. Either they'll take us to a table, or we find our own, and sit down. A waitress will bring us a menu, or it will be printed on a sign. We choose what we want to eat, order, and wait for them to bring our food to the table."

"That sounds easy enough," she said with a smile. "But, I can see how a woman might get lazy with food so easily obtainable. There would be no standing over a hot stove, and no cleaning afterwards."

A man dressed as a fisherman met them at the door, led the way to a table, and placed menus on the table. Man chose the seat with his back to the wall. The fisherman looked at the Walker Colts on Man's thigh and frowned. "Not many men carry pistols anymore. We're civilized in Portland."

"Where we just rode in from is far from civilized," Man replied. "We saw four men, a woman, and a child murdered. The killers are here in Portland."

The fisherman gasped and hurried away.

"What does salmon taste like?" she asked.

"I have no idea," he said. "I know it's a fish and very popular in the northwest."

"I'll try it," she said. "Chicken for me," Man said. "I haven't had chicken since I left home. As we discussed earlier, maybe we can have chickens and hogs next winter at the cabin."

She offered him a wistful smile of approval.

The meal was delicious, and Kate enjoyed the salmon. "What now?" she asked.

"We can walk around Portland and look, that is, if you want. We can go back on a different street and you can window shop in more stores." As they walked, Kate often stopped and looked inside the windows, especially the shops featuring women's clothing.

Man opened the door to their room and Kate immediately went to the bed to check their rifles. They were where they left them.

"Tomorrow, when we're out exploring, do you mind if we find a church?" he asked, sheepishly.

"Do you still want to marry me?" she teased.

"Yep, I want papers on you, and a ring on your finger."

She hopped on the bed. "Would having papers on me and a ring on my finger make this better," she asked as she watched him undressing.

"I don't know about being better, but I want the world to know that Kate and Man are a married couple."

She offered a contented sigh of contentment as he settled between her legs. "If it's any better after we're married, I'm not sure I could stand it," she said as her first peak began to burst.

***

The next morning they found a small café for breakfast. They again wore their city clothing as not to be so conspicuous. They finished eggs and ham and sat back, sipping another cup of coffee. "What do we do today," she asked. "That is, besides letting me walk through the shops and stores to look."

"The way I see it," he said. "We can do some more sightseeing and shopping, pack up and go on west to the coast, or go hunting."

"Hunting, for what in Portland? I doubt there's a deer anywhere close." She knew what he meant, but wanted him to say it before she did.

"Hunting for Bull and his gang," he offered, and then sipped his fresh hot coffee before continuing. "It just isn't right to let those killer thieves walk away to continue their murdering ways. But, from the feeling I got after we talked to the police, I have the distinct feeling they weren't concerned about what happened outside Portland. But I can see it from their point of view. If they arrested them, what could they charge them with? Our story that they robbed and shot George Bowman, killed Martin Quinn in cold blood, shot three men in a posse trailing them, and murdered Rachel and Junior Knox. Any two-bit lawyer would have them out in minutes. There's no evidence or eye witness to any of their crimes."

Kate sat in thought. "Just suppose we find them and put them down, we could be charged with murder. We aren't law, and have no authority to do anything."

"Are you saying we pack up and move out and forget it?" he asked.

"Yes and no, a proposal, or just a thought," she said. "We go hunting and find them if they're still in Portland. They don't know us. When Bull shot at you, it was dark, and you were behind the tree. We keep an eye on them and see what they do, and where they go. Once out in the territory, it would be like the slave traders, us against them."

"There's five of them," he said. "We know they shoot from ambush, and killing is nothing to them. It could be dangerous if they spot us."

"Are you suggesting we do nothing," she said with a frown he understood.

"Nope, I'm thinking we need to find a church and get married, and then worry about Bull and his men."

"Wow, what a deal," she laughed. "We marry and go hunting Bull and his gang for our honeymoon, how romantic."

"Kate McAlester, I know you too well. You're not about to ride away without doing anything about them. I saw the determination in your eyes, the same as I saw the morning you offered yourself to the slave traders in exchange for the Indian girls."

"I can't help it," she said. "I grew up believing right is right and wrong is wrong. I believe the only law should be what's right, and it's wrong to let those killers off without anybody doing anything."

"So do we go hunting for a church first?" she asked, making eye contact to let him know that was what she wanted. "Besides, I need papers on you, you handsome devil. I've seen women looking at you and I don't share well. Homer Manchester, you belong to me, only me. Is that understood?"

He laughed loud enough that a few people at other tables turned to stare at him. He noticed and almost whispered. "Yes ma'am, I understand. Shall we go change your name?"

***

They were walking down the street when a family in a buggy approached them. The driver suddenly pulled back on the reins and shouted, "Man, is that you?"

Startled, Man approached the buggy, trying to recognize the couple. Suddenly, it hit him. "Morgan, Fredrick Morgan, Mary Ann and is that little Lucy Lou?" he said. "You were on the wagon train a few years back. You were the settler that had trouble keeping the water barrel on the side of the wagon."

"That's me. What brings you to Portland," Fred asked.

"Passing through, but at the moment we're looking for a church and preacher to get married." He reached from Kate's hand. "This is my bride to be, Kate McAlaster."

Mary Ann spoke for the first time. "We belong to a small church not far from here. We have a nice young preacher named Brother Powers. We would be happy to introduce you and stand at your side."

Man glanced at Kate. She was nodding her head.

"Hop in with us," Mary Ann said. "We go by the church. We were in town buying a few things."

Man helped Kate into the buggy and they sat beside Lucy Lou. Fred slapped the reins on the rump of the horse and Mary Ann turned where she could talk to them. "Is it true that Jake and Slats were killed? We heard a rumor that Indians wiped out the entire train, killing everybody."

"It's true, with one exception," Man said. "Kate was the only survivor. Jake, Slats, and her father hid her in a cave before the battle. They knew what would happen if she became a captive."

Mary Ann turned to face Kate. "I hope we have time to talk. I would love to hear about that. I worried the entire time we were on the Oregon Trail. We saw Indians, but it was always a small bunch, and they didn't bother us."

"There weren't many wagons on our train," Kate said. "Jake and Slats said it was a large band of Indians on their way to their winter campground. The men on the train were outnumbered by so many, they didn't have a chance."

Fred stopped the horse in front of a small white building. God's Church, was on a sign in front. Fred and Man stepped out first and helped the women down. "My you have grown," Man said to Lucy Lou. "I remember you as a skinny little girl with long pigtails. How old are you now?"

"Sixteen," she said. Mary Ann cleared her throat.

"Mom, I'll be sixteen in twelve days. That's close enough for me to tell people I'm sixteen."

"I remember those times when I was a teen," Kate said. "I wanted to be grown so much."

"How old are you?" Lucy Lou asked.

"Lucy Lou," Mary Ann scolded. "It's not polite to ask the age of a woman."

"I don't mind," Kate said. "I'm not a teen anymore." But that was all she would say.

A man wearing a black coat came to the door. "Welcome, Mary Ann, Lucy Lou, and Fred. May I help you with something?"

Fred made the introductions of Kate and Man. "This couple wants to be married. I met Man on the Oregon Trail; he was one of our guides on the train. We saw them on the street and brought them to meet you."

"Come inside out of the wind and we can talk,"

Reverend Powers said with a gesture toward the inside of the church.

He led the way to his office and sat behind a desk. There were only two chairs and Fred gestured for Kate and Mary Ann to sit.

"When do you want the ceremony?" Powers asked.

"I was thinking of Sunday afternoon," Mary Ann put in quickly. "This Sunday is dinner on the ground after our morning service. Everybody will be here, and we could start this couple off in the proper manner. We could properly welcome them into God's fold."

Kate turned toward Man. "Can we stay that long? That's two days from now."

"Unless, they move out and we decide to follow, it would be fine with me."

"What are you talking about?" Fred asked. "Who moves out?"

"We'll tell you later," Man replied. "Sunday will be fine for now. If we have to leave, we can get word to you somehow, and postpone the wedding."

"Dinner on the ground," Kate said. "We did that at home before we came to Oregon. Every family brought a dish and we ate under the trees on blankets."

"It's the same here," Mary Ann said. "But the men built tables for us. We do this once a month."

"Then the wedding is set for Sunday afternoon," Brother Powers said.

"We'll be here," Man said. "That is, if at all possible."

They walked out to the buggy. "Do you have a dress?" Mary Ann asked.

"Every dress I had burned on the train. The night before the attack, my father hustled me out, and all I had was men clothes. We stopped at The Fort and I bought four dresses. One is almost white, but a housedress. It certainly isn't a wedding gown."

"If you two aren't busy," Mary Ann said. "Can you come with me to my shop? I think I have one that will fit you. A woman should be married in a white gown."

51

Kate was beaming in excitement at the prospect of wearing a real wedding gown.

"I can help," Lucy Lou said. "Mom is teaching me to sew and do alternations."

"That would be nice," Kate said. "You said shop, what kind of store do you have?"

"We have a General Mercantile, from planting seed, plows, to clothing," Fred said. "Not the size of George Bowman at The Fort, but as Portland grows, so are we. Business has been good and I have plans for moving to a larger building."

***

Man and Fred went to the storage room and unloaded the supplies Fred bought in town while the women were busy in the sewing room. "What was that about having to leave?" Fred asked. "You said something like if they move out. Are you after somebody?"

"Five men robbed George at The Fort and shot him. He'll survive, but they stole the furs he bought from trappers and four wagons. They murdered Preacher Quinn in cold blood, and killed three men in a posse. On top of that, they murdered a woman and her son. We followed the wagons here, but lost them."

"Did you report it to the police?" Fred asked.

"That was the first thing we did when we got here. They didn't appear to be that concerned, and I can see why. They have nothing to charge them with except our word, and we were not eyewitnesses. The leader is called Bull and he shot at me as they were leaving The Fort. But it was dark and I couldn't put my hand on a bible and swear I could identify him."

"So you two are tracking five killers? In my opinion, that's plain stupid."

"Maybe so, but what if it was Mary Ann and Lucy Lou that were murdered in cold blood after they had their way with them?"

Fred's face turned white as that thought struck him like a bolt of lightning.

"If we don't stop them, they'll kill again. That's their lifestyle." He paused, and then said, "Can I ask a couple of questions?"

Fred was regaining his composure from thinking about his wife and daughter, and he took a deep breath. "Ask away."

"If Bull and his gang had four wagon loads of stolen furs to sell, where would they go? They have the four wagons and three horses they stole at the Knox homestead. Where would they sell them without questions being asked?"

Fred was fast with his reply. "I know one person that would buy stolen goods without batting an eye. In fact, he'll buy anything at a bargain. Ace Harper is his name. His place is on River Road, a rundown warehouse. His name is on a sign in front. The wagons and horses, there's a stable at the edge of town on North Road. Bingham Brothers Stable, but be careful at either place, they both play rough. I heard that Harper and Bingham came west because they got into serious trouble back east somewhere."

"We intend to be careful. Bull shoots from ambush, and as they say, birds of feather flock together."

"I'll ask around and see if any of our friends knows anything," Fred said.

"Make sure the word doesn't get back to Bull and his gang. If they suspect anybody is after them, they'll be cautious, and watch their back trail."

"I know who to ask, and they can keep their mouth shut."

The women joined them and Kate was beaming in excitement. "It's beautiful," she said as she hugged Man. "I can't wait for you to see it on Sunday," she said.

Kate turned to Mary Ann and Lucy Lou. "Thank you so very much, but I know you have work to do, and we need to get going. We'll see you Sunday morning at the church."

Chapter 3

As Man and Kate walked back to the hotel, he told her what Fred said. "What do we do?" she asked.

"You can shop on the way back to the hotel. Check out all the stores along the way. Then we put our trail clothes on and have a look-see at Ace Harper's Warehouse and the Bingham Brothers Stables."

"I'm with you," she said as she stopped to look in the first store. It took an hour for them to window shop and get back to the hotel, but Kate was happy. She had seen inside so many shops and stores and enjoyed seeing the merchandise on display.

They put on their riding skins and strapped their Walkers on their hips, took their rifles, and went to the stable for Redbird and Arabian. Brock met them and saw the way they were dressed. "Pulling out?" he asked.

"Nope," Man said. "We're going to do some riding and exercise the horses. We'll be back and plan on staying until Monday."

"Expecting trouble," he asked, eyeing the weapons they carried.

"We hope not," Kate said. "But, we never go out without our guns. It's a violent country out there."

Brock nodded agreement. He has been a mountain man before his age drove him into town.

"How do I find River Road?" Man asked.

Brock gave him directions, mostly by pointing.

They followed his directions and found Ace's Warehouse without trouble. They rode by looking, but could see nothing. When they were past it, Man turned the horse's head and they circled behind the warehouse, again seeing nothing of interest.

"I wish I had a peek inside," Man said.

"How could we manage that?" Kate asked.

"I don't know. If workers are there, we would have no excuse to go inside."

"Could I go in and ask for directions to the Morgan store?" Kate asked. "A lost woman shouldn't cause any concern."

"If you want to risk it, I'll wait here and be ready if you need help."

She circled back to River Road and stopped in front. Nobody seemed to be around. She boldly walked inside the warehouse. It was almost dark inside, and she didn't see anybody, so she went farther inside.

There was huge pile of furs on top of a tarpaulin to keep them from the dirt floor. She saw the warehouse was packed with merchandise, from hardware to furniture. A voice startled her. A man with a scar on his cheek came from the darkness.

"I'm lost," Kate said. "I'm looking for Morgan's store, and I guess I took a wrong turn. I just got to Portland yesterday, and Fred and Mary Ann Morgan are friends."

"How do you know them?" Scarface asked.

"I was on the wagon train with them," she fibbed. "I knew they were going to settle in Portland and open a store."

He gave directions without any apparent alarm at her being inside the warehouse. Kate thanked him and hurried outside and mounted Redbird. Man was waiting out of sight of the warehouse.

"I saw a huge pile of furs," she said. "I had no way of knowing if they were George's pelts. But the amount seemed about right. One man was inside. He didn't give his name, but he had a scar on his face." She outlined the location on her cheek with her finger.

"Maybe we'll have better luck at Bingham Brothers Stable," he said.

They circled behind the stable to look. Four wagons were parked behind the barn. "There they are," Man said. "I saw them in George's warehouse."

"Want to go in and try to buy one?" he asked.

"Is that wise?" she asked. "What if Bull and his men

are inside."

"We'll ignore them as if they are strangers and haggle with Bingham on the price of a wagon," he said.

They went back to the front and walked inside the building. A short fat man met them. "We were told you might have a wagon for sale that we can afford," Man said.

"Who told you that?" the fat man asked.

"Well, I don't know his name, but he works at the stable where we have our horses. We lost our wagon to fire."

He seemed to accept that explanation. "I have four in stock, but I'll tell you upfront. Nine hundred and no haggling, I want cash on the barrelhead."

"That's out of our price," Kate said.

"Sorry for your trouble," Man said. They turned and walked out.

"We know where Bull sold the skins and wagons," Man said. "I want a peek at his livestock." They circled the corral, but there was no Chestnut in the bunch, but there were two roans with freshly altered brands. "Somebody used a running iron to change the brand. I would bet my hat those horses belonged to Knox. Bull or one of his men took the Chestnut. It was probably of better quality than what he was riding."

They kept an eye on the Bingham's Stable until almost dark with no sign of Bull and his men. "We better get back to the hotel," she said. "I doubt they'll make an appearance this late. In fact, they may be a long way from Portland by now."

***

Sunday morning, they were up early, anxious for their wedding day. Man paid for the extra days and ordered another bathtub brought to their room. They both took a bath and he dressed in his new clothes and put on his dark coat. Kate watched as she dressed in one of her new dresses. Mary Ann would have her wedding dress at the church.

"Do we take our rifles and pistols?" she asked.

56

"Yes," he said. "Put the pistols in the saddlebags. Our rifles will be on the saddles. It pays to be careful. But we can leave the other two here as before. I'll put the tub outside the door."

"I've never ridden a horse wearing a dress before," she said. "Somehow, it seems unladylike."

"We have three choices," he said. "Walk, wear pants, or ride in a dress. "But, it'll be a very long walk to the church from here."

"I'll wear pants and take my dress. I noticed a room where I can change when we get there. I expect that's where Mary Ann will have me change into the wedding dress. It's so beautiful; I know you'll love it."

The Morgan family was waiting when Man and Kate dismounted. Lucy Lou and Mary Ann took Kate's hand and led her inside the church while Man tied the horses to the hitching rail.

"Did you have any luck on locating where Bull sold the furs and wagons?" Fred asked.

"Kate saw a pile of pelts in the warehouse belonging to Ace. We can't prove they belonged to George, but from the size of the pile, it fits. The four wagons belonging to Bowman were parked behind the barn at Bingham Brothers Stable. I recognized them. Two roan horses were in the coral with freshly altered brands. I suspect they belong to Knox."

"Bull kept the Chestnut for himself," Man speculated. "Well, that's our guess. The Chestnut was probably a better horse than he was riding."

"So far, nobody I have talked with knows anything about where Bull may be hiding out," Fred said. "But, I'll keep asking, hopefully somebody has seen them."

Church members began to arrive and Fred was kept busy introducing Man. They went inside when Brother Powers came to the door. That seemed the normal procedure as the men immediately fined inside and went to seats beside their wives and family. Fred led Man to a pew. Mary Ann and Lucy Lou will bring Kate here

57

shortly," he said. "I'm sure Mary Ann is busy with last second alterations on the dress."

As he predicted, they came out of the room and hurried to join Fred and Man. Kate was wearing the green dress. "I expected to see the wedding dress," Man teased.

"Not until the actual wedding," Mary Ann said. "Kate is so beautiful in it. I know you'll love it."

Man held Kate's hand during the service. Proud they were finally going to be legally married in a church.

Before Reverend Powers ended his service, he made the announcement about the wedding of Man and Kate to follow dinner on the ground. "I hope everyone stays and welcomes this young couple. Maybe someday, they'll move to Portland, and join our church."

The women hurried to their wagons and buggies and brought bowls and platters of food to the tables. The men walked to the trees to talk while the women were busy. When they were ready to eat, Mary Ann motioned for the men to come to the tables.

Reverend Powers offered thanks and led Kate and Man to the table first. He gestured to the Morgan family to be next. "I want them to go through the line first," he announced. "As soon as they finish eating, Mary Ann will take Kate inside to dress for the wedding."

Kate was too excited to be hungry and only nibbled at her food. Mary Ann noticed. "Relax, everything will go smoothly. Fred and I will be there with you."

"Thank you," Kate said. "I appreciate it. But, I'm nervous and excited. It's not every day a woman gets married, and I've never seen one."

"Just relax and the preacher and I'll make sure you do the right things."

As soon as Mary Ann finished eating, she led Kate toward the church. The men went back to the shade of the trees to talk where a few rolled cigarettes and lighted up. A few others took a bite of chewing tobacco.

The children went to the riverbank to play. The boys were throwing rocks making them skip on the water, and the girls were playing a game with a ball.

Suddenly, a terrified scream came from the children. The men looked and saw a man with Lucy Lou under his arm carrying her toward a horse.

Fred and Reverend Powers raced toward the man as fast as they could run. Man saw they were going to be too late to stop him, and ran to where Arabian was tied. He jerked him loose and leaped in the saddle, pulling his rifle. He jacked a shell into the firing chamber, and raced toward the man now on a horse with Lucy Lou in front of him on her belly. He was holding her down with one hand and turning the horse's head with the other.

Reverend Powers was several yards in front of Fred because he was much younger and could run faster. The man on the horse pulled his pistol and aimed at Powers. "Back off if you don't want a taste of hot lead in your belly," he shouted.

Powers didn't slow his pace and kept running toward the kidnapper. "Put her down," he yelled. He grabbed for the reins of the horse and the man fired down at him.

The force of the bullet caused the preacher to fall in front of the horse. This gave Fred time to grab at the reins. The man shot Fred as he jerked the horse's head around and spurred the horse into a run.

Man was closing fast on Arabian. The kidnapper saw him and turned and fired twice. The bullets went wide and Man pulled up and aimed his new Winchester 1873 rifle. He knew he had to shoot high, or risk the bullet passing through and hitting Lucy Lou.

His aim was true, the back of the head exploded, and the kidnapper was thrown from the horse. Man raced on and pulled the frightened horse to a stop and reached for Lucy Lou. She was crying, and put her arms around Man's neck as he put her in front of him on the saddle.

Mary Ann was running as fast as she could with Kate at her side. Man gently handed Lucy Lou down to her mother, and reached for Kate's hand, she put a foot in the stirrup, and swung up behind him. She was wearing the wedding dress.

They hurried to where the men were putting Preacher Powers and Fred on a blanket under a tree. One of the men said, "Both are alive. Powers has a hole in his arm above the elbow. Fred was hit in his side. Somebody went for the police."

Kate jumped down and took charge. "I need my saddlebags," she said.

Man went for them and hurried back. With the help of one of the women, they cut the clothes away to give them access to the two wounds. "The bullet went through Powers," Kate said. "But, it's still inside Fred. He needs a doctor to remove it. Somebody bring a wagon and we can take them. He needs attention as soon as possible. I have most of the bleeding stopped, but he may be hemorrhaging inside."

A policeman stopped his horse and stepped down to look at the two men on the blanket. "Who shot them?" he asked.

Man pointed toward at the body of the outlaw. "That man tried to kidnap Lucy Lou Morgan and shot Fred and Brother Powers when they tried to stop him. I took him down."

The policeman and Man led their horses to the man on the ground. The policeman rolled him over on his back with the toe of his boot. "Erick Venal," he said. "He was released from jail this morning after serving six months for beating a woman. He's been in jail more than out since he's been in Portland, good riddance."

As they walked back to the people gathered around the preacher and Fred, the policeman was looking at Man. "Aren't you the man that reported George Bowman was robbed and shot? You said it was a gang led by a man called Bull. They also murdered a woman and her son?"

"That's me. Has anything been done?"

"We have nothing to go on except your story," the policeman said.

"I can understand that," Man said. "We found the

furs stolen from George in Ace Harper's Warehouse. The four wagons belonging to George are behind the barn owned by Bingham Brothers Stables. Two horses fitting the description of the horses stolen from Knox are in the Bingham corral with freshly altered brands."

"What are you doing investigating?" the policeman demanded.

"Apparently doing your job," Fred said. The entire congregation heard the exchange.

"Thanks to Man," another man said, "he stopped the kidnapping and stood his ground as the abductor was firing at him after he shot Preacher and Fred."

The policeman mounted his horse and rode away without another word.

Reverend Powers and Fred were loaded in the back of a wagon and Mary Ann and Mrs. Powers got in with them. A member of the congregation jumped on the seat of the wagon to drive.

"We'll bring your buggy and Lucy Lou," Kate said. "But I need to change first." She hurried back inside the church to change into the pants she wore riding to the church.

Man waited for her and drove the buggy with their horses tied behind. Lucy Lou huddled beside Kate, and she put her arm around the frightened girl's shoulder.

They found several of the congregation in the front yard of the doctor's office. He had a clinic beside his house, but it was much too small for the visitors.

"Any update?" Man asked.

"Mary Ann is inside with them," one of the women replied. "When she knew anything, she said she would tell us. About all we can do is wait."

Man tied the buggy and their horses to a tree and joined the friends of Brother Powers and Fred to wait. Lucy Lou clutched Kate's hand as Kate proceeded to tell them why they were in Portland, other than to locate a preacher to marry.

"If anybody sees a Chestnut horse with a blaze face,

and he may have a newly altered brand," she said, "we would appreciate knowing the location. We think Bull took the horse, as it was a better quality than he or one of his men was riding. If a man with a full bushy beard dressed mountain is riding the Chestnut, give him a wide birth. There may be five of them together, and they are killers."

One of the men stepped forward. "I saw such a horse and man like you described a couple or three days ago. I was crossing Clay Street and a man riding a Chestnut almost ran me down. He didn't pull up at all, and I had to jump out of the way. The ruffian laughed and shouted for me to get out of his way."

"That sounds like Bull," Kate said. "Do you know anything more? We want to locate them."

"Nope, he went on down Clay Street and I went into a store. I didn't see where he went."

"If you find them, what are you going to do?" a woman asked.

"We'll have to evaluate the situation and make a decision. The law doesn't appear to be concerned, so if anything is done, it'll have to be us."

"That would be five against two," somebody said.

"We know the odds," Kate said. "We've faced bigger in the past. If we attempt to take them down, we have to be smarter than them to even up the numbers."

Mary Ann came outside with a smile on her face. Lucy Lou raced to her mother and grabbed her hand. "Is daddy going to be okay?" she asked.

"The doctor removed the bullet from Fred," Mary Ann said. "It didn't do any major damage to his insides. The doctor is working on Reverend Powers now. He said he would be fine, and he can go home when he finishes. The bullet missed the bone. Fred will be moved to a room and kept here for several days."

She hurried to Man and hugged his neck. "Thank you for saving Lucy Lou. We all know what that heathen would have done to her, and probably killed her afterwards."

She then went to Kate and reached for both of her hands. "If you hang around for a couple of days, Reverend Powers said he would be up and about, and ready to marry you and Man."

"If we're still here, that's a deal," Kate replied. "I left your beautiful dress at the church."

"If we don't have to move out in a hurry on our other mission, we'll be ready. But, if we do leave, we may be able to come back. It depends on if we locate Bull, and which way he goes."

Chapter 4

The next morning, Kate and Man were seated at a table eating breakfast when a big man came inside and looked around. He had a full beard and was dressed for the cold. He had a rifle under his arm and a pistol on his hip. He spotted Man and Kate and walked to their table as if he knew them.

They both saw a badge on his vest under his long coat. Man stood to greet him and offered his hand to shake. He gripped Man's hand in a vice-like squeeze. "My name is Joe Meek, Chief United States Marshal for the Oregon Territory. Can I join you for a cup of coffee?"

Man motioned toward a chair beside him. "This is my bride to be, Kate McAlaster," Man said.

Joe nodded at her with a smile.

A waitress brought him a cup of coffee and he swallowed over half of the scalding hot liquid without flinching.

"I know a great deal about you two," he said. "Correct me if I'm wrong on any part of it."

He had Kate and Man's attention with that comment.

"You rode with Jake and Slats for a few trips on the Oregon Trail. You and Kate put Truman Vincent and Bedford Leach, the slave traders down."

"Yes," Man said, "with the help of Indians. They stole several of their women and girls. We didn't know Leach's first name, only Leach from documents on his body."

Joe went on. "I have a report on the incident at The Fort. It came from George Bowman and the report on the killings of Rachel and Junior Knox from the local police. Also, you stopped a kidnapping at a church yesterday. That also came from the local police."

"All true," Man said.

"Is it also true you two are in pursuit of Bull Blevins?"

"Yes," Man said as Kate nodded her head in agreement.

"There are five known murderers in the Blevins gang," Joe added. "Three of them are brothers and two cousins. We had a report of a couple of trappers murdered and their furs stolen. One of the trappers was shot, but made it to a small settlement, and identified the men before he died of his wound."

"Tell me about spotting the furs stolen from George," Joe said.

"Fred Morgan, a local merchant and friend gave us the lead," Man said. "I met him on the Trail when I was with Jake and Slats."

"He and his wife Mary Ann own a store here," Kate added. "I walked into the warehouse belonging to Ace Harper and saw a pile of furs. I can't swear they were the furs taken from George, but it's a safe bet. From what we learned, Ace will buy anything of value, and is a known fence for stolen goods according to Fred Morgan."

Joe sat listening to her report.

"We circled behind Bingham Brothers Stable," Man added. "The four wagons belonging to George were there. I saw them in George's warehouse at The Fort and can identify them. Two roan horses were in the stable with altered brands. They fit the description of the horses stolen from Knox."

"Since you two are about to be married," Marshal Joe said, "why are you risking your lives?" He was addressing Kate.

"Those killers need to be stopped for this wonderful territory to progress as a State and become civilized. We intend to live here and raise a family. Their kind must be in prison or dead."

"That's why I'm here," Joe said. "I have several marshals working for me, but we're spread too thin. This is a big territory and travel is hard, especially in the winter."

Joe glanced around to see if anybody was listening.

Seeing nobody, he continued. "If you find them, you need authority to arrest or do what's necessary to stop them."

Kate gasped at that statement.

"Homer Manchester," Chief Marshal Joe Meek said, "will you accept the job of temporary deputy United States marshal?"

Kate turned toward Man for his reaction. He met her steady gaze for a few significant moments, and she raised her eyebrow slightly, giving him her approval.

"Yes, I'll accept," Man said.

Joe turned to Kate. "There's nothing I can offer you, except partner with Man. I would be booted out of my job if I appointed a woman as a deputy United States marshal. Times are changing, but we're nowhere near that place yet."

"Yes, I'll partner with Man and understand. As soon as we find a preacher, he'll be my husband."

"Congratulations, Homer Manchester" Joe said. "I have to move on, but will you accompany me to the police station where I'll swear you in?"

"Of course, how long does the position last?" Man asked. "You said temporary."

"Until the Blevins gang is buried, or in custody, or until I see fit to withdraw the appointment."

Man paid for their breakfast and Joe's coffee and followed him out to his horse. "Ours are at the stable behind the hotel," Man said.

"I'll follow you," Joe said.

The three tied up in front of the police building. Joe walked in first and Chief Forest Kline and three policeman instantly stood at seeing Meek.

Joe spoke to the men. "Forest, you've met Homer Manchester and Kate McAlester?" He already knew this, as he read the reports.

"Yes, I met them when they first arrived in Portland," Kline replied.

"I need to borrow your bible. I'm about to swear in Homer Manchester as a temporary deputy United States marshal. His first assignment will be Bull Blevins and his gang."

Chief Forest Kline pulled a bible from his desk and offered it to Joe.

He proceeded with the swearing in ceremony. Chief Joe then took a document from his pocket and handed it to Man. "Please read and sign this."

Joe watched Man read it, and then sign. Joe then offered it to Kline. "Forest, I need you and your men to sign this as witnesses that Homer Manchester is now officially a temporary deputy United States marshal. This will assure me that there's no misunderstanding between us. You will give Man your complete cooperation and support. Is that clear and understood, Chief Kline?"

Kline nodded without an expression. "Say it out loud so your deputies will understand how it is," Joe said. "I'm not in the mood to put up with a turf war between us. Apprehending Bull and his men are too important."

Kline said, "Deputy Marshal Homer Manchester will have our support and assistance as needed." He didn't put in the temporary; he suspected if Man proved to be capable, the job would be permanent. Almost all men in law enforcement go through the probationary period. Joe just used the word temporary, leaving him room to withdraw the appointment at any time. Man must prove himself first.

Chief Marshal Joe signed the document, and put it in his pocket. "I'll take it to the Governor for his signature. He read the reports and sent me to recruit Man. Leach and Vincent were a thorn in his side for ages."

He proceeded to pin a badge on Man.

Kate and Man followed Joe Meek outside.

"What do we do now?" Man asked.

"Tomorrow, or the next day, a marshal will be here. His name is Augustus Schweitzer, but few people know that, call him Gus. He has his orders to find and arrest or kill Bull Blevins, and his gang of cutthroats. You'll work with him. He'll be in charge, follow his orders."

"Gus is getting on in years," Joe added. He took a bullet in his leg from Bull and walks with a severe limp. That's one of the reasons I appointed you to work with him. He needs help on this one, and there were no deputies I could send. Gus has trouble writing detailed reports, but he's one of my best deputies. Watch and learn from Gus. I want you to send reports to this address. At times, I get a report from Gus that only says he's dead, or I got all of them. I want a few more details."

He handed Man a sheet of paper, and an identification card. "Use the telegraph if available. Make your reports short, but complete enough for me to know what happened, or is going on. Always include where you are and where you are going. If I need to tell you something, I can get the word to you. Always report to the locals you are in town and check the telegraph office."

Show your ID to any law enforcement person, and if they don't cooperate fully, notify me immediately. You're authorized to use any equipment, personnel, and jail for prisoners." He pulled a package from his saddlebags and handed it to Man.

"Handcuffs, but you must use your own weapons and supply your own ammunition. Where do you want your salary sent?"

"George Bowman, at The Fort," Man replied.

Joe touched spurs to his horse and turned toward the river and rode out of sight.

Kate looked at Man and almost giggled. She reached for his badge, looked at it a moment before blowing her breath on it, and polishing it with her sleeve.

"What now, Temporary Deputy United States Marshal Homer Manchester, Sir, and my partner?" she asked.

"Shall we go visit Fred first, partner? And then check on Reverend Powers and see if he's ready to perform the ceremony. We can marry, and then start our honeymoon you mentioned, going after Bill Blevins."

Kate playfully thumped him on his chest.

***

They found Fred in his bed propped up on pillows with Mary Ann feeding him with a spoon. She saw them and almost dropped the bowl of broth.

"What's that on your shirt?" she exclaimed. She put the bowl on a table and hurried to Man. "Fred," she said. "Man is a deputy United States marshal."

Lucy Lou had been reading a book, but put it down to look at the badge.

"Tell me about it," Fred said. "How did you get that honor?"

"A man named Joe Meek came to us," Kate said. "He asked Man if he would be a temporary deputy marshal, and asked me to partner with him. We went to the police station and he was sworn in. Our first assignment is Bull Blevins and his gang."

"Joe Meek," Fred said. "He's famous in Oregon. He's the chief United States marshal for all of the Oregon Territory. But how did he know about you two?"

"George Bowman sent part of the information to him, and the local police Chief Kline made reports," Kate said.

"Chief Joe said Marshal Augustus Schweitzer would be here tomorrow or the next day and we'll go with him after Bull and his men," Kate said.

"I want to find Reverend Powers and marry before he gets here," Man said. "If we rush off chasing Bull, we may not find another preacher if the trail leads us into the wilderness."

"Let me finish feeding Fred," Mary Ann said. "Then Lucy Lou and I'll go with you to Reverend Powers home. We have our buggy tied up behind the doctor's office."

As she fed Fred, Lucy Lou came to Man and gave him a hug. "Thank you for saving me," she said. "I was too scared to remember to thank you yesterday."

"I'm glad I was there," Man said. "I know it was a frightening experience for you."

"I couldn't see much," she said. "It happened so fast

and he had me over the front of the saddle with my head down, but I heard you shoot and he was thrown off the horse. I was so happy. I knew what happened, then you lifted me off the horse, and I knew I was safe when I saw that awful man on the ground."

Fred and Mary Ann were smiling as they listened to their daughter.

Chapter 5

Reverend Powers came to the door at Man's knock. His arm was in a sling. "Who is it?" a woman asked from the rear of the house as she came through a door wiping her hands on a towel.

"It's Mary Ann, Lucy Lou, and the man that saved Lucy Lou. You saw them at the church. Homer Manchester and Kate McAlaster, the couple that want me to marry them."

"I'm Grace Powers," she said. "I was so busy at the church, I didn't have time to meet you, but I witnessed what you did. We all thank you."

"It's nice to meet you, Grace," Kate said.

"When do you want the ceremony?" Powers asked.

"As soon as possible, and you're able," Kate said. "We're expecting a U.S. marshal, and we may be on the move in a hurry. We have an assignment.

Both the preacher and Grace saw the badge on Man's shirt for the first time. It had been hidden by his coat.

"I didn't know you were a marshal," Powers said.

"He wasn't until a short while ago," Kate replied. "Chief Marshal Joe Meek swore him in just a few minutes ago."

"Congratulations Marshal Manchester. Would two o'clock be alright?" Powers asked.

"Yes," Man and Kate replied as one.

"I was hoping we could have a more formal wedding for them," Mary Ann said. "Maybe we can round up a few of the congregation to be there. Kate, I'll meet you at the church at one to help you dress."

***

Man and Kate went back to the hotel and Man stretched out on the bed and watched Kate. She was busy arranging their clothing. "In case we have to leave suddenly, I'll have everything ready to pack and load," she said.

A knock startled them. Man hurried to the door. One of the local policemen was at the door. "Chief Kline needs you at the police station immediately," he said. He turned and almost ran from the hotel.

Kate frowned. Man said, "Damn, not again."

Since they didn't know what to expect, they changed into their working skins, buckled their Walkers around their waist, put their rifles under their arm, and went to saddle the horses.

Chief Kline met them on the porch of the police station. "We just got a report that Knox was in town vowing to kill the men that murdered his wife and son. I have only one policeman on duty that's available. The others are on assignment and it would take too long to get them back here. Will you side us?"

"Of course," Man replied. "Do you know where to start?"

"I was advised somebody mentioned the two horses fitting the description of the horses stolen from him were seen at Bingham Brothers Stable. I hope that is where he went and we can get there in time to stop him from being killed."

The four mounted and rode to the stable as fast as they could on the crowded streets. "Take the back," Chief Kline said. "We'll give you time to get in place, and we'll go in at the same time."

Kate and Man spurred their horses, circled behind the stable, and hurried to the back door. Man peeked through a crack. "I can see inside, it's dark, but I see three men."

They pulled their pistols and waited for Kline and his deputy to enter the front door.

"Now," Man said when he saw Kline open the door. He pushed the rear door open and hurried inside with Kate close behind. As soon as Man was inside, he stepped to the right, Kate went to the left.

The three men saw Kline, jerked their pistols, and fired. One of the policemen went down with a bullet through his arm. Kline leaped behind a stack of hay. Man shouted, "I'm a deputy marshal, throw down the weapons. You're under arrest."

The three men turned trying to sight their pistols on them. Man and Kate fired as one. Two men went down as bullets ripped through their chest. The other scrambled for cover, but Kline was ready and fired. The man sprawled on the floor with a bullet through his heart.

Man and Kate hurried to the supine men and kicked their weapons away. One was alive.

Kline rushed forward and searched him. He took another pistol from the wounded man's pocket as well as a skinning knife. "We need to get my man, and this scum, to the doctor," he said. The policeman was standing, holding his arm. The bullet went through the fleshy part of his upper arm between his elbow and shoulder. The wound wasn't serious.

"I wonder why they started shooting," Kline said. "Apparently Knox isn't here."

"But, for whatever reason, they started it," Man said. "I see a wagon." He hurried to harness a team. Kate followed Man to help and heard a moan. She walked to an empty stall and saw a man on the floor. She hurried to him and knelt down. It was too dark in the stall to identify him.

"Man," she shouted. "Help me. A man is here."

Kline and Man hurried to her. Together, they pulled the man from the stall. As soon as they could see, Kate exclaimed. "It's Melvin Knox."

Knox had a long gash on the back of his head, and his arms and legs were bound. Man pulled his knife, cut the rope, and Kate found a water bucket and wet a towel. She bathed Melvin's face and neck with the cool water until Knox opened his eyes.

He immediately started swinging his fist. "Calm down," Man said. "It's Man and Kate. The men that did this are either dead, or in custody."

Comprehension gradually returned. "What hit me?" he asked.

Kate was still bathing his neck and face with the wet towel. "We found you tied in a horse stall," she said.

"I remember now," he said. "I walked into the stable, and recognized my two horses. I was standing there petting them when everything went blank."

"You have a heck of a gash on your head," Man said. "I expect one of them bashed your head with something hard. We need to get you to the doctor. We have two wounded men to take as well."

"Is it one of the Bingham brothers?" Melvin Knox asked.

"Yes," Chief Kline said. "Thaddeus was wounded. Hector and Abner are dead."

"I hope Thad dies as well," Melvin said. "They knew those horses belonged to me. When we came to Portland, we stabled them here. I saw somebody altered my brand. What about my Chestnut? He wasn't here."

"We suspect Bull or one of his men are riding him," Man said.

"We can talk about this later," Kline said. "We need to get them to the doctor's office."

***

The Doctor examined Knox, gave him pain medication, and released him. "Be careful for a few days. You have a slight concussion, but you'll be okay, just take it easy."

They waited for the doctor to examine the wounded policeman. He cleaned the wound, and put in a few stitches to close the gash. A nurse bandaged the arm, and helped the policeman put it in a sling.

Thad Bingham was next. The doctor looked at the wound and motioned for them to follow him outside.

"The wound did a lot of internal damage. I'm not skilled enough to repair the organs. It's only a matter of time. He's hemorrhaging inside and I can't stop it. I expect him to expire within a few minutes."

"Good," Melvin said.

"When you're able, come to the police station," Kline

said. "We need to fill out reports on the incident."

"When can I get my two horses?" Knox asked.

"Probably, it will be tomorrow, or the next day, it's dependent on the judge. Why do you want them so fast?"

"I'm riding a mule, and I want the two horses to find Bull and his gang. They murdered my wife and son, but then you know that."

"Let us handle it," Man said. He showed Melvin his badge. "Another marshal will be here soon, and we're going after the Blevins gang."

"I'm going with you," Knox said. "I have nothing to live for now. I gave my place to Lucas Musick and his wife Richelle, that is, if I don't go back."

"You do have something to live for," Kate said. "I know it's hard for you now. I lost my mom and dad, but life goes on. It'll take time, but there may be another woman come into your life. She may never replace Rachel, and your son can never be replaced. But, in time, you may have more children. You're young enough to start over. Don't sacrifice your life. Let us take the Blevins gang down."

"I'm going after them, with or without you," Knox said.

***

They walked out of the doctor's office. "What time is it?" Man asked.

Kline looked at his pocket watch. "Two-thirty," he said.

Kate and Man raced to where their horses were tied. "We were going to be married at two," Man shouted over his shoulder.

They found several people at the church when they dismounted. "We heard about the shooting at Bingham's Stable," one of the men said. "Is it true you killed two of them and Kline got the other?"

Man nodded. "I'm sorry we're late for the ceremony, but Chief Kline asked us to assist in the arrest."

Mary Ann grabbed Kate by the hand and she and

Lucy Lou hurried her inside with three women following.

"Are you going to marry dressed like that?" Powers asked.

"My marrying clothes are at the hotel. I don't see that I have a choice."

Grace Powers stepped forward and reached for his hand. "Come with me. You're larger than my husband, but you would look better than wearing skins."

When he came back, he was wearing black pants that were ankle high and unbuttoned at the waist. The coat was much too tight, but he left it unbuttoned. The white shirt was so tight, the buttons were about to pop across his massive chest. But, at least, he wasn't wearing mountain man skins.

Mary Ann led Kate out wearing the wedding dress. She was beautiful. She saw Man and wanted to chuckle, but held it in check. After all, she was about to marry and agreed, he looked better than before.

The small group followed the bride and groom into the sanctuary. Suddenly, the door opened and Melvin Knox and Chief Kline walked in.

"We decided to come to the wedding," Kline said. He and Knox hurried to a seat.

Reverend Powers and Mary Ann placed Man and Kate in position. The preachers arm was still in a sling, but he managed to open the Bible to the proper place.

Mary Ann and Lucy Lou were standing on Kate's side, and one of the men was standing on Man's side.

"Do you have a ring?" he asked.

Man pulled his wallet from the pants, searched inside, and handed a ring to him.

Kate was watching, wondering where he got it. Since they met, he hadn't been any place to buy one that she wasn't at his side.

Reverend Powers started the ceremony. A man opened the door and stepped inside. Everybody stopped to look. Kate and Man recognized him from Chief Marshal Joe Meek's description. It was Marshal Gus.

He recognized what was happening, removed his fur cap, and took a seat beside Chief Kline.

Powers continued with the ceremony. Both said, "I do," and Man took the ring, placed it on Kate's finger, and then kissed her.

He smiled and said, "Finally. Hello, Mrs. Homer Manchester."

Kate kissed him again.

The guests were waiting to congratulate the happy couple. Gus was the last in the line. He took Man by the hand, and then reached for Kate. "I'm Deputy Marshal Augustus Schweitzer. They told me at the police station where to find you two. I hate to rush you, but we need to get moving. I have a lead on where Bull and his gang are hiding out."

Kate rushed toward the room for her clothing with Mary Ann following. Grace led Man to their home to change into his skins.

They met and hurried to where their horses were tied. They saw Chief Kline with Knox, restraining him from following. "You would only be in the way, and probably get yourself killed, or cause one of them to be injured or killed trying to protect you. You're going with me, even if I have to put cuffs on you."

They killed my wife and son," Knox protested.

Gus swung up on a big gray gelding, and spurred into a lope. Kate and Man followed staying close behind.

Man looked back and saw Kline and Knox riding the other way, back to the police station."

Gus pulled back on the reins and waited for Man and Kate to join him. "Joe got a wire from one of his contacts that Bull is hiding out in a cabin belonging to a cousin or some kin. From what I learned, that's it below us, near the river."

He pulled field glasses from his saddlebag and looked at the house. Man did the same. "No horses in the lot," Gus said.

"No smoke from the chimney either," Man added.

"They're not here now. I expect they have moved out. I'm sure everybody in town heard about the shooting at Bingham's Stable. They may have decided Portland wasn't safe anymore. I'm sure the Bingham brothers knew where they were holed up, and Bull was afraid they would talk."

Deputy Gus nodded agreement, touched spurs to his horse, and led the way down toward the cabin. He pulled his pistol and dismounted. He gestured toward the two sides with his left hand. Kate went to the left and Man to the right with Walkers in their hand as a precaution.

Gus opened the door and quickly moved to the side in case somebody fired. However, the cabin was dark. He stepped in swinging his pistol from side to side in case somebody was there. Man and Kate followed him as he went deeper into the cabin.

Kate saw a lamp on the table and lit it so they could see. Five bunks were against the wall with a table in the middle. Nothing else of importance was in the cabin. Whoever was living here was gone.

Gus knelt and felt the ashes in the fireplace. "Cold," he said. "I suspect the last fire was yesterday, or before. I can't tell."

They walked outside and Gus went to the lot and examined the horse droppings. "Yesterday," he said.

"What now?" Kate asked.

"Go to the hotel, and I'll get a room. There's no need knocking ourselves out when we don't know which way they went. We have to wait until we get a lead. I'll send Joe Meek a report, and he'll wire us when something breaks."

Man was grinning. She saw and returned a smile. The hotel would be better than sleeping on the cold ground tonight. After all, this is their wedding night.

Gus saw their exchange. "I'll see you two for breakfast."

As soon as they were in the hotel room, Kate examined the wedding ring on her finger. "It's so beautiful," she exclaimed. "But where did you get it? We haven't been apart since we got to Portland."

He pulled her close and kissed her upturned lips. "It belonged to my mother. I took it after I found her body. She had hidden it in her shoe. She knew the Yankee soldiers would take it."

***

It was late in the morning before Kate and Man went to the café to eat. Gus wasn't there, but that was expected. He probably ate a couple of hours before.

They were finishing their third cup of coffee after eating when Gus limped in, smiling, but didn't make a comment about them being late.

"Nothing from Joe as yet," he offered. "I went by the police station and Chief Kline had a policeman take Knox to the edge of town and watch until Melvin was out of sight. Kline got his two horses released and Knox rode one, he led the other and mule he rode in. I think he finally got the message he wasn't going after Bull, and went home where he belongs."

Kate and Man nodded they were happy at the news.

Gus gestured at the waitress for a cup of coffee. Man waited until Gus took his first sip of the hot coffee before speaking. "Kate saw a pile of furs at Ace Harpers warehouse," Man said. "She couldn't identify them as belonging to George Bowman, but I was thinking. I sold my furs to George the day before the robbery. I could identify mine, if that would be beneficial. If mine are in that pile, it would be a proof they came from George."

Gus finished his coffee in one gulp and stood.

Kate and Man hurried to the front to pay, and followed Gus outside. His gray gelding was tied at the hitching rail. "Our horses are behind the hotel," Man said.

"I'll go with you to get them," Gus said.

As they walked to the stable behind the hotel, Kate whispered, "Gus is a man of few words."

Man nodded agreement.

Chapter 6

Kate and Man rode on either side of Gus as he made his way to the warehouse belonging to Ace Harper. "How do we handle it?" Kate asked. "When I went in before asking for information, I saw a short man, I don't know if that was Ace, or a man that works there."

"It wasn't Ace," Gus replied. "Ace is tall and thin."

"It's possible anybody there will recognize us," Man said. "Since we've been in Portland, we've seen and met a lot of people. Too many people know about us with the attempted kidnapping of Lucy Lou and the shooting at Bingham's Stable. Every time we go out wearing our working skins with the Walkers, people stop to stare."

"They'll know me on sight," Gus said. "I've had several run-ins with Ace. Side me and we'll walk in and see if the furs are still there. If they are, Man look through them, and if you can identify yours, I'll place Ace under arrest for having stolen property. Be cautious and ready, Ace may choose to fight rather than go back to jail. He spent several years in prison and has vowed he would never go back."

They checked their weapons and Gus led the way inside. Kate looked and pointed at the place where the furs were located. They were gone. The three searched the warehouse with their eyes and saw no evidence of the stolen furs.

Gus turned and walked out without anybody seeing them. He swung up on his gelding, touched spurs to the sides of the horse, and rode away with Man and Kate in his wake.

He stopped when he was out of sight of the warehouse. "Ace has already sold them. My first guess would be to the Hudson Bay Fur Company. Let's go there next. However, finding your furs with the others may prove difficult. I expect they were separated into categories as soon as they arrived."

A large woman with her hair pulled back in a tight bun was seated at a desk and greeted them. "Hello Gus," she said, when he walked through the door.

"Hello, Fanny Mae, I'm here to look at the furs you bought from Ace Harper. We think they were stolen from George Bowman."

Fanny Mae stood and gestured toward chairs. "I'll go get Bernard."

She hurried through a door located behind her desk. Kate and Man went to the chairs to wait, but Gus quickly walked behind Fanny Mae's desk and began looking at papers stacked in a neat pile. He shuffled them quickly and picked up a sheet and read. A smile crossed his face and he gave Man and Kate a nod of satisfaction, but didn't explain what he found.

He heard people approaching. He put the paper in his pocket and hurried to where Man and Kate were seated. "I found the invoice," he said. "I was right. Ace sold the furs to Hudson Bay."

"Do we need to be ready for a battle?" Kate asked.

"Naw, Bernard is a pussycat and may wet his pants when I accuse him of buying stolen property."

Bernard came through the door with a frown on his face. Gus stood to meet him.

"Fanny Mae tells me you think we bought stolen furs from Ace Harper."

"I know you did," Gus said. "Don't bother to deny it. I found the invoice on Fanny's desk. You paid Ace two thousand, about two-thirds of the value. You knew they were stolen property. Otherwise Ace wouldn't have had them. He's not a fur buyer and you know it."

Bernard was grimacing, and shifting from one foot to the other. Fanny Mae was looking at the floor, not meeting the gaze of Gus, Man, and Kate.

"Ace brought the furs in early this morning," Bernard explained. "He said he bought them from a trapper. I examined them and asked what he wanted for them. He told me and I bought them. Besides, how do you know they belonged to George Bowman?"

Gus gestured toward Man. "He sold his furs to George at The Fort. That night, Bull Blevins, and his gang stole the furs and four wagons from George and shot him during the robbery. We found the wagons behind Bingham Brothers Stable. Man can identify the furs he sold to George. Show us the furs you bought."

"I can't do that, they're already separated and mixed with other furs."

Gus reached for Bernard and marched him through the door to the warehouse. Man and Kate stood and followed.

They saw several large containers with furs separated by kind and quality. "Look around, and see if you see any of yours," Gus said.

Man went to a container and quickly sifted through them. He held up a pelt. "This is one of mine. My skinning technique is different from most. I sold it to George Bowman. I can stand in court and swear this was one of my pelts I sold to George Bowman. And, that it was with the others that were stolen."

"That's all I need," Gus said. "A jury will buy that as proof Bernard purchased stolen property. I'll get a warrant and shut this warehouse down until the trial. I expect Hudson Bay can open for business again in about three or four months. But, you'll be in prison Bernard."

Bernard's face paled and he coughed as sweat popped out on his face. "Gus, be reasonable. I run a business here. Hudson Bay will fire me, and they have enough money to fight this in court. Let me make you an offer. I'll pay George Bowman a fair price, and swallow the loss of what I paid Ace."

"A fair price plus twenty percent for his anguish," Gus demanded.

Bernard gasped, but nodded. He knew he was in a tight spot and Gus had him by the shorthairs. Gus had the upper hand in this negotiation and Bernard knew he held a losing hand.

Gus pulled the invoice from his pocket and sat behind Fanny May's desk and compared the prices paid for similar furs from the other invoices on the desk. He began to write numbers on the page.

He finished and handed the figure to Bernard. He started to protest at the amount. "This is outrageous," he moaned.

Gus pulled his handcuffs from his belt and reached for Bernard's wrist. The fur buyer jerked his hands back and quickly agreed with the amount as being fair. Gus led him to the desk and waited. Bernard signed a voucher and told Fanny Mae to write a check payable to George Bowman. Bernard gave her the invoice where Gus made the calculation. "For this amount," he said.

Gus took the check and turned to Bernard. "If I ever have to come back because you purchased stolen furs, you won't get another chance. You'll be frog-marched in cuffs to the jail for everybody in Portland to witness you being arrested. Hudson Bay will have the reputation of being another Ace Harper and fur dealers will find other places to sell their pelts. I expect Hudson Bay will find another manager for this buying station when that news spreads. Do I make myself clear?"

Bernard was pale and nodding his head vigorously. Sweat was now dripping from his nose and his shirt was wet.

"I'll never buy anything from Ace again," Bernard said.

"Or from anybody else where you have the slightest suspicion they are stolen," Gus added. He turned to Fanny Mae. "I can also take you in as an accessory. Should Bernard have a relapse when greed gets the best of him, it will be your duty to remind him that buying stolen furs will get both of you thrown in jail."

He had both of their attention.

Man and Kate followed Gus out the door and mounted without another word being spoken. Gus pulled to a stop when they were out of sight of the warehouse.

"Bernard was right. Hudson Bay would have beaten it in court. They have too much money, and getting a conviction would have been slim to none. This way, right prevailed, and you can bet ol' Barney and Fanny Mae learned a lesson. He'll never knowingly buy stolen furs again. There's no proof Ace bought stolen furs. He got by this time, but his operation will be under surveillance, and we'll get him sooner or later."

Kate and Man were smiling, they were learning from Gus. The more they knew about this man, the better they liked him.

"What now?" Man asked.

"I'm going by the telegraph office to see if we have anything from Joe on the whereabouts of Bull. I'll send him a report the Bowman part of the case was resolved. Then I need a bath, shave, and haircut. The coffee I had earlier is gone, and I'll find a place to eat. Where will you be if I need you?"

"At the hotel," Man said.

"You want more private time with your beautiful bride," Gus teased.

"Yes," Kate said. "My husband's wife needs some loving," she said without blinking.

Gus cackled at her remark. "Damn Man, you picked a fine woman to marry. And I saw her shoot those Walkers she carries on her hips. Kate's a keeper."

He reached in his pocket for the check Bernard gave him. "What can I do with this? We need to get it to George. And his wagons and mules that are at Bingham's stable?"

"I'll take the check to the bank," Man said. "I expect George has an account here as he purchases and sells here in Portland. I'll make arrangements to get the wagons back to The Fort. I expect Fred Morgan can help with that. He knows everybody and owns a store. He'll know where to get drivers for the wagons."

"Do it first. You two may take too long at the hotel, and we may be on the move if Joe has any information for us. If you go to the hotel first, Kate may not let you out of bed in time to get to the bank, or pick up the wagons."

She playfully punched Gus in the stomach as she chuckled. "You may be right," she said with a teasing chuckle.

They stopped at the bank and talked to the president. He allowed George Bowman had an account and deposited the check for them. He had heard about the robbery and shooting, and asked the condition of George.

Next, they went to visit Fred. He was seated in a chair when they entered. Lucy Lou and Mary Ann weren't there and Fred was glad to see them. He asked Man to help him back to the bed. "I asked Mary Ann to get me something to eat, and thought I could sit up until she returned, but I was wrong. My wound is hurting sitting up."

Man and Kate helped him and waited until he relaxed. It hurt more when he moved.

"I've been asked by Deputy Marshal Gus to get George's four wagons back to The Fort," Man said. "Do you know anybody I could hire to drive them? I think the two empty wagons could be hitched together, and would need only two drivers. The extra teams could be led behind the wagons."

"I'll see to it," Fred said. "As soon as Mary Ann gets here, I'll have her send for Alfonzo; he works for me from time to time. I'm sure he and his son would like to drive the wagons home. I sometimes send him and his boy to Seattle for supplies. He's a good man with stock, conscientious, and will get the wagons safely back to George."

Man reached into his pocket and gave Fred the deposit receipt. "Have Alfonzo give this to George. It's for the sale of his furs to Hudson Bay. Ace sold them to Hudson, but Gus negotiated with Bernard and got the money for the furs."

Fred asked, "How did Gus ever get money out of Bernard? He's as tight as the bark on a tree."

Man let Kate tell him what happened.

He laughed at the way Gus handled Bernard.

"Keep that between us," Man said.

"I can keep my mouth shut," Fred said. "And I won't tell Mary Ann."

"Won't tell me what?" Mary Ann asked as she and Lucy Lou came through the door with two sacks of food.

"That I said you are an Angel to take care of me while I'm in bed," Fred said.

She accepted it with a frown, knowing Fred was fibbing.

Kate greeted Mary Ann and Lucy Lou with a hug as a greeting. "We have to go," Kate said. "We stopped by to tell you and Fred that we'll be on the move soon. We're waiting for a wire from Joe Meek on the location of Bull. When it comes, we'll be hitting the trail with Gus."

Man and Kate went to the police station. Chief Kline was seated at his desk and stood when Man and Kate came in.

"We came by to tell you the Bowman robbery has been resolved by Gus," Man said. "Ace sold the stolen furs to Hudson Bay, but Gus got the money for them from Bernard. I deposited it at the bank in George's account."

"How did he manage that?" Chief Kline asked. "I mean, how did Gus get anything from Bernard?"

Kate went through the brief description and Kline laughed.

Fred Morgan is arranging for Alfonzo and his son to take the wagons back to The Fort."

"Al can pick them up here when he is ready to leave," Kline said.

"Anything more on Knox," Kate asked.

"Nope, after he was read the riot act and assured he would spend a few days behind bars if he attempted to interfere, he went toward home. My man watched and Knox didn't turn back. He left Portland."

"Thanks," Kate said. "He needed to go home and

start over. Time will make it easier on him. I know his cabin will be lonesome, but he has friends close to help him through this tough time."

Chapter 7

George Bowman was seated on the porch of the store when he saw four wagons enter the gate at The Fort. He yelled for Maude. She came to the front and saw the wagons.

"Ain't those our wagons?" he asked. "I can't see too well with the evening sun in my face."

Maude was holding her hand to shade her eyes staring at the wagons approaching. "It's them," Maude said. "But who's driving?"

The first wagon stopped in front of the store and Alfonzo jumped down and walked toward the older couple waiting in front of the store. "I'm looking for George Bowman," he said.

"You found him mister," George replied. "I see you brought my wagons home, which were stolen. I'm anxious to hear about it."

A young man joined Alfonzo holding his hat in his hand. "My name is Alfonzo, and this is my son, Al Junior. A man by the name of United States Marshal Homer Manchester paid us to bring the wagons to you. Man, as he's called, sent this to you." He reached into his pocket and handed George a receipt for the deposit at the bank.

Maude leaned over her husband's shoulder to read and gasped. "It's for the sale of the furs that were stolen from me when they took the wagons," George said.

"I know," Alfonzo said, "from what I heard. Man and his wife, Kate took down the Bingham Brothers in a gunfight. That's where your wagons and teams were found. They recovered your wagons and located the stolen furs in Ace Harper's warehouse, but by the time they went to recover them, they had been sold to Hudson Bay. A couple of marshals went there and Bernard paid you for the stolen furs. That's the money Man put in the bank in Portland for you."

"Did you say Kate and Man married?" Maude asked.

"Yes ma'am, at the church there in Portland. Fred and Mary Ann Morgan arranged the wedding. I work for Fred. That's how I'm delivering your wagons, Fred sent Man to me."

"Where do you want the wagons and teams? Me and my boy will put them away for you. Man said you were shot during the holdup."

"In the warehouse, turn the mules loose in the lot, and if you would, toss hay in the rack, and give them a ration of oats. I'm not up to taking care of them as yet."

"Do you intend to go back today?" Maude asked.

"Yes ma'am, we need to get back. Fred was shot and he needs me."

"How was he shot?" Fred asked.

"A man was kidnapping their daughter, Lucy Lou. Fred and Reverend Powers attempted to stop him, and both were shot. Man went after the kidnapper and knocked him right out of the saddle with a head shot. The kidnapper had Lucy Lou over the front of his saddle trying to get away, but he wasn't fast enough to escape Man's bullet."

"You said that Man is a deputy United States marshal," George said.

"Yes ma'am, Chief Marshal Joe Meek came to Portland and swore him in. From what Fred said, another marshal named Gus, plus Man and Kate, are going after Bull Blevins and his gang."

"Bull is the outlaw that shot me and stole my furs," George said.

"So I was told," Alfonzo said. "Man and Kate must be good friends of yours."

"They are," Maude said. "You and Junior put the wagons away and come inside. I know you must be hungry; you had hard days on the trail to get here. I'll have a hot meal on the table by the time you finish."

Junior was nodding his head.

As they were eating, George asked, "You said Man paid you to drive the wagons here. I need to know how much. It ain't right for him to foot that bill."

"He gave me and Al Junior twelve dollars each. He was very generous, and we needed it. It was a hard winter, and I didn't get in much work for Fred."

"From the talk around Portland," Al said, "that couple is making a name for themselves, especially that Kate. She's the brains and wears those two Walker Colts on her hips. From the talk, she can shoot faster and better than that deputy marshal she married."

Maude walked out and watched the two men ride out the gate. She went back inside and found George on the bed. "Did you see the amount Man sold the furs for?" he asked.

"I saw, isn't it more than you said they were worth?"

"From what I figure, it's about twenty percent more than I expected. I wonder how Man and Kate pulled that off from Bernard at Hudson Bay. Bernard is as tight as Dick's hatband."

***

Gus banged on Man and Kate's door the next morning early. "It's time to move out. Get packed and load your mules. I'll meet you at the café in an hour. I'll have grub ordered for us. Take warm clothes, we're headed into the mountains."

Gus was waiting when Kate and Man walked in the café wearing their skins with their Walkers on their hips. Both brought their rifle inside, rather than leave them on the horses tied to the hitching rail. Everybody looked up and watched the pair walk to Gus.

"I already ordered a big breakfast. You two had better eat hardy, we'll noon on the go. We have a lot of ground to cover today."

A pot of coffee was on the table. Kate poured for them and they quickly had food in front of them.

Gus finished first, paid, and went out to his gray gelding and swung up. He had a loaded pack mule behind him. Kate and Man wolfed down the remaining breakfast and followed Gus. Man led their two mules. People lined the street to watch as the trio rode down Clay Street.

Somebody said, "When those marshals and Kate find Bull Blevins and his gang, I would like to be perched on a limb watching the battle. Bullets will be flying. It'll be three against five, but my money is on the marshals and Kate. I heard one of the policeman say that Kate was firing those twin Walkers with both hands faster than the eye could see when they took down the Bingham's."

Gus turned his horse and followed a road parallel to the Willamette River until they were out of Portland. He pulled back on the reins of his gray horse and stepped down and stretched his back and legs. Kate and Man dismounted and stood beside him under a huge tree.

"Bull was sighted at Washougal," Gus said. "A local lawman sent a telegram to Joe. The word is out all over the territory to be on the lookout for the gang. The local didn't make contact. He's the only policeman there, and the five Blevins were heavily armed. Bull is riding a Chestnut horse with a blaze face."

"That would be the horse they stole from Melvin Knox," Kate offered.

"I expect you're right," Gus said. "What's worrying me, where are they going? There's a lot of unsettled wilderness in that direction. They must have a destination in mind. I would have thought they would have gone to Seattle, or on to Vancouver. They have money in their pocket after selling the mules, horses, wagons, and furs."

"Do they know you're after them?" Kate asked. "They could be trying to lose you off their trail."

"I'm sure they know," Gus said. "They have contacts and family around Portland. I suspect almost everybody heard about us, and Bull would suspect that Joe sent me after them. I owe him one." He tapped his gimpy leg. "Bull ambushed me, and put a slug through my leg. It broke the bone and it wasn't set right. Every change of the weather, I sure feel it."

"He may be setting up an ambush for us again," Man offered. "If he suspects we're on his tail, that would be his style, shoot from ambush. Any man that kills a woman and child has no conscious or moral fiber. He ambushed the posse that went after him after he stole the wagons, and shot George and the preacher in cold blood. Neither was armed."

"From this point on, keep distance between us," Gus said. "If they shoot from ambush, we don't need to be bunched together."

He mounted and took the point as they followed the road. Kate stayed on the left as far from Gus as the trees allowed. Man was doing the same on the right.

They rode into Washougal without incident. A man with a badge on his vest stepped from an office and walked out to meet them. He had an old .45 on his hip.

"Hello Gus," he said.

"Hello Elmo, the wire didn't give the name of the man that spotted Bull, but thanks for the lead. What can you tell us?"

"Come inside out of the wind. With the sun about gone, it's a little nippy out here. I have a warm office and a fire burning."

The three followed Elmo into the office and saw chairs around a wood stove. The heat was welcome to the riders.

"Elmo Stoddard," Gus said, "meet Homer and Kate Manchester. Man is a new deputy marshal. Joe put him on to go with me after Bull. This is his first official assignment, but he has experience, besides he rode with Jake and Slats on the Trail a few times."

Elmo offered his hand to shake with Man and Kate. He offered cups and poured coffee from a gallon pot on the stove.

"I was outside of town investigating an incident between two lumberjacks and saw Bull and four others on the road. I recognized him right off. I had dealings with him before. He didn't see me though. If he had, I expect we wouldn't be having this conversation. Anyway, I tailed them keeping well back. They went to an abandoned cabin about a half mile from here. They knew where they were going. I watched for a while, and saw they put their horses in a lean-to and saw smoke from the chimney. I hurried back and sent the wire."

"Are they still there?" Gus asked.

"I rode out and checked this morning, and again an hour ago. The horses are still there, but I didn't see nobody. I wasn't about to go knocking on the door."

"We have time before dark," Gus said. "Maybe we can end it here and get back to Portland tomorrow."

Gus led the way and mounted. Elmo went around the back of the police station and met them on his horse. He took the lead with Gus, Man, and Kate behind.

Elmo reigned in and waited for the others to stop at his side before speaking. "The cabin is just around the bend. I suggest we split up and each of us take a side. If they bust out, they could go in any direction. It could be five against one, but I don't recommend riding up to the front of the cabin. They'll start shooting the second they spot us."

Gus took charge. "Kate to the right, Man the left, Elmo the rear and I'll be in front. Take cover, and I'll bring them out. Elmo and Man, find a place so you can see the horses. That'll be the first place they go. I'll be in position to cover it as well. "Kate I expect if they get the horses, they'll run in your direction, so find good cover, and be ready.

Man and Kate pulled their second rifles out and left the other in the scabbard. Elmo eyes the rifles.

"Aren't they the new Winchester Model 1873 rifles? I saw one in Seattle."

"We each have two," Man said proudly. "Smooth as silk action and more accurate than any rifle I've ever fired."

"How come you have two each?" Gus asked.

"We bought them from George Bowman at The Fort. He had four and Kate and I have been in scrapes when the need for more firepower was needed."

"I also saw both of you are wearing twin Walker Colts," Elmo said. "How did you afford such expensive weapons?"

"We picked them up along the way. The men using them had no more need of them, and they would have rusted away if we left them on the bodies."

"Anybody I know?" Elmo asked.

"Truman Vincent and Bedford Leach were two of them," Man replied.

"You took down those slave traders," Elmo exclaimed.

"We had help from Indians," Kate said.

"Get in position," Gus said. "You can talk later, and it'll be dark soon. When I think you've had enough time to be ready, I'll start it."

Gus sat on his horse and waited until he was sure the others were in place, then urged his gray to walk forward, slowly. He had his rifle ready. The moment he was in sight of the cabin, he pulled up and dismounted and went behind a tree.

"Give it up," he shouted. "Bull, we have the cabin surrounded."

"The horses are gone," Elmo shouted. "I have a good view of the lot."

"Damn," Gus said. "Cover me, I'm going to the cabin."

He worked his way forward, keeping close to cover in case it was an ambush. He pushed the cabin door open and it was dark inside. He stuck his head through the door, and jerked it back quickly. Nothing happened, he stepped inside. The cabin was empty.

He walked out where Man and Elmo could see him. "Empty," he said. Kate came from the back of the cabin. "I saw tracks going east," she said.

She and Man went for their horses. Elmo was taking with Gus in front of the cabin. "Thanks for your help," Gus said. "We're going after them. Wire Joe Meek and give him a report on what we found here. If you learn

94

anything more, let Joe know, and he'll get it to us."

Elmo nodded and watched Gus leading the way following the trail of Bull and his gang.

"My old eyes ain't what they once was," Gus said. "Man will you take the point and follow them? It will be too dark in a few more minutes, but we can be on their trail."

"Check out places for an ambush," Kate warned. "I'll be close watching as well." She rode to his right side and focused on every possible ambush site. Gus was off the left, leading the pack mules.

"Too darn easy to follow their trail," Man said. "Either they don't care, or don't know we're back here. As long as Bull has been riding the outlaw trail, I would think he would check his back."

"Hopefully, just cocky," Gus said. "But, that worries me as well. He knows me too well and knows Joe and me won't give up."

"Bull didn't last this long being careless," Kate put in. "I have an uneasy feeling in my gut. I think we're riding into an ambush. There are too many places to hide in the trees and rocks. We could ride into five rifles and wouldn't know until they fired. We would all be dead before we heard them. Remember the posse from The Fort rode into an ambush."

"What are you suggesting?" Man asked.

"It's too dark now for us to see," she said. "We need to get off the trail and find a place for the night. Early tomorrow morning, we circle around and pick up their trail up again. If we can't find it, we ride back this way and surprise them from behind. That worked well with the slave traders."

Gus listened to what Kate said. "I agree, it's getting late in the day, if they have an ambush in mind, they'll know we packed it in for the night and be ready tomorrow. I hope they are not far in front of us, you can take them from the rear, and I'll have the front."

"I don't think we would have to ride more than three

or four miles," Kate said. If we find their tracks, we go on, if we don't, we set up a surprise for Bull and his men."

Gus nodded agreement and they rode almost a half mile off the trail and found a place to spend the night. "I'll take the first watch," he said. "Divide the night into three parts." He rode several yards to a large bolder and climbed on top. Kate took a couple of extra blankets from the mule and tossed them to him. "It'll get cold there tonight."

***

They sat eating a cold breakfast as a fire might attract attention from Bull. Gus stood and stretched his aching back. "I thought about it during the night. I'm for going on. In these mountains, the odds of one or two of us making a circle and finding their trail again would be difficult. If you lost it, and had to come back here, we would lose half a day."

"We would lose a lot more than half a day if they catch us in the open," Kate said. "We could lose our lives."

"Point well taken," Gus said. "I know you two are rookies, but from the reports, you didn't take out Vincent and Leach by doing stupid things. But, we need to close the gap. I think they have a destination in mind and are going to be moving on. I think Bull knows he can stay well in front of us, that is, if he knows we're back here."

Since Gus was in charge, neither Man nor Kate offered an objection.

They rode back to the trail and started following the tracks again. Man was riding point and stopped Arabian under a tree after three hours on the trail. He waited for the other two to come to him. "What do you propose?" Gus asked.

"I've seen one set of tracks veer off the trail and go to a likely ambush site. On three occasions, they did that, but each time the tracks come back to join the others. In my opinion, Bull is looking for the right place."

"I recommend we do it this time," Kate said. "Man

96

and I can make a circle as we discussed, you wait here. We'll come back and meet you if I'm wrong. But, if you hear shooting, charge from this side, and we'll have them caught in a crossfire between us."

"You have a devious mind Kate. But, I like your style. "I'll be waiting here, ready, if you start it from their backside. If not, we can move on again. I know this area, circle to your right on the trail around a hill, the trail they are on goes to the left of it. When you get to the other side, turn back west and you'll pick up this trail. I think it's no more than two miles."

Man turned Arabian and Kate urged Redbird to his side. It was easy riding and they spurred the horses into a lope. They were both anxious for the run and covered the ground in a hurry. When the terrain worsened, they pulled the horses back to a trot. There was no need of risking injury by one of the horses falling.

They circled the hill as Gus suggested and quickly found the trail they had been on and Man stepped down to look. "I see tracks of horses, but they are older. Bull didn't pass this way. Hopefully, we have them between us."

Man mounted and pulled his rifle and jacked a bullet into the chamber, and added another so he would have a full magazine. Kate did the same. He pulled his spare rifle and did the same with it and dropped it into the scabbard. If the need for extra firepower were needed, he would have the second rifle ready for action.

Kate was busy doing the same with her two rifles. They spread out and carried their rifle across the saddle in front of them, and started back toward where Gus waited. They walked the horses, making as little noise as possible, keeping the horses hooves on turf when possible. Surprise was essential to make the ambush successful. They rode in silence, both watching in front, alert for any movement, or sight of men or horses.

As they got closer to where Gus waited, they became more cautious. Man raised his rifle up to the port position to be ready. Kate saw and lifted hers as well. Both horses sensed the situation and had their ears pointed forward and often sniffed the air. Neither detected other animals.

They rode on, slowly, anxious. Kate leaned forward, searching, ready should she spot Bull and his men. Man whispered, "There are no tracks on the trail. Either they are in front of us or have left the trail."

They were within a hundred yards of Gus when Man pointed to the east. "There are tracks leading off that way."

Kate veered Redbird over where she could examine them. "It's them, they left the trail."

"Gus," Man yelled. "We found where they left the trail."

"I'm coming," he replied. He reined up beside them and looked at the tracks. "I wonder why they did that," he exclaimed.

"They're going to a particular place, or saw us split up and suspected what we were doing," Kate said.

"Could be," Gus nodded. "But if they saw us, they knew they had me five to one. They could have waited until you two were out of range to help, overrun me, and turned back to meet you."

"Good point," Man agreed. "But for whatever reason, they left the trail moving east."

"I'm sorry I suggested circling," Kate said. "It gave them another couple of hours lead on us."

Gus was studying the area with his eyes. "You had it pegged right. I see where they tied the horses behind those trees out of the line of fire." He pointed with his finger. "The grass is trampled behind that rock," he said with a gesture. "Two were there, another two were behind those trees on the other side of the trail. The third was probably waiting in front. They would have had us in a deadly crossfire. The trail is narrow here, and we would have been bunched close. Kate you saved our lives. We would have ridden into the ambush, and with five rifles firing, the odds are none of us would have survived."

Man was gesturing his head in agreement, as he looked at where Bull and his men were stationed. "We must be cautious as we follow. They know we're after them. They know our strength. I'm surprised they didn't try to take us or you out. What possible reason caused them to move on rather than end it here?"

"We may never know," Gus said. "I doubt we'll ever have the chance to ask. Dead men don't talk much."

The trio went for their pack mules and moved out as before, spread out, following the Blevins gang. Man again took the point following the tracks.

Two hours before dusk, Kate signaled for the others to stop. "Redbird senses something. I've seen it before. Either they're in front of us, or something else alerted him."

"Look in the north," Gus said. "I think we're in for a spring snowstorm from the looks of those clouds. We're high enough in the mountains that ain't uncommon. In fact, this time of the year heavy snow is common. Warm moist air is met by a cold front and heavy snow is the result in the high elevations. I think your horse knows it."

"I've been in this area before and seen such a snow," Gus added. "There's an abandoned trappers cabin about two miles ahead. There's shelter for the horses with ample grazing. The settler cleared a nice area of brush and trees and the grass grows tall and strong."

He spurred his gray gelding into a lope. Kate and Man followed, as the dark clouds looked more menacing.

Gus stopped his horse in front of a log cabin. It was small, but sturdy. He dismounted and began to unload his pack mule. Man and Kate did the same with their two mules and followed him inside.

The cabin had a rock fireplace, a sturdy table made of a split log, and two bunks. This would beat sleeping on the ground in the rain or snow.

"I'll care for the animals," Gus said. "They need to graze should it snow tonight." He left Man and Kate to work on the cabin. Man brought wood inside and built a fire. Kate was busy with their food supplies and putting the bedding on the bunks.

Man grabbed the ax and went outside. "We need more wood if we are forced to stay here a few days."

As soon as Gus finished fashioning a temporary fence for the animals, he came to help Man with the firewood.

They stacked ample wood beside the cabin door. Kate came to the door and watched them place the logs in a neat stack. "Hot food is on the table."

The two men walked to a nearby stream to wash their hands and faces. They found Kate was already seated at the table when they entered. She handed Man the one pot of food. That was the only cooking vessel they carried on the trail. They each had a tin plate and a fork.

As soon as they finished, she handed Man a bucket that was in the cabin and said, "I need water."

He came back a few minutes later with the bucket of fresh spring water. "The horses and mules finished grazing and were huddled together. I led them to the creek to drink and put them in the shed. It's getting colder and I spotted a few light show flakes, but the heavy clouds look like they're about ready to dump on us."

Gus was seated in a chair, leaning back against a wall. If it snows, the tracks of Bull and his men will be lost. We have no idea where they are headed in these mountains. The odds of finding them will be next to none. If it snows, we'll need to turn back and wait for them to appear again. Joe will notify us when they're spotted."

Man was agreeing. "Since they left the main trail, they seem to be winding around following the valleys. I haven't decided which direction they're going, but if I had to guess, I would say, northeast. What town is in that direction?"

Gus scratched his chin in thought before speaking. "The largest town is Coeur d'Alene. Wherever Bull is headed, it's generally east and Coeur d'Alene would be closer. We can send a telegram to Joe from there, and wait for a break. In fact, that would be better than backtracking."

***

They woke to a foot of snow on the ground, but the sun was shining brightly and the snow would soon melt. However, the tracks would be lost. Gus went out to move the animals out of the shed to graze. Spots of grass were already appearing from under the snow.

Kate was busy making breakfast while Man put their supplies and gear into bags ready to be loaded on the pack mules.

Gus came in, took his seat, and waited for Kate to bring the cooking pot to the table. "It's nice having a woman on the trail," he said, "and such a pretty one at that. May I ask, are you enjoying your honeymoon?" he said in a joking tone.

Not to be outdone, she said, "It would be better if you weren't with us. A little privacy would be nice."

"When we get to Coeur d'Alene, you and that husband of your can get a hotel room, and enjoy that privacy until we get a lead."

They let the horses graze for an hour, saddled them, and put their packs on the mules. This time Gus took the point and pointed his gray gelding toward the north-west and Coeur d'Alene."

Chapter 8

Kate pulled Redbird to a halt under a tree to view the town below. "Coeur d'Alene is beautiful," she exclaimed. "And the lake is so blue." Gus stopped beside her. "When I retire and hang up my saddle and toss my badge on the desk, this is where I hope to live. The winters get cold and there's snow of course, but the summers are mild. A cool breeze off the lake keeps the temperature just right."

"I can understand that. I suppose the melting snow from the mountains keep the lake full," Man put in. "But, what is the major occupation here to support Coeur d'Alene? I expect there are trappers, some agriculture, but there aren't enough of them to support a town this size."

"There are several silver and gold mines," Gus said. "It's a trading center for people living near. However, in my opinion, Coeur d'Alene is too close to Spokane to become a large city. However, a few immigrants from the Oregon Trail end up here."

Kate took the point and guided Redbird down the trail leading into town. She saw a sign, 1st Street, and walked Redbird as people were crossing in front of them. Most stopped to look at the trio dressed in skins with pistols on their hip. She saw a hotel that looked the best she had seen since entering Coeur d'Alene.

She glanced back at Man and Gus and pointed. Both were nodding agreement. They tied their horses to a hitching rail and went inside. All three had their rifles under their arm. Gus walked to the counter and said, "Two rooms, please." The clerk stuttered something, which could have meant they had no rooms. Gus put his rifle on the counter and pushed his coat back to show his badge. Man saw and did the same.

"Yes sir," the clerk said. "He turned the registration book around for them to sign."

"This is the first time I've been to this fine

establishment," Gus said. "Where can we stable our horses and pack mules?"

"Around back," the clerk replied nicely. "Stabling the horses goes with the price of the room. It also includes a bath tub brought to your room."

Kate had to choke back a giggle as the clerk rubbed his nose. But, then they had been on the trail for several days without a bath."

"How long will you be here Mr. Marshal Augustus Schweitzer?"

"Just call me Gus. I don't know, but we'll be here until ordered to move out. You may have heard of Chief Marshal Jo Meek. He'll be sending us orders."

"You must be after some bad ones. Do you think they're here in Coeur d'Alene?"

"Maybe, we lost their trail in the mountains; a sudden snow took their tracks away. They were headed this way when we lost the trail."

The clerk quickly glanced around as if he suspected the outlaws were hiding in the lobby.

"We'll take our animals around to the back and go to our rooms," Gus said. "The tubs will be appreciated, plenty of hot water, soap and towels, I trust."

"Of course," the clerk replied. But, I must ask, how you will be paying your bill?"

"With a United States voucher," Gus replied. "That's acceptable, isn't it?"

"Of course, we don't get many, but it's acceptable."

"I see a café next door, can we put our meals on the bill here at the hotel, and pay with one voucher. That would simplify the bookkeeping for us."

"Of course, the café is owned by this hotel."

Gus led the way outside to where the horses were tied. "In about an hour, meet me at the café. "I'm going to take a bath first, and then go to the police station. I also need to check in so Joe will know we're in Coeur d'Alene and we lost their trail. Always let the locals know you're in their town. At times, they can be of assistance, and we may need their jail."

***

Gus had finished eating a steak when Kate and Man entered the café. They were wearing their store-bought clothes. Gus stood to greet them with a nod of appreciation at seeing Kate in a dress. He was wearing denim pants and a gray shirt. "It took you more than an hour to take a bath," he teased.

Kate stuck her tongue out at him. "As you said, we're on our honeymoon."

Gus laughed. "I was married once, a long time ago, but I understand." He didn't elaborate on what happened, but Kate detected an expression of sadness.

They joined him at the table. "I didn't know you were married," Kate said.

"As I said, it was a long time ago. I lost Marge soon after we married. A fever came through and half the town was sick with pox. Somehow, I didn't catch it."

"I'm sorry," Kate said. "You've never considered marrying again?"

"Nope, Joe Meek hired me as one of his first deputy marshals. I've been on the move so much since then, I haven't had time to meet a woman. Maybe when I retire and have time, a pretty woman will look back at me."

He changed the subject. "The steak here is tolerable, not the best, but it beats trail grub even though you're a good cook, but your choices of food are limited when you have to use what's on the pack mules. The potatoes and beans are very good," he added.

***

The next morning, before they dressed, Man asked, "Town clothes or working skins?"

"Skins," Kate said. "I have a gut feeling we'll be working today." They buckled their Walkers on their hips and picked up their rifles before walking to the café for breakfast.

Gus was also dressed for the trail. He nodded approval. "Sit and have breakfast and I'll tell you what I learned." He waited until they ordered before speaking. "I had a wire from Joe this morning. One of the men with Bull is Nelson Watson. Nelson is a cousin or something of Bull's. Anyway, Nelson's parents live near here. I got the location from the telegraph man. They have a cabin not far from town. If Bull and his men are here, maybe they visited, or hopefully, staying there, but I doubt that. The telegraph man said Don and Thelma Watson have a cabin. I doubt it's large enough for five guests. Don is a miner."

They finished and Gus mounted his horse and followed Kate and Man to get Redbird and Arabian.

The cabin was about a half mile from town located in a grove of tall trees. Gus pulled up and studied the cabin with his binoculars. "There's a barn behind the cabin. I'll circle around and see if there are horses. Stay here until I signal you. If they're here, we must be careful. It could be six guns to face. If there are no horses, I'll go to the door and ask questions. Find a good place and cover me if I walk into a hornets' nest."

"If there are horses here, what do we do?" Kate asked.

"You two watch while I go get help. If they're forted up in the cabin, it'll be hard to get them out. There's no need to risk getting killed when help is close. About a dozen policemen could get them to come out with their hands in the air."

"Wishful thinking," Man said. "They face the rope dance if arrested."

"I know that, but we can say we tried, and followed Joe's rules. Never engage the bad ones alone if help is close. Joe said he hated funerals for his deputy marshals and would fire me if he had to attend mine." He was chuckling as he rode away.

Man and Kate tied their horses to a tree and circled to a place they had an open view of the cabin. They soon saw Gus ride around the cabin and dismount. They knew the barn and lot didn't indicate Bull and his gang was here.

Gus knocked loudly on the door and a woman opened it with a shotgun in her hands. They spoke loud enough for Man and Kate to hear. They both had their rifles aimed at the door should somebody start shooting.

"Are you Thelma Watson?" Gus asked.

"Could be, who are you?"

"I'm Augustus Schweitzer, United States Marshal. I'm looking for Bull Blevins. I was advised your son, Nelson is riding with him."

"What has that no-account Bull done now?" she asked. "He led our boy off with the promise of a lot of easy money, and a fun time with the whores. His dad had him a good job at the mine and he up and walked away."

"They robbed and killed several men. They also killed a young boy and raped and murdered a settler woman."

"Well, I ain't seen Nelson or Bull is several months. What makes you think they're here?"

"I was tracking them through the mountains and lost their trail due to a sudden snow. They were headed this way."

"He didn't tell them about us," Kate whispered. "Keeping us in reserve in case of a fight later on?"

"Could be," Man replied in a low voice as not to be heard. "The woman may be bolder if she thinks Gus is alone."

"Well, I ain't seen them and they ain't here," Thelma said with malice in her voice. She slammed the door of the cabin.

Gus walked out to his horse and mounted. The woman opened the door a crack, watched until Gus was away from the cabin, and then shut the door. Gus rode by where Kate and Man were hiding. He vanished from sight and Kate and Man slipped back to their horses and joined him waiting in the trees. They made sure Thelma didn't see them.

"I think she's lying," Gus said. "They're not here, I could see inside the cabin. There were tracks in the barn,

106

but it might be only one or two horses belonging to the Watsons. But then, the tracks may have belonged to Bull and his men, there's no way to tell."

"What do we do?" Kate asked.

"Since we don't have another lead, we stake out this cabin and watch. You two go back into town and do whatever, come back and relieve me about mid afternoon. There was no horses in the barn, so I doubt Mrs. Watson will be going anywhere, but somebody may come here."

Man and Kate turned their horses back toward town. "Enjoy your honeymoon," Gus teased.

As they rode back into Coeur d'Alene, Man asked, "Mrs. Manchester, what do you want to do today?"

"Mr. Manchester, we could go window shopping, or go back to the hotel and play Mr. and Mrs. Manchester games."

He touched his spurs to Arab and the laughing couple loped toward the hotel."

***

They went back to the Watson cabin about three in the afternoon and found Gus stretched out on his bedroll taking a nap. He jumped when he heard the sound of the horses. He sat up and welcomed Man and Kate. "Not a darn thing here. I spent the day resting and napping. The woman never went outside, and nobody came here."

"We can take over the stakeout if you want to go into town," Man said. "You must be hungry."

Gus stood and stretched his back and legs. "I expect Don Watson to be coming home from work before dark. That is, if that's where he is today. The telegraph man said he works in a mine."

"Watch and see if he comes in and if they have visitors. Don't do anything, just watch. If they have company, one of you come get me fast. I'll be at the hotel or café."

He went to his horse, put the saddle on his back, and tied his bedroll in place. Man and Kate watched him ride toward town. She went for the bedrolls and Man unsaddled both horses and staked them out to graze.

When he came back, she had the bedrolls ready where Gus had his. He had moved the rocks away and a soft carpet of grass offered a comfortable place to rest.

Kate put her head on his shoulder and relaxed. Man had his head on his arm watching his lovely bride. "I love you," he whispered.

Her eyes popped open and she kissed his lips and said, "I love you."

The sound of a running horse caused them to jump and grab their rifles they had leaned against a tree. Gus raced to where they waited.

"Several riders are coming this way. I counted ten, but they were in the trees and there could be a few more. From the way they were riding, they mean business."

"Saddle up and be ready."

Man hurried to the horses as Kate rolled up the bed and tied it behind the saddles. Gus dismounted and walked closer to the house and was crouched behind a rock where he had a good view of the Watson cabin.

Man and Kate joined him. "Before they get here," Gus said, "one circle to one side of the cabin, and the other go the other way. We don't know what's going on. I don't think the men are the Blevins gang. They weren't dressed like them, and there were too many, but we need to be ready if trouble erupts."

Kate hurried to the left and Man went to the right, but keeping out of sight of the cabin in case Thelma Watson was watching.

They took positions and waved at Gus as the sound of horses caused them to look at the trail. Ten men went toward the house, and pulled to a stop in the trees in front of the house. The obvious leader of the men said something, but they were too far away for Gus or Kate to hear.

The leader pulled a red bandana from his pocket and put it around his face. The others did the same, and pulled their hats down low on their heads.

108

Gus gestured toward Man and Kate with his arms as if to say, what the hell. He jacked a bullet into the firing chamber and replaced it with another in the magazine. Man and Kate did the same and added a bullet to the Walkers. There could be big trouble brewing.

The men went toward the cabin with the leader in front. Thelma opened the door wide enough for her head, and aimed the shotgun at the man in front.

"Beasley, that mask is silly," she shouted. "Don ain't here, and I ain't seen him in three days. So take your goons and get out of here before I put a load of shot in that oversized belly of yours."

"Thelma," Beasley shouted. "Tell that stupid husband of yours if he keeps on riling up the miners, he's going to be fish bait in the lake."

"He knows that, and if he was here, I expect you and your henchmen would be blasting away at the cabin. But, you can tell your boss that threat goes both ways. You may well be fish bait if you try to kill Don. If you kill him, his friends will get you."

She added gruffly, "You won't find him alone and defenseless like the six miners you murdered in cold blood."

"Do you think that worthless Bull Blevins will risk being killed for nothing," Beasley shouted. "The miners don't have enough money to pay him and his men. We know your boy Nelson is riding with Bull, but money will override any loyalty they have for you."

"I heard the Mine Owners Association was trying to buy Bull off," she said. "But it didn't work, and they're ready to have it out with you and those bar scoundrels you have behind you. It'll be like shooting fish in a barrel when the war starts. Your men will turn tail and run like scared rabbits when the real shooting starts. They're only brave when back shooting or gunning down an unarmed miner."

Thelma fired a round over the head of Beasley. The gang turned their horses and rode toward the trail in a lope. Thelma stepped out on the porch and watched the riders leave, and then went back inside the cabin.

Man and Kate circled back to where Gus waited.

"We seem to have a feud brewing between the miners and the mine owners," Gus said.

"It sounds more like a war is about to be started," Kate said. "If what Thelma said is true, there's already been six men killed. The fighting has already started. And now we know where Bull and his men were headed when they left Portland in a hurry. I expect the miners contacted Bull and offered him money to side with them. That's why they were on the move so fast and ignored us."

"We need to get back into town," Gus said. "I'm going to the police station and ask Chief Kincaid why he didn't tell us about this situation. I'll send Joe Meek a wire letting him know what's brewing in Coeur d'Alene. He may want to send reinforcements. This could get out of hand in a hurry if the Mine Owners Association turn their army loose on Bull and the miners. It could turn into a blood bath."

"What do you want us to do?" Kate asked, as the trio rode back toward town.

"Go with me of course. I want you to hear what Chief Kincaid has to say about the problem between the Mine Owners Association, and the miners. It sounds like they're trying to form a union, and the Association is trying to stop it by getting rid of the leaders of the several mines. I had picked up on rumors they were trying to band together, but when I heard it, it wasn't this serious. Mostly talk about the need for a miners union."

"If Bull and his men are siding with the miners against a group like we saw at Don and Thelma Watson's home, it could get bad in a hurry," Man put in. Bull would put Beasley and his men down in a heartbeat."

"I know," Gus said and touched spurs to his gelding. The three rode into town at a lope. Gus stepped down in front of the police station and tied his horse to the rail. Kate and Man followed him inside.

Gus pushed the door open and walked inside. A clerk at a desk stood to greet Gus. "Is Kincaid here?" he demanded.

"No," the clerk replied. "We had a killing about an hour ago. Chief Kincaid has gone to the crime scene."

"Who was killed?" Gus asked.

"A miner named Watson. He was shot in the back by ambushers."

"Would that be Don Watson?" Gus inquired with a quick glance at Kate and Man.

"No, the man that was shot was named Jon, they were brothers. But how did you know about Don?" the clerk asked.

"We were at Don Watson's home and overheard a man named Beasley threaten to kill Don. From what we heard, we suspect he works for the Mine Owners Association."

The policeman whistled in apprehension, but didn't comment. Gus followed up with a statement. "That's what we're here to discuss with your Chief Kincaid."

"Does that make the seventh murder of miners?" Kate asked.

The clerk nodded his head, but again didn't reply. It was obvious he didn't want to talk about it, or was under orders to keep his mouth shut.

"Where is the murder site?" Gus asked.

"On the north road out to the Coeur d'Alene Mine, do you know how to find it?"

"I know," Gus said, turned, and left the police station.

Gus led the way from town and they soon saw a cluster of people, horses, and a hearse wagon in front. Gus rode to the center of the group of onlookers and watched as men were carrying a body to the hearse. He spotted Chief Kincaid, but motioned for Kate and Man to stay behind him. "We'll wait until we can talk to him in private."

He gestured to his right. "Do you see the man in the

fancy suit, standing off to Kincaid's right? Gus asked.

Kate and Man both nodded.

"His name is Charlie Siringo," Gus said. "He's a Pinkerton agent. I wonder what he's doing here in Coeur d'Alene."

As soon as the hearse was pulled away by two draft horses, the crowd of spectators began to disburse. Gus waited until only policemen remained. "Do you see Charlie Siringo?" he asked. "He seems to have disappeared, see if you can spot him."

Kate and Man stayed mounted at Gus's order and began to circle the area. Kate pointed with her index finger. Man rode to her side and looked at the direction she was gesturing. He grabbed his binoculars and focused. "It's Siringo with three men riding toward the mine," Man said.

Gus saw them returning and waited. "He and three men are going to the mine," Kate said.

"Thanks," Gus said as he eased his horse closer to Kincaid and dismounted. Kate and Man dismounted and walked behind Gus to where Kincaid was standing under a tree away from the other policeman. Gus gave a hand gesture for them to stay back. It was easy to see Gus was irritated, and was poking a finger in Chief Kincaid's chest as they talked.

Gus finished with Chief Kincaid, hurried back to Kate and Man, but went on to his horse. He mounted and turned toward town without saying a word. Kate noticed his face was red, his eyebrows were arched, and his lips were shaped into a hard frown. Something had ruffled his feather, big time.

Gus rode for a time, then turned from the road, stopped, and waited for Kate and Man to come to him. She noticed they were out of sight of the road now and he had cooled down and had his emotions in check.

They wanted to hear what Gus had to offer from his talk with the Police Chief Kincaid.

"Kincaid said there's a big conformation brewing

between the Mine Owners Association, and the Western Federation of Miners. The miners have joined together and are attempting to form a union, which is now referred to as, WFM. Kincaid said Charlie Siringo, and other Pinkerton agents were hired by the MOA to infiltrate the WFM and suppress their activities to organize."

"When a union member is indentified, he's fired by the mine operator. If one of the union organizers is identified, what they call a rabble rouser, he's killed."

"What brought this on?" Kate asked.

"Kincaid said the mine owners claim that due to the rising cost of mining as the shafts go deeper, more equipment and ventilation is needed. That is expensive. That coupled with the fall in silver prices, they're cutting cost. Wages paid to miners was reduced, a ten-hour day was ordered, with no increase in pay for the extra hour or two each day. The miners claim safety measures are ignored and they are not being treated fairly."

"It appears both sides are gearing for a war, so to speak," Gus said. Apparently, the miners hired Bull Blevins and his men to back them. The Mine Owners Association hired gunfighters to battle back."

"This sounds a lot like the range wars in the southwest," Man said. "The big ranchers fought the land grabbers moving in and taking part of their range. Sodbusters, as they were called. Both sides hired guns and a lot of innocent people were killed."

"That could happen here," Kate offered. "What can we do to stop it?"

"We need help on this," Gus said. "It's too big for us to handle it alone. Hell, it may take the army to stop the war if it should break out. I don't know how many miners are involved, but I expect thousands spread over the area. There are several mines and they all hire a lot of men. Not only the men in the shafts, but the men outside, and the smelters have numerous employees. That added to all the wagon drivers. The numbers add up in a hurry.

Chapter 9

Kate and Man went back to the hotel thinking about the developing situation in Coeur d'Alene. From tracking a gang of murders, it had escalated into a much more serious situation.

"What an initiation into being a temporary deputy United States marshal," Man said in his joking tone. But, she saw from his expression, it wasn't a joking matter. There was the potential for a lot of bloodshed before it was over. If a shooting battle between the two sides erupted, it could cause untold numbers of deaths. It could turn into a little civil war and he had witnessed the killing and bloodshed and didn't want to be involved in it again. He lost his entire family in that war.

Gus rode ahead of them, his head down, obviously troubled by the situation. He veered his horse to the telegraph office. Kate and Man remained seated on theirs mounts while Gus went inside to send a wire to Joe Meek.

"Gus never told us why Chief Kincaid didn't tell him about this trouble when we first got here," Kate said.

"I know," Man agreed. "When he comes out, I'll ask."

Gus came limping out and mounted his gray gelding. "They'll let me know when a reply comes in," he said. "I'm going to the café and eat and then to the hotel and get some rest while I can."

"May I ask a question?" Man said.

Gus turned toward Man. "Of course ask."

"Why weren't we told about this when we first got here? Was it a secret, or were we invading their turf?"

"I don't know, Kincaid evaded that question, and I didn't push that point. We needed what was going on more than why they kept it from us. But, I suspect you were right, deputy marshals coming into his city. Professional pride, I hope, and nothing more. I hope he isn't on the payroll of the Mine Owners Association, or a sympathizer with the Western Federation of Miners, where it's affecting his job. As this plays out, I suspect we'll find out which."

"But from this point forward, until we know for sure, we keep Chief Kincaid out of the loop, and in need to know category. We don't want our activities known by either side. We must remain natural in our every action."

Kate and Man were nodding agreement.

They dismounted at the café, put their rifles under their arm, and walked into the café. As usual, the patrons in the café all turned to look at the trio as they went to a table at the rear. Man and Gus selected chairs facing the rest of the room so they could see the front door. That was considered prudent judgment in light of the seriousness of the situation. It was possible either side could want them out of the picture.

As they were finishing the meal, a man came inside and stood by the door looking around. His eyes focused on Gus and he walked to their table.

Gus motioned to the vacant chair. "Hello Charlie," he said. "I recognized you at the site of the killing today."

"I saw you as well," Siringo said. "What brings you to Coeur d'Alene?"

"We're on the trail of a known killer, Bull Blevins, and his gang. We tracked him here from Portland. What brings you here?" Gus asked.

"Gus, I know you already know the answer to that question just like I knew what brought you here. My boss sent me here on an assignment. Just following orders, just like you."

"Who are your people?" Siringo asked. "I see the man is wearing a deputy marshal badge. What's a beautiful woman wearing skins and Walkers on her hips doing with you?"

"Long story," Gus said. "And we don't have time to discuss that now. Why was Watson murdered? Did you or your henchmen do it?"

"None of your damn business," Charlie said. "You

115

and your cohort keep out of this matter. It's between the MOA and the WMF. Federal Marshals intervention is not needed. I was sent to tell you that."

"Tell your boss at Pinkerton Agency and the MOA bosses that murder of anybody is our business. We understand there have been seven already, so we're involved whether they like it or not."

"Don't get riled up at me," Siringo said. "I'm just the delivery boy in this instance. Since I knew you, it was thought you might listen to me, but I see you're as hard headed as ever. I told them that before I came here. I also told them you wouldn't back off and let well enough alone."

Siringo stood to leave.

"Tell your bosses to back off," Gus said. "A shooting war over this, we don't need."

"It may be too late for that to happen," Charlie said. "The fuse may already be lit. The miners and owners are both determined."

"Then you had better stomp the fuse out before it explodes," Gus warned.

Charlie left without comment. Gus looked at Man and Kate, but didn't offer a comment. Almost everybody in the room heard the exchange. Several customers were hurrying to finish eating, and get out of the café. Trouble could erupt at any time.

"We had better watch our backside," Kate whispered where only Gus and Man could hear. "If the Mine Owners Association feels we're a threat, they may try to deal with us like the union organizers, a shot to the back."

"Or if the WMF thinks we're here to back the MOA, the same could be true," Man added. "We may be between them when the shooting starts."

***

A banging on Kate and Man's door brought Man out of bed with his pistol in his hand. He went to the door and stood to the side and asked, "Who?"

"Gus," was the instant reply. Man opened the door

116

and stepped back. Gus came in, and eyed Kate with the quilt pulled up to her chin. "There was an explosion at one of the mines," he said. "I don't know the details as yet, but get dressed and saddle up. We'll be on the move as soon as I get the details. A wire has already been sent to Joe Meek for reinforcements to hurry. I think the war has started."

Man and Kate dressed in their skins, pulled on their heavy coats, and retrieved the two extra rifles. This could be the beginning of the first battle between the MOA and the WMF. They packed their saddlebags and rolled up their bedrolls. Kate checked the room to make sure they weren't leaving anything, and they went to the stable for Redbird and Arabian. The holster already had them saddled.

"Mr. Gus came by and told me to get them saddled. The whole town is up already as the news of the explosion at the mine spread."

"Thanks," Man said, and tossed the man a quarter. He caught it in the air and smiled. "Good luck Deputy, I'm afraid you two will need it, a lot. I witnessed a similar feud down New Mexico way."

They mounted and rode out toward the street and saw Gus coming at a lope. There was enough light from the sun even though it wasn't time for the ball of fire to appear over the eastern mountains.

He led the way from Coeur d'Alene at a lope. As soon as they were out of town, he pulled back to a walk and Kate and Man rode to his side.

"Here's what I know at this point," Gus said. "There was a gunfight at the Frisco mine. From the first report, the miners claim the guards fired first. Of course, the guards accused the miners of shooting first. The miners dropped a box of powder down an air vent into one of the mine buildings. The building exploded, killing one company man and injuring several others. The miners fired into another structure where the guards took shelter. Another company man was killed. Then, about sixty

117

guards surrendered. The miners took them prisoners, and marched them to the union hall. That's all I know about the explosion and what transpired."

"What are we going to do?" Man asked.

"I don't know until we get there," Gus replied.

***

It was chaos when they rode into the Frisco mine compound. Men were scurrying around; nobody seemed to be in charge. A man Gus knew hurried to them.

"Hello Julian," Gus said. "I didn't know you were here."

"I got here about an hour ago. Joe sent me."

"Meet our new temporary deputy, Manchester, but called Man. This is Julian Fielding, another deputy."

The two shook hand. "I'm glad you're here," Julian said.

"I was told about the explosion, and the shooting between the miners and the mine guards," Gus said.

"Have you heard what else happened, I mean after that?" Julian asked.

"No," Gus replied.

"After the explosion here, the miners searched for the man that was in charge. They intended to hang him, but didn't find him. A gunfight took place at the Gem mine. I was advised a man on a bridge was killed, probably by miners. Company men retreated from the mine. Another report said that miners went to the Bunker Hill Mine. That mine was evacuated, and non-union miners were ordered to leave the area."

"I also heard Governor Frank Steunenberg ordered the Idaho National Guard to come here to contain the insurrection, as it was labeled. President William McKinley is sending army troops. They are expected as soon as they can get here. That's all I know."

"Have you heard anything about Bull Blevins and his men being involved?" Gus asked. "He's what brought us here, we trailed him from Portland."

"I'm sorry," Julian replied. "But, from the reports

and information I have, his name hasn't been mentioned. If he and his men were among the miners, I don't know it. But from accounts, from five hundred to a thousand miners are involved. The numbers vary depending on who you're talking with."

"I understand that," Gus said. "But more importantly, what do you need us to do?"

"At this point, I don't know," Julian replied. "As I said, I haven't been here long enough to know who's really in charge. I expect when the National Guard and army arrive, they'll take over. It appears the violence has ended for now, or at least, I hope so."

"Have you heard anything about Charlie Siringo?" Gus asked. "He came into the café where we were eating and warned us to back off. He said that order came from Pinkerton and the MOA."

"I didn't know he was here. What are Pinkerton Agents doing here?"

"We were advised they're working for the Mine Owners Association," Gus replied. "From what we've learned, they were hired to infiltrate the miners and report union sympathizers, organizers, and members to the Association. Union members were fired and seven WMF organizers were murdered before you got here."

"Damn underhanded by the Pinks, if you ask me," Julian said.

**

Since the situation appeared to be resolved for now, Gus turned his horse back toward Coeur d'Alene. He motioned for Man and Kate to ride close. "The National Guard under the direction of Governor Frank Steunenberg and the army will take over now. Our mission is Bull. I suggest we go back to the Watson cabin and stake it out again. When Don shows up, we can tail him to where Bull is hiding out. I expect they're together in this."

He led the way. "I'm glad we weren't called on to get into a gunfight between the MOA and the WMF," Kate said. "In this case, who's right, and who's wrong? There was violence on both sides. I would think that both were in the wrong, and both were in the right, it depends on how you look at it. If I spent my money establishing a business, and I was the owner, I don't think my employees have the right to interfere with the way I manage it. If they don't like it, go find another job. It's not right to shoot and burn the business because you don't like company policy."

Gus nodded, but didn't comment.

"But, on the other hand, the miners have to go down in those awful shafts every day, and safety precaution should be taken and they deserve to be treated fairly. But, violence rarely, if ever solves a problem. If the mine owners are forced to operate in the red, the businesses will folds, and everyone is affected. The miners are out of a job, and their families suffer. The owners could be faced with loans they got to start the mines in the first place. With no income, they can't repay the loan, and the financial institutions are harmed. A solution must be reached in the middle where both sides get part of what they need and want, a safe work environment for the miners, and a profit for the mine owners, which allows money to be used for improvement of the working conditions, and keep the mine operating."

Again, Gus nodded, but didn't comment.

They rode in silence until Gus stopped at the place they watched the Watson cabin before. "Let us take it today," Man said. "If Watson shows up, we'll tail him if he leaves. If he leads us to Bull, one of us will go get you."

"I'll be at the hotel getting some shuteye," Gus said. He turned his horse toward town. Kate pulled their bedrolls from behind their saddles.

"What do we do while we wait?" Man said with that special grin on his face and a twinkle in his eyes. "After all, we're still on our honeymoon until Bull is arrested or killed."

***

120

It was dusk when a lone rider approached the cabin from the opposite side of the road. The rider went into the back of the barn and Man and Kate watched him cautiously run to the side of the cabin. He looked around, and then peeked around toward the front of the cabin.

"Is it Don Watson?" Kate asked.

"I don't know, since I've never seen him. For the moment, let's watch and see what he does."

The man must have said something they didn't hear, because Thelma came to the door, walked out on the porch, and looked around. She turned and walked to the side of the cabin where the man waited and they saw them talking. They both rushed back to the cabin door, and the man closed it behind them after looking around.

"That has to be Don from the way Thelma acted," Kate said. "I suspect there were worried somebody was watching their cabin from the way he acted."

"I expect Watson knows the so called enforcers hired by the MOA are looking for him. If they find him, I think he would be murdered."

"I agree, but he must be awfully stupid. If I approached my cabin, suspecting somebody was watching, I would have made a couple of circles around it first, a wide one first, and then a closer one. If he had done that, he would have spotted us, or our horses."

"True, but then you are more experienced than him, and a lot smarter. I don't know, but I doubt he's anything more than a simple miner."

They saw the white smoke from the chimney turn to a gray, and then it became darker. "Thelma or Don put wood on the fire," Kate said. "I expect she's cooking supper."

"There's nothing we can do, but wait and see what develops," Man said. "He may be settling in for the night. After the violence at the mines today, he may be exhausted, and it's possible the usefulness of Bull and his men has ended. They're not about to take on the National Guard and army."

The temperature began to cool, as the sun no longer offered its warming rays. Man and Kate huddled together, using their bedrolls to keep warm.

The sound of a horse alerted them and they both scrambled for cover to wait. A gray horse came into sight on the road. "It's me, Gus," a low voice said from the trail.

"We see you," Man said. "Come on in."

Gus tied his horse and their mules loaded with their supplies. He tied them to the picket rope beside Redbird and Arabian and came in to camp wearing a heavy coat. "It's getting colder," he said.

"So we noticed," Man said. "About dusk, a man came to the cabin from the other side. He put his horse in the barn and Thelma came out to meet him. We think it was Don, from the way they acted. We haven't seen them since he got here."

A faint light was evident through cracks around the door. "It appears they may have settled in for the night," Kate offered. "Is there any news from the mines?"

"The National Guard and the army arrived. I heard they rounded up about six hundred miners and have them confined in a stockade. As far as I know, there has been no more violence."

"That's good to hear," Kate said.

"I did some investigating and talked to several people that should be in the know. If Bull participated in the so called uprising of the miners, nobody is admitting it."

"Maybe they came here for another purpose," Kate suggested. "Like what?" Man asked.

"I don't know, maybe for Nelson to visit his parents. Or, maybe knock over a bank, a mine payroll. I expect either would be sizeable a few days before the miners are paid."

"Good point," Gus said. "I doubt Bull would ride here from Portland for Nelson to visit his parents. I like your idea, if they didn't come here to hire out to the miners, something else is brewing. But what and when is

122

the big question? Bull seems to have two things on his mind, money, and women. And to ride this far, it has to be money."

"We may have to wait until it happens to know," Man said. "At least we'll be close and ready to take the trail after them."

"I hope you're right on that," Kate said. "They have to know we're in Coeur d'Alene. Somebody would have gotten word to Nelson and Bull that we're here. The miners are probably close, and if any of them learned we were chasing Bull, we must assume they know."

"That brings us to what we do tonight," Gus said. "The way I see it, we stake out the house tonight, and see if Don leaves or somebody comes here. If not, we'll be in position tomorrow morning should he go to work. However, I doubt the mines will be operating tomorrow and Don may be one of the miners that were fired, since he's one of the union organizers."

"Back to square one," Kate said.

She went to their bedrolls and put them together under a tree. Gus and Man went to move the horses to a place to graze during the night, but close enough should they be needed.

***

It was midmorning when Kate and Man saw the man that entered the cabin the evening before open the door a crack and peek out. He spent at least two minutes looking in every direction, and then hurried toward the barn. Thelma came out and stood on the porch with her shotgun.

Man and Gus hurried to saddle the horses, as it appeared the man was going to leave the cabin. Kate watched using the binoculars. The man rode to the porch, and Thelma handed him a bundle, which he put in his saddlebags. She then helped him tie a bedroll on the back of the saddle.

Kate hurried to where the men were saddling the horses. "The man appears to be preparing to take a trip.

Thelma gave him a package that I expect was food and a bedroll ready to be strapped on the saddle. When I came to find you, he was kissing her."

They put their bedrolls on the horses and mounted. Kate led the mules and Gus took the lead. He and Man circled to higher ground so they could see which way the man went.

He left the way he came in the night before, the opposite direction from the road to the cabin. Gus hung back out of sight of the man they all assumed was Don Watson.

After riding over a mile, Gus said, "He's not going to the mine. I hope he's leading us to where Bull is hiding out. If he is, they'll have out sentries. Spread out and keep your eyes open for any movement."

The trio rode for another mile before Gus stopped and motioned for Kate and Man to join him. "Watson is making it easy to follow. He has kept the horse on soft ground the entire way. A blind man could follow his trail. It's as if he wants us to follow. I suspect he could be leading us into an ambush."

"When we were trailing the slave traders'," Kate said. "We circled around and came back at the ambushers from the opposite direction. It worked great that time. But then the situation was different. They were in a narrow valley between mountain peaks and that was the only place they could go. Where we are here, the man could turn in either direction, and we could lose him or we might not circle far enough to assure we were on the other side of where they are waiting, if an ambush is their plan. I know we tried that before and it didn't work."

Gus sat his horse in thought. "We'll do it like we did before. You two circle and come back to meet me. Surely, where Bull is hiding can't be that much farther. We're several miles from Watson's cabin. I know it's a gamble, but safer then riding into six rifles shooting from hiding."

"I'll keep the mules so you can move faster. Use

124

caution and don't let them surprise you."

"We'll be careful," Kate said. Man and Kate veered to the right and urged their horses into a lope. Man took the point and Kate stayed behind him, watching in every direction for something out of place, or a movement. She saw nothing suspicious as they rode hard hoping to get on the other side of the killers.

Man rode for about two miles and turned back to the trail. He stopped and waited for Kate. "I think this is far enough and there are no fresh tracks of a horse. Are you ready?"

She pulled her hat down and drew her rifle from the scabbard. Man did the same, and they rode abreast, about ten yards apart. Kate jerked to attention at movement in the trees, but they saw a deer race away when he caught their scent, or saw the approaching riders.

"He wouldn't have been here if riders were close," Man said. Kate nodded.

They rode for another mile, nothing. "Where could they be?" Kate whispered.

"I don't know," Man replied. "There are still no fresh tracks on the trail. Maybe he went in another direction. Another half mile or less and we'll be back to where Gus is waiting."

"I'm up here," Gus said. They looked up and saw the Marshal standing on top of a large bolder. "I'm glad it was you," Kate said. "Otherwise, we would have been in the sights of their rifles."

"Either the man turned off the trail, or isn't using the trail. There're no tracks," Man said.

Gus climbed down, went to his horse tied behind the bolder, and rode out to meet them. "We'll have to backtrack searching both sides of the trail looking until we find where he turned off of the trail."

They found the tracks of the man they were tailing, and where he turned off the trail. He was on a path of water polished rocks and the tracks vanished. Man went to one side and Gus the other searching for any sign where he left the rocks. They rode for another mile before Gus motioned for Kate and Man to join him.

"He gave us the slip. Either intentionally, or he turned off the rocky trail, and we missed seeing his tracks. That stretch of rock was where it had to happen. There's nothing to indicate he went on after the rocks ended. It was soft ground and he didn't go on that way. Our best option is to go back and search every possible place he could have gone."

"I agree," Man said. "Going on seems to be a waste of time. You would have picked up his tracks if he was in front of us."

They rode back to the place they lost the man and each started making a circle out to the sides. Kate took the inside, Man the next and Gus the outside. They stayed about a hundred yards apart, riding, looking down at the ground for any sign a rider passed.

The riders made a complete circle and met where Gus came back to the starting point. Kate and Man were shaking their head. "Not a damn thing," Gus said. "His tracks have to be here somewhere. Make another circle as we did before, but farther out."

He turned his horse and rode away constantly looking down. Kate was the first to complete her circle as she had the shortest distance to travel. She was waiting when Man joined her. Again, he was shaking his head. They rode to the point Gus would meet them. "He didn't see anything either," Kate said, looking at the expression on Gus's face.

"Where the hell could he have gone?" Gus said in disgust. "It appears he flew away, or there would be something. We should be able to spot a mark on the ground, a broken twig, or something. It's as if he turned into a ghost."

"I suggest we make one more circle, but wider," Kate said. "Going back to Coeur d'Alene seems to be a waste of time. All we could do there is stake out his cabin, and wait for him to return."

Gus nodded and spurred his gelding into a lope. He

was getting impatient and frustrated.

As the two other times, they met with the same results. Not a sign a rider had passed. "I saw a large valley to the west. There's a hill we can use and scan the valley with our binoculars. If he went this way, he might still be in sight, but I doubt it. He should have had ample time to get to the other side by now. We wasted so much time making the circles, but it's our last hope to spot him."

Gus led the way, they climbed to the top of the hill, and Man and Gus pulled their binoculars to look. They made a careful search from side to side of the valley. The only thing they saw was several deer and a female bear with two cubs.

"If the man we are following is Don Watson, he's a miner, not a skillful rider capable of not leaving one sign or track," Gus lamented. "When we catch him, I'm going to find out how he managed to elude us."

"Could Watson have tied burlap sacks on the hooves of his horse to prevent leaving tracks?" Kate asked.

"That's an old trick to hide a trail and it's possible," Gus said. "That would explain how he escaped without leaving a track. If he avoided brushing against bushes or trees, that would account for no broken twigs. Somebody did a heck of a job coaching him, or the man we are tracking is not Watson."

"Bull may have been that coach," Man said. "But, regardless of how he escaped, he did. Now, what do we do? As you mentioned, go back and stake out his cabin and wait could prove to be a long wait."

"Unless you have a better option," Gus said. "We don't have a clue which way he went."

"Is there a larger town close to us?" Kate asked. "If so, we could go there, and have access to a telegraph. Joe Meek could notify us if Bull and his gang strike again. I hate to say it, but he may have to kill or rob again for us to pick up his trail."

"Missoula is east of us," Gus replied.

They rode into Missoula and found a bustling town.

127

New homes and businesses were under construction. Gus led them to a hotel located on Front Street. It was an older building, but appeared to be well maintained. Gus gestured at a café. "We can make our headquarters here. The telegraph office is in the next block. I'll report to Joe and meet you here in an hour or so. I'll also check in with the locals to let them know we're in town and why."

He walked in front of them to the desk, got two rooms, and paid for one night with a voucher. "I don't know how long we'll be here," he said. "I'll keep current on the payments, as we may have to move out in a hurry, day, or night."

"I understand, Marshal," the clerk said. "I was a deputy before I took a round in the leg. I can do this job seated. Your horses are welcome in our stable behind the hotel."

"Thanks," he said as he turned to leave. Man and Kate carried their saddlebags up the steps. They found they had a room overlooking the main part of town. Kate began putting their things away and Man stood looking out the window.

"I see Gus put our horses in the stable and is walking down the street toward the telegraph office. He seems to be limping more. Maybe he's spending too much time in the saddle."

Kate came to look and put her arm around him. "Gus is happy doing what he does. I think being a Marshal is all he cares about, and will keep going as long as he's able."

They were still watching when they saw Gus hurrying back as fast as he could walk. "Something's wrong," Kate said. They rushed down to the lobby to meet Gus when he stormed through the door breathing hard."

He saw them and motioned them outside where they could talk in private. "I've been ordered to go back to Coeur d'Alene. It seems the WFM hired one of their henchmen, Harry Orchard, to kill the Idaho Governor, Frank Steunenberg. The report said Orchard was a paid informant for the Cripple Creek Mine Owners' Association."

"What are our orders?" Man asked.

"Keep after Bull and his men. Joe Meek said that it was reported Bull, with Watsons help, kidnapped a mine owner for ransom. They paid twenty-five thousand in cash to get him back. Watson collected the money, met Bull and they disappeared. Apparently, Bull was holding the mine owner, and when Watson met them at a hideout, the miner was released unharmed, except scared out of his skull. Apparently, it was Don Watson we followed and he gave us the slip and met Bull and his gang with the ransom money."

"Anyway, I have to get moving. You two are on your own. Every deputy U.S. marshal is tied up on a case, or in Coeur d'Alene, due to the miner uprising. They're taking the report that Orchard will make an attempt to assassinate Governor Frank Steunenberg seriously. Apparently, I was wrong to think the violence was over. But, you would think the National Guard and army could take control and stop the killings."

"But back to you, Joe said to stay here until something breaks on Bull. Check the telegraph office several times a day or make arrangements for them to deliver any urgent telegram to you at the hotel."

He turned to go to the rear to the stable, and then stopped and came back. He handed man several pieces of paper. "Here are vouchers for your expenses. Keep the receipts. They audit the expenses as if the money was coming out of their pockets."

They watched Gus hobble around the hotel and he came by a few minutes later with the horse in a fast trot leading his pack mule. "Enjoy your honeymoon," he said with a wave and disappeared down the street.

***

The next morning, a wire was delivered to their room. Man tore it open and read it to Kate. "Bull, Watson, and gang spotted on the road to Seattle. Proceed post haste."

"Will we ever get a chance to enjoy a real honeymoon," she teased as they packed their saddlebags. They went by the clerk and told them they were leaving and went to the stable for Redbird and Arabian. Before they rode out, they stopped at a general store to replenish their supplies.

The clerk eyed the voucher Man handed him in payment, and then carried it to the back. An older man came to the front carrying the voucher and eyed Man. "You're new," he said as he eyed the badge on Man's shirt.

"Yes sir, we were riding with Gus, but he was called away by Joe Meek."

"And how is Joe these days? I haven't seen him in a month of Sunday's."

"He's doing okay as far as we know. We only met him once, which was in Portland when he hired me as a deputy marshal."

"You said you were riding with Gus. I was with him when he took a round in his leg. Bull Blevins shot him from ambush. In fact, I pulled him off the trail and took one in the shoulder. That was when I hung up my gun belt and gave my badge to Joe."

"Gus was here and rode out this morning," Man replied.

"Damn, he doesn't know I moved here. I've been intending to send him a letter, but never got around to it. I would have liked to see him and chew the fat over a few beers."

"I'll tell him when we see him. I didn't catch your name. I'm Homer Manchester, but go by just Man. This is my wife Kate."

"When did they start letting wives tag along with deputy marshals?"

"Well, Joe said he couldn't hire a woman, but she could be my partner. We work as a team."

"I got you pegged now, you rode with Jake and Slats on the Oregon Trail, and I heard about a man and woman taking out the slave traders. That was you two."

130

Man nodded.

"Now it makes sense. My name is Casey, Jeffery Casey. Most call me Casey."

"Nice to meet you Casey," Kate said and offered her hand to shake.

Man was waiting to shake Casey's hand.

"Who are you tailing, if you can tell me?" Casey asked.

"It's no secret, Bill Blevins, Don Watson, and gang. Gus and us have been on his trail from Portland to Coeur d'Alene. Now here. As I said, Joe Meek pulled Gus away, and sent orders for us to go to Seattle. Somebody reported they saw them on the Seattle road."

"Damn, I hope you get that bastard, excuse the language Kate. As I said, I was with Gus and it was Bull that shot both of us from ambush. He's a back shooter and has no regard for human life. I don't know anything about Watson."

"Watson and Bull kidnapped a mine owner at Coeur d'Alene for ransom," Kate said. "We need to get going though, we stopped for supplies before moving out. It was nice meeting you Casey."

"Take care and mark my words, Bull is a back shooter."

***

Kate and Man rode hard and camped at sundown, and were back on the trail at first light. They wanted to be in Seattle fast, and hopefully make contact with the police before Bull arrived and had time to go to ground in a hideout, if that was his plan. He and his men had money in their pockets after receiving the ransom and hopefully, in a mood to spend it in the local saloons and brothels.

The next evening, Man pulled up and motioned for Kate to come closer. "I caught a flicker of light through the trees. It may be a campfire. Dismount and let's check on foot. It could be Bull."

She tied Redbird to a tree and followed Man toward where he saw the light. As had become their custom, she moved off to the side several yards.

Kate saw the campfire first and dropped to her knees. Man saw her and did the same. She was pointing to the right of where they had been going.

Man circled in that direction in a crouch with both Walkers in his hands. Kate saw him and pulled her two pistols and together they approached the camp.

Suddenly, a bullet smashed into a tree not more than two inches from Man's head. He instantly dove behind the tree before the second bullet drilled into the ground where he had been walking.

Kate reacted the instant she heard the shot, and was scrambling forward, using rocks and trees for cover. She reached a point where she could see ahead and saw several men rush for cover. In the near darkness, she couldn't identify any of them; they were only outlines in the fading light.

She saw a flash from a rifle. The shooter was on a boulder not more than twenty yards in front of her. The sentry was aiming at where Man disappeared. Kate waited until she was sure of her target and pulled the trigger on the Walker in her right hand. The man was knocked backward off the rock with a bullet in his chest.

This caused a barrage of weapons to be discharged toward her. She saw Man backing away from his hiding place, and she began moving backward keeping her pistols aimed at the shooters. Somebody bellowed an order. "Get the horses and circle around them. We can cut them down in a crossfire."

Both Kate and Man scrambled as fast as they could manage back to where they had tied the horses. She was the first in the saddle and spurred Redbird into a run. She glanced back and saw Man was close behind. They left their two pack mules, as they needed to move fast before Bull's men got behind them.

Man pointed toward the west and she veered in that direction. They heard shouts from where their horses were tied.

Redbird understood the urgency and was racing at full speed, but being cautious of the trees and rocks. Man's Arabian was keeping within five yards of the horse in front of him.

Kate found a place between two huge boulders and pulled Redbird to a stop. Man stopped beside her. "Good shot," he said. "I could barely see his image in the darkness. We finally found Bull. But, if not, the gang was sure anxious to shoot. Putting out a sentry that fired without speaking proved they were outlaws on the run."

"What do we do now?" she asked.

"It's too dark to engage them tonight. This is as good a place as any to bed down until dawn. I doubt they'll follow in the darkness, but I'll keep watch if you'll get our bedrolls and find a palace for the horses."

She stepped down, took the saddlebags and bedrolls to a smooth place under a tree. She had to work in the darkness as any kind of fire could attract Bull and his men. She then led the horses to the rear and put the picket rope between the trees. This would give the horses room to graze on the tall grass that grew beside a small spring seeping water from under the face of a rock wall.

Man waited and listened for any sound of horses hooves. There was nothing but the sounds night in the mountains. He found Kate seated on their bed, and she offered jerky and parched corn. "Supper is served," she whispered. "I'm afraid the wine and candles will have to wait for a more appropriate place."

He took a bite of the jerky and said softly, "You over cooked the steak again, it's tough."

She playfully punched him on his chest. "Try the corn, it may be better."

He crunched on a few kernels and said, "Hard as a rock, but it's just the way I like it."

"Wash the jerky and corn down with water, it helps," she said with a teasing grin.

They finished eating in silence before she said, "What do we do tomorrow morning?"

"I'll go out before dawn and scout to see what they did. They may be camped nearby, or moved out during the night. I hope they missed our pack mules and they're where we left them. If you'll take the first watch, I'll relieve you, and be ready to check their whereabouts as soon as there's enough light."

She picked up her bedroll and walked toward the opening between the two rocks. She found a place to sit about ten feet up and settled in to watch. Only the normal sounds reached her ears. It was too dark to see anything, as the moon was only a sliver in the sky.

Man found her by whispering, and she guided him to her. "Nothing," she said. "Not one sound of humans."

"That's the way we want it," he whispered. "I'll take it from here and be back after dawn."

She left her bedroll for him, and went back to where he slept and crawled inside the warm bedding. She was asleep in a matter of seconds.

At the first hint of light in the east, Man slid down the rock and walked back toward where they encountered Bull. He walked for several yards and stopped to listen. Then he would move on forward and stop to listen. It took almost an hour before he found the place Bull and his men camped. It was deserted. Only the ashes of their campfire remained.

He walked to the place where the sentry had been and found a dark stain on the ground, but no body. They took him with them, either the body, or he was only wounded. He had no way to know. The sound of Kate's bullet hitting flesh was a deep satisfying thud, the sound made when a bullet hits a body in the chest, and he hoped it was a kill shot. There would be one less to deal with.

It was light enough to see now. He walked to the place the outlaws horses were tied and looked at the tracks. He moaned when he spotted the tracks of ten horses and two mules. Either they had extra mounts, or Bull had added four more men. With Watson, his gang had grown to ten.

He circled around the campsite looking for any evidence they left behind. There was nothing, but the ashes, and the dark spot on the ground.

He went back to where they left the mules. They were where they were tied. Thankfully, Bull and his men missed them in the darkness.

Man hurried back to where Kate waited. He found her huddled in the bedroll for warmth as the sun hadn't had sufficient time to overcome the chill of night in the mountains.

She saw him and stood, waiting. "They're gone," he said. "I'll make a fire and we can eat a warm breakfast. I found our mules and supplies."

"I'll do it, if you'll care for the horses," she said.

As if Arabian and Redbird heard her words, they both nickered. Man took a ration of oats from the packsaddle to feed them.

As soon as they finished the oats, he saddled and brought them to where Kate waited with a pan over the small fire. They ate as the horses and mules grazed on fresh grass. They had eaten all the grass within the length of their stake rope during the night.

"It was easy to pick up the trail of Bull and his men. "But, I counted ten horses," Man said.

"She groaned at the significance of his comment. "What about the man I shot?" she asked.

"He wasn't at the campsite."

"I'm sure I got him dead center of his chest," Kate said. "I'm surprised they took his body. I expected them to leave it, stripped of anything of value on him. That seems to be the way of the outlaws we have dealt with."

"Me too," Man said. "But for whatever reason, they took him with them."

They rode until almost noon when Man pulled up when Arabian turned to look and sniff the air. He gestured to his left and turned his horse toward whatever his horse saw and smelled. They found the body of a man. There was a bullet hole in his chest, dead center between

135

his man nipples. He was naked except for long underwear. They dismounted and walked to the body and Man turned him over on his back. They had never seen him before.

"I wonder why they brought him this far?" she asked.

"Who knows, maybe he wasn't dead, but died and they ditched the body. You were right about what they would do; they took everything but his filthy underwear."

They rode on, leaving the body. Human trash like the men traveling with Bull doesn't deserve a decent burial. Besides, Man wanted to make up lost time, and be as close to the gang as possible if they continued toward Seattle.

***

As usual, they attracted attention riding in wearing their working skins with the twin pistols on their hips. A man wearing a badge stepped out and motioned them to stop. Man reined Arabian in and waited for the man to approach them.

"I spotted your United States Marshal badge. Welcome to Seattle, I'm Assistant Chief of Police, Delmar Summerfield. If I may ask, what brings you here?"

Man leaned down to shake the offered hand as he spoke, "Homer Manchester, but called just Man by my friends." He gestured at Kate. "This is my lovely wife and partner, Kate."

The policeman touched his hat in respect to the introduction.

"Delmar, if you would, show us to your headquarters, we need your assistance." He noticed several onlookers had walked to within hearing distance.

The assistant chief also saw the bystanders and motioned with his hand. "Go to the next street, that's Columbia, and hang a right. You'll see the sign on the left. I'll follow you. Chief Winkle is in his office, or was when a left a few minutes ago."

Man and Kate tied up in front of the building and waited until Delmar joined them before going inside the police station. A man was seated at a desk, and was openly watching the unusual couple with Assistant Chief

Summerfield. Their attire and weapons got his attention.

"Is Winkle still in his office?" Delmar asked.

"As far as I know, unless he went out the back door. But, I saw him go for coffee a couple of minute ago."

Summerfield led the way down a hallway and stopped at an open door. "Chief, a deputy U.S. marshal to see you."

"Bring him in," Winkle said.

Delmar made the introductions of Man and Kate, and then went to a chair at the side of the room. Chief Winkle motioned to chairs in front of his desk. "What brings you to Seattle?" he asked.

Man gave the Chief a brief rundown on Bull Blevins. Joe Meek sent us after him. We think we caught up with him a few miles out of town. A sentry shot at me, but Kate took him out, but there are nine more in the gang. They took off during the night."

"I've been reading about the chase on the wire. Since you have been on the trail for a while, you may not have heard the latest. A man by the name of Orchard assassinated Governor Frank Steunenberg? Orchard got him with a bomb from the first report. A deputy marshal arrested Orchard."

"We hadn't heard that, but Augustus Schweitzer was with us when Meek pulled him off when he got a report that could happen. I guess Gus didn't get there in time to prevent it, but Gus may have made the arrest of Orchard."

"But, back to Bull," Man said.

"What can we do to help?" Winkle asked.

"We need help locating him. We have no clue on why he came here, or if he is here. Maybe he thinks Seattle is a goodtime town. With the ransom money, and other loot he has in his pockets, I expect he can do almost anything he chooses."

"There are plenty of places he could do that," Delmar put in. "I can put the word out to our men, make a few contacts, and see if anything turns up."

"We would appreciate it," Man said.

"Do you two plan on taking on Bull and his gang alone?" Chief Winkle asked.

"Not if we can help it," Man said. "But the circumstances will dictate our actions."

"If we locate him," Delmar said. "We'll have men available and hopefully, in a place to keep innocent bystanders out of harm's way."

"We do as well," Kate said.

"Could you recommend a good hotel for us to use while we're waiting until we get a lead on Bull and his gang? We need a place to take a bath and a café that serves a good steak. We've been on the trail for several days, a good bed and hot tub of water would be welcome."

"I would recommend the Potter House. It's clean and has a bathhouse, as well as a place to stable your horses. Delmar can guide you. One of my men will know where to find you if we get a lead."

"Where is the telegraph office?" Man asked. "We need to report to Joe Meek we're here, and have made contact with you."

"Delmar can point it out to you on the way to the hotel. You go past it. Give Maurice, the telegraph man my regards. I'll provide what assistance you may need if we turn Bull."

"Thanks Chief, we appreciate it."

***

For two days, Man and Kate enjoyed the opportunity to do nothing except walk the streets and shop for things Kate wanted. But, she knew she couldn't buy much since they would be leaving on horseback, and what she bought must be small enough to add to their supplies on the mules. Man tagged along behind her, watching and smiling. He considered himself the luckiest man alive to have met a woman like Kate. It was as if they were made for each other.

On the third morning, Delmar found them finishing breakfast at the café located beside the Potter House. "Chief Winkle asked me if you could come to the station house."

"Of course, we are finished and can go now," Man said. He dropped money on the table for their meal, and he and Kate followed Delmar out on the street. "What's up?" Kate asked. "Is there any news on Bull?"

"I don't know. The Chief asked me to find you, and ask you to come to the station."

They found Chief Winkle seated at his desk with a frown on his face. He looked up and saw Man and Kate, and stood to greet them. He motioned toward the two chairs in front of his desk.

"Delmar, close the door please."

"Do you want me to stay?" he asked.

"Yes, we have a situation brewing and you may be a part of it."

Delmar closed the door and then walked to his chair.

Chief Winkle waited until they were seated and picked up a folder on his desk. "I sent a request to the Washington State Attorney General for assistance on a very sensitive situation. I informed him that a deputy marshal was in town, and requested your help. The attorney general contacted Meek and he gave his approval. In fact, they agreed you would have the lead on this one."

Man and Kate exchanged glances. They both suspected political ramifications, and the attorney general and the chief of police wanted somebody else to take the heat. Namely, a temporary deputy United States marshal named Homer Manchester.

"Meek is wiring your orders," Winkle added. He walked around the desk and handed Man the folder he had in his hand. "Read this, and then we'll talk." He gestured at Delmar to go with him. "Do you want coffee while you read?" he asked. "I'll have cups brought to you."

"Not now, thanks," Man said. "We ate breakfast only a few minutes ago."

Kate moved her chair close to read with Man. They finished and Man put the folder on the desk. "A real hot potato," he said.

"What will we do?" she asked.

"We need to read the wire from Joe before doing anything. I want to know our specific orders."

She nodded. "Do you want me to go to the telegraph office while you talk to the Chief?"

"I don't know if he would give you the wire since it will be addressed to me, but give it a try. The telegraph man is named Maurice. Delmar knows him; maybe he'll go with you."

The door opened and Chief Winkle and Delmar came inside. They both had a coffee cup in their hands. Winkle saw the folder on his desk and asked. "Well, what do you think?"

"We want to see our orders from Meek before discussing it," Man replied. "Do you think they would give Kate the wire if Delmar goes with her, or should I go?"

"Maurice knows us, and if Delmar asks for the wire, he'll give it to Kate, but he might not if Kate goes alone. Del, go with her," he said.

Man waited until they left before speaking. "This could get hairy in a hurry," he said. "I can see why you and the A. G. wanted to shift the lead to me."

"Heavy politics is involved," Winkle said. "I expect the attorney general is trying to shift the responsibility, and make it a federal investigation. And, to be honest, I'm up for election this fall. People will take sides, and there'll be no political winners."

"Since I'm a rookie deputy marshal, I'm expendable if it goes bad," he said. He didn't add the fact that he was only a temporary marshal.

"A marshal is not elected like the rest of us. You guys are appointed and your boss is Joe Meek. He can weather a lot more heat than the rest of us. But I agree, this could well be a career maker, or a career killer for you."

Man chuckled, softly. He liked Winkle, he was upfront and honest and felt he would offer as much support as he could without sticking his neck in the noose.

Kate and Delmar came in and she handed Man an envelope. He tore it open and Kate stood at his side to read.

Jackson Maus, Attorney General, Washington State, requested federal assistance on the State Senator Logan situation. You'll take the lead with cooperation from Chief Winkle and Attorney General Maus. Wire reports to me. Until Bull is located, give the Logan case your full attention.

He handed the wire to Chief Winkle and Assistant Chief Delmar to read. They finished and Winkle put it in the folder, and handed it to Man. "What are our orders?"

Man swallowed hard. It startled him that the Chief of Police of Seattle was asking a temporary marshal for orders.

"We need to study this report and talk to the boy," he said. "We need to get a feel for the situation before doing anything." He opened the folder and read before speaking. "Where can we find Jebediah Spencer. It says he's with foster parents. What's his age? It doesn't say here."

"Jeb is maybe sixteen, I don't know his exact age. He's currently staying with friends of mine. I felt it prudent since his life could be in danger. I'll make arrangements for you to meet Jeb."

"Can you give us more information?" Kate asked. "How did you get evolved. The report says you obtained information."

"I deliberately left that part out of the report. Too many people have access to it, and I'm afraid word would get back to Logan. If the allocations are true, the boy could be in extreme danger."

"As you read in the report," Winkle added, "a woman's body was found in the river and identified as Jane Spencer. A couple of my men went to the home of Jane and Jeb was there, alone, hiding. From the report, he was in a state of shock, and ran to hide when my men went

141

into the house. They brought him in, and I chatted with the boy. When I got him settled down enough to talk, he said State Senator Logan murdered his mother."

"Did he witness it?" Man asked.

"No, but he followed his mother to a house in the old part of town and saw a man enter the house a few minutes later. He hid and watched. He said he saw the man come out with his mother over his shoulder and load her in his buggy. Jeb followed and saw the man throw his mother in the river. He said the man had a pistol on his hip and he knew if he tried to do anything, he would be killed."

"He followed the man back to Logan's home. He had no idea who lived there, but after he took my men to show them the home, they identified the owner as State Senator Logan. That didn't surprise Jeb when he was told the owner of the home."

"Jeb said his mother told him that his father was Senator Mitchell Logan. Jeb said his mom went to meet Logan every Tuesday and Thursday afternoon, and always came home with money. Logan was supporting them. Apparently, she was Logan's mistress."

"Jeb also said that his mom was worried and told him that they were going to move to California as soon as Logan gave her a large sum of money. Jeb followed his mother to the house because he knew his mom was scared, and he was afraid for her."

"We have no idea the identity of the man that murdered Jane. It was not Logan from Jeb's description. He was young. From what I got from Jeb, the killer was in his late twenties, dark long hair, tall and thin. I know that isn't much to work with, and that description doesn't fit any of the known hired killers we know about. Logan may have brought him in from somewhere else."

"How do you know it wasn't Logan?" Kate asked. "What does Logan look like?"

"Logan is short, hefty, and nearing fifty. That's all we have now. I'll make arrangements for you to meet Jeb tomorrow."

142

Man and Kate went back to the hotel and sat on the bed. "Damn, damn it," Man said. "Going after known killers that shoot back is better than this case."

"What will we do? Where do we start?" she asked.

"Do you have any thoughts, comments, or suggestions?" he asked.

"Not at the moment, I need to think about it for a while. Maybe something will pop into my mind."

She started undressing and gave him her special grin. Maybe some loving will stimulate my brain. It has worked in the past."

***

Kate kissed Man awake and waited until he spoke, giving him time to gather his thoughts. "I have a couple of thoughts on how to proceed," she said.

He pulled her closer and she rested her head on his shoulder. "We can stake out the home of Logan and see if a man fitting the description of the killer goes to the house again."

"And what else?" he asked. "You said you had a couple of thought roaming around inside that pretty head of yours."

"We interview Jeb and see if he knows more than he told Chief Winkle. He's alone now, in protective custody, he has to be depressed after seeing his mom's body thrown in the river. Maybe I could become his mother, so to speak. It appears he has never had a father he knew, it might help if he got to know you as well. Maybe a bond could develop between you two and he would add more information."

"Besides, a boy needs a man to learn from."

"A suggestion," Man said. "We ask Chief Winkle to put a surveillance team on the home of Logan. It would free us up to investigate more. They could watch the house around the clock."

"I like that," she said. "I hate stakeouts." She giggled. "Well, there were times on the last one I really did enjoy."

143

Chapter 10

An hour later with her head on his shoulder, making tiny ringlets with the hair on his chest, she was in deep thought. She pushed up to see his face. "Here's the way I see it. We need to meet Jeb Spencer and hear his story first hand as soon as possible. Chief Winkle said he would arrange that today. As I said, maybe I can get more out of him than Chief Winkle. Hopefully, a boy of maybe sixteen will confide in a woman more than a man since that is all he has ever known. He's alone now, and I know he's lonesome for his mother. She was all he had, and he's never experienced having a man to talk with. That is, that we know about."

"Jeb was jerked from a very traumatic experience, and that has to be hard on a teenage boy. That being coupled with being placed in a foster home with strangers has to be difficult on the young man."

"I agree," Man said, "and the sooner we get going the sooner we can dig into this case. He stood and started to dress. Kate saw what he was doing and slid from the bed and saw he was dressing in his working skins. She did the same. "Do we go armed?" she asked. "I assume so, since you're dressing for work."

"Yep, if Jeb is in danger, we need to be prepared in case something happens." They buckled their Walker Colts on and went to the door. When they reached the lobby, Man turned toward the back door of the hotel. He walked swiftly to the stables. "We have no idea where the boy is being kept. It may be close, or across town. Either way, mounted will make it faster."

Chief Winkle listened to Man's request and turned to Delmar. "Put a team to watch the Logan house and tell them to report to only me or you and keep their mouths shut. Set up a schedule and select a place where they'll not be discovered. I don't want the newspaper printing that Logan is a murder suspect."

Delmar stood and started toward the door, but stopped and turned back to talk to the Chief. "I'll take two men and see what's available as a place to observe from. As large as that house is, I expect there are side doors as well as a back door, shall I split the men?"

"You're right, there'll be more than two entrances, put as many men as you need watching the house. Two to a team so one can report if a man fitting the description goes to the house again."

"I'm sure Logan will leave his home every morning, do we put a tail on him? He might meet the killer somewhere else. He's smart and I suspect he doesn't want to take the chance of being seen with the assassin if anything ever happens."

"I agree, this is too important, have a backup team ready to follow Logan," Winkle said. "Tell them if they are spotted, they'll hear from me."

Delmar left the room. "Thanks Chief Winkle," Man said. "Will you have somebody take us to meet Jeb?"

"I'll do that myself. The boy is with a friend of mine. May I ask, what do you intend to do with the boy? The arrangements I made were only temporary, the couple keeping him are elderly, and should Jeb decide to leave, they couldn't stop him. But, I hope that isn't the case. Hopefully, Jeb knows he could be in danger, and where would he go? He and I talked about going back to his house and he knows that could be dangerous. He's a sharp kid and I explained if Logan had his mother murdered that he would be a lose end. I mentioned Logan knows he's capable of causing him trouble when he announces he's a candidate for the Washington job. His opponents would really work that angle."

Chief Winkle had one of his men saddle his horse and bring it to the front. Man and Kate mounted and followed the Chief to an older home, but with well-kept grounds. He circled to the rear, dismounted, and tied the horse to a hitching rail.

An older man dressed in tan pants and a blue shirt

came out to meet them. He was red cheeked, with a pleasant smile was on his face. He offered his hand to Kate first. "Maxwell Curtis," he said. "Are you a deputy marshal as well? I saw the badge on the man with you."

"Hello, Mr. Curtis. Nope, I only partner with him, and he's my husband. May I introduce Homer Manchester. Chief Marshal Joe Meek said they weren't ready for a female deputy marshal."

"I know Joe, and that sounds like his personal belief. Times are changing, but ol' Joe is of the old school."

The two men shook hands.

"I expect you came out in regard to Jeb," Maxwell said. "I'm worried about the boy. He only comes out of his room to eat and a growing boy should eat much more than him. He only picks at his food. I know he must be hurting inside after the traumatic painful experience he went through. He has to be deeply depressed."

"Deputy Manchester wants to interview the boy," Chief Winkle said. "Max, can we go inside, or had you rather bring the boy out?"

"Mr. Curtis, which do you think would be better for Jeb?" Kate asked. "You've been around him more than us since the tragedy."

"I don't rightly know," Curtis replied. "As I said, he only comes out of his room when we call him to eat. Belle is worried about him, she thinks he needs to be doing something to get his mind off the terrible situation."

"Belle is your wife?" Kate asked.

"Yea, we've been married for fifty-four years. She raised four boys and understands them a lot better than me," Curtis said.

"Do you have a horse he can ride for a few days?" Man asked. "Maybe a change would be beneficial. Kate and I'll take him with us and hopefully, he'll relax somewhat and open up and we can learn more details of what transpired."

"I don't know if he has any experience horseback," Max said. "But, I have a gentle gelding he can ride and keep as long as you need him. I got the horse from a puncher down on his luck and needed money fast. I loaned him twenty and he put the horse up as collateral, but never came back. That was a couple of months ago. He's a good quality horse and if the boy wants him, he can keep him. I have no need for him, and if it'll help, I'll be proud to let Jeb have him for his own horse. I doubt the boy has ever had anything of his own."

Curtis left and went into the house. A woman hurried out dressed in a long gray dress with her almost white hair was tied with a ribbon.

"I overheard Maxwell. I hope you can help Jeb. He ate only part of a biscuit for breakfast. It's almost lunchtime. I'll send along something for the young man to eat and pack everything he brought, which is very little."

She hurried back inside.

Max and Belle came out with Jeb between them. He was taller than Curtis, but very thin. He was dressed in city clothes. They were old, but clean. He had a cloth cap on his head. Belle handed him a sack with food, and another with his spare clothes.

Kate stepped forward to greet Jeb. "I'm Kate Manchester," she said. "This is United States Deputy Marshal Homer Manchester. But you can call him Man. Everybody does."

Man stepped forward and offered his hand to Jeb. The boy took it awkwardly. It was obvious he was unaccustomed to shaking hands with a man. Man gripped his hand firmly, but not hard enough to be painful

"Jeb, Mr. Curtis has a horse you can ride. Do you want to get out of here for a while and see the country?"

Jeb nodded his head up and down.

"Come with me Jeb, and help saddle the horse," Max said.

Chief Winkle hadn't spoken since the introductions. He was leaning against a tree letting Man and Kate take charge.

Kate and Man followed them inside a barn and to the

147

rear to a corral. A sorrel horse stood in the corner. Curtis handed Jeb a rope and pointed toward the horse. "Go put the rope on him," Max said.

The boy walked toward the horse making a loop. He tossed it over the head of the horse with a smooth motion, and led the horse into the barn.

Kate glanced and Man and smiled. Jeb wasn't a novice with horses.

"He's a beautiful horse. What's his name?" Kate asked.

"Darned if I know," Max said. "The puncher never told me. But then, I expected to keep him only a few days. Jeb, you can name him."

The boy didn't reply, only nodded. They watched Jeb brush the horse and carefully put the saddle blanket on his back. He tossed the saddle on the horse with ease and began to chinch it.

"Where did you learn that?" Kate asked.

"I worked in a livery stable after school, and on weekends," Jeb said.

"I exercised the horses that were kept there. Mr. Brewer had me ride each of them about a mile every day."

He put the sack of food in the saddlebags and tied the bag of containing his clothes on the back of the saddle. He led the horse outside the barn. Man and Kate went for Redbird and Arabian. "I don't know when we'll be back," Man said as they rode past Chief Winkle, Belle, and Maxwell.

"Bye," Belle said. "Enjoy your day."

"Thank you for everything," Jeb said. "I appreciate you letting me stay with you."

"It was our pleasure," Belle said. "Your room will be ready when you need it."

"Any place special you want to go?" Kate asked.

Jeb nodded and turned his horse toward the west. Man and Kate let him lead the way. He rode for over a mile and reined up on top of a hill overlooking the ocean.

He dismounted and walked to a rock shelf in the side

of the hill. They instantly saw a rock fire circle, and evidence somebody had camped here.

"You've been here before," Kate said.

"Many times," Jeb said. "This is my camp. When I needed to get out of the house, I often came here." He went to the rear and behind a rock and brought out a wooden box. They saw it had an assortment of things such as food and clothing, but more important, they saw an old pistol.

"Does it shoot?" Man asked.

"Yes, and I'm pretty good. I practice when I can buy bullets. If I had it when that man killed my mom, I would have used it on him. Mom wouldn't let me keep it in the house. She was afraid of guns."

Jeb brought the old pistol to Man. "It won't compare with the Walker Colts you have," he said.

They were surprised he recognized them. Man pulled one of the pistols from the holster and handed it to Jeb. The boy gasped at the beauty and workmanship of the weapon. "Will you let me fire it someday?" Jeb asked.

"Sure, now if you want. Have you practiced here? We don't need somebody hearing and investigating."

"It's safe, follow me," Jeb said as he turned to walk the other direction still inspecting the weapon. He went down the hill toward the ocean and stopped near the bottom. He pointed the Walker toward a rock about the size of a man. A dark circle was painted on the bolder about the size of a man's chest.

"I only have four bullets left, and was saving them if I ever see the man that murdered mom."

"Shoot mine," Man said.

Kate stood back, watching Jeb and Man, inwardly smiling. It was working as she hoped, they were bonding.

Jeb fingered the weapon again and pulled it up and fired with one smooth motion. A hole appeared dead center in the circle.

"Fire four more," Man said.

Jeb pulled the trigger four times in rapid succession

and the pattern could be covered with a coffee cup.

"Darn good shooting," Man said.

Jeb smiled.

"Why did you want to learn to shoot?" Man asked.

"I knew someday I would need to know."

"Why is that? What happened to make you think you would need to learn to shoot?"

"I had rather not talk about it," Jeb said and handed the pistol back to Man.

Man didn't ask more. Instead, he loaded the pistol and put it in his holster.

"Where did you get the pistol?" he asked.

"I found it," Jeb said quickly looking toward the ocean.

"The character of a man is earned," Man said. "Be honest with us and we'll always do the same. I'm not here because of the pistol. But, since I brought it up, do you know why we came to see you?"

"Sure, Logan would have me murdered if he knew I saw the man that murdered mom, and then go to his home. And I could be a threat to him being elected to go to Washington. Chief Winkle told me that was why he hid me out with Mr. and Mrs. Curtis."

"So where did you get the pistol?" Man asked.

"It was about two years ago," Jeb said, meeting Man's gaze. "A man came to our home." His face turned red and the leaders in his neck extended and his hands curled into a fist.

"He hurt mom. She was fighting him and hit him with her fist. His nose started to bleed. He pulled this pistol and tried to shoot her. It misfired and he threw it at her. It hit her in the chest and knocked her to the floor. I hit the man on the head with a piece of firewood."

Mom helped me drag the man outside, and we locked the door. It was raining. We watched at the window until the man came to and staggered away. He was too drunk to remember the pistol, and probably didn't know what happened. We never saw him again."

"Mom told me to get rid of it. But, I took the pistol to a gunsmith and cleaned his shop for a week in exchange for working on the pistol and a box of bullets. I cleaned the shop every Sunday night after I got off at the livery stable for a box of ammunition."

"Thanks for being honest," Man said. They walked back to the camp and Kate went for wood and built a fire. She pulled food from her and Man's saddlebags and began to cook. Jeb went for the sack that Belle gave him. Kate took it and added it to the food she had, and soon had a hot meal ready.

They sat on rocks to eat. Jeb ate as if he hadn't eaten in days. Kate smiled. The therapy was working. He needed to get outside and think about something besides him mom.

Man waited until they finished and Kate took the tin plates away. "Tell me what you know," Man said. "The more information we have, the better our chances are of helping you, and finding the killer."

Jeb paused in thought before speaking. "Where do you want me to start?"

"Anywhere you want. No matter how insignificant you may think a detail may be, tell us. Something you may think is of no importance may be the clue we need find the man that killed your mother, and we can put Logan away."

"That I doubt," Jeb said. "Logan is too powerful and has influential friends in high places."

Neither Kate nor Man commented on that statement. He could be right.

"I'm going to start with my grandparents," Jeb said. "I never met them, but mom told me about them. My grandfather was a lumberjack, his wife was the cook in a lumber camp. Both were uneducated, real backwoods people. My mom was born in the camp and never went to school. She didn't know how to read or write."

"Her father died and her mom brought her to Seattle. She was about twelve or so. Her mom got a job with Logan's parents as a maid. When mom was a late teen,

151

well, Logan, you know. Mom got pregnant with me. Logan moved her to the house we live in, I mean we lived in. I can never go back there."

"Mom told me that Logan gave her money. He came to our home often when I was young, but I remember. She put me to bed, but I heard them. At first, I didn't understand. Later, when I was older, well, I understood what was going on. I heard mom and Logan arguing when I was about ten. She said he couldn't come back anymore. I was getting too old and it wasn't right."

"After that, she started going to him at another house. I followed her at times. I knew why she went, but she refused to discuss it with me. She kept saying I was too young to understand."

"She always came back from seeing Logan with money. It wasn't much, but with what she got washing dishes at a café, we did okay. As I said, I worked after school and on weekends."

"Mom was very determined I learn. Every night, we sat at our table and studied. She joined me and learned to read and write. She said the only way for me to get out of our situation was an education."

He paused and sat staring at the ground.

"Go on," Kate encouraged, wanting him to talk freely without interruption.

"I love to read and got every book I could find. I often found discarded newspapers and read every word. One of my teachers loaned me books to bring home."

"Going back to Mom and Logan, she told me that he told her he was going to run for political office and go to Washington. He said seeing her had to stop. If his opponents found out about mom, it would ruin his chances of being elected. He promised her a large sum of money if she would leave Seattle and never tell anybody about us. She agreed and went to meet him for the last time. She was going to get the money and we were going to leave that day. That was when she was murdered."

"I think Logan had her killed for two reasons. First,

he wanted to keep from paying her, second, to eliminate any chance of a scandal from arising because of us. I'm smart enough to know I'm a threat to him as well. Chief Winkle hid me out with the Curtis family. He thought Logan would find out I was taken to the police station, and I would be in danger."

"Chief Winkle could be right," Kate said. "That's one of the reasons we came for you. Do you have any money?" Do you have any thoughts on what to do, or where you want to go?"

"I have less than two dollars. And, no, I haven't decided what to do or where to go. Mom was talking about San Francisco. I can't go back to work at the livery. Logan knows I work there. He could send the man after me there. As has been said, I can't go back to where we lived. That house belongs to Logan and the man that killed mom might be watching it."

"Would you like to stay with us until this is resolved?" Man asked.

"Yes, very much," Jeb replied.

"The hotel may not be safe, a shooter from the top of buildings would have a clear shot at you coming or leaving. We could camp here."

"It would be safe here," Jeb said. "Nobody knows about this place, and we can see anybody approaching. The ocean protects us on one side, and the steep cliff on the other side, so nobody could circle us."

"Man," Kate said. "Stay here with Jeb and I'll go to the hotel for our things, and buy supplies. I can go by and tell Chief Winkle we'll be in contact with him for any updates. I hesitate on giving our location. Logan may have ears in the police station."

"Good thinking," Man said. "Watch for a tail when you leave the police station and hotel and bring the mules." Man said. "There's ample grass on the hillside for them and our horses. Jeb and I'll work on the campsite until you get back."

She went to Redbird and stepped into the saddle.

153

Man walked to her. "Stop by the gunsmith and buy a better weapon for Jeb and a supply of ammunition. You never know when he'll need it. He's old enough to join us in a fight if necessary. Also, see what they have in a quality rifle. He may as well be outfitted properly. Get him some better clothing to wear. He'll need a warm coat."

She nodded and rode away.

Jeb heard the exchange. "Why?" he asked.

"For the obvious reasons, you can help us if the need arises."

"I didn't mean that. Why are you doing this for me?"

"We like you and want to protect you and get whoever killed your mother. I was left an orphan after the war, and a man took me in when I was younger than you. I lived with him until he died. I believe we should help others. Maybe someday, you can take in a young man that needs your help."

Jeb nodded.

They staked their horses out to graze and got busy improving the camp while they waited for Kate to return. Man cut wood into fire length and Jeb stacked in beside the fire ring. They tossed rocks away making a smooth place to sleep.

***

Kate went to the hotel first and loaded their belongings on the mules and then went to the gunsmith. She explained what she wanted.

"Are the weapons for Jeb?" he asked.

Kate nodded.

Jeb worked for me some, he cleaned my shop in exchange for bullets for that old antique. "My brother is a policeman, and he told me about Jeb's situation. Sad business and Jeb is such a good kid. He's a hard worker and honest. I never worried about him taking a thing and gave him a key to come in on Sunday night to clean. He always did a great job and put up things I left scattered around."

"I'm glad you're helping the lad," the gunsmith

154

added. "He never had a chance before in the environment he was raised in, but hopefully, he can have that chance now. But that will be away from here. People know about him and his mom, and they have labeled him. I've heard comments made about that bastard son of Jane Spencer. I know the kids heard and teased him. But, I never saw Jeb lose his temper and that was more than I can say for me and I wasn't the one being talked about."

"I had one customer tell me I shouldn't let that kind of kid work for me. I asked the customer to get out of my store and never come back and that Jeb had never been in trouble or in jail like the customer had."

The gunsmith went to a rack and pulled down a Henry. I can vouch for this rifle. I sold it to the man that used it. He was a merchant and I doubt it has been fired a hundred times in its life. When he died, his wife brought it to me to sell for her. He opened a case and took out a pistol. "A Colt," he said. "It shoots the same ammunition as the Walkers you carry. It won't compare in quality, but it's a good weapon and reliable. I've worked it over and it won't let Jeb down in a fight."

She picked up six boxes of ammunitions and put them on the counter.

He went to a rack of holsters and found one that would fit the pistol and Jeb's slim waist. "Does he need a saddle holster for the rifle?"

"Yes," she replied as she looked at the selection. "Man and I each have two rifles, another scabbard would be better than keeping the extras in our bedrolls."

She selected two rifle scabbards made for the left side of the saddle. The gunsmith put the purchases in a cloth sack for easy carrying. She paid the charge and turned toward the door.

"As I said, Jeb's a good lad," the gunsmith said. "I hope you get the man that killed his mother. That was a low thing to do, even for her. I mean, her lifestyle. However, I have to admire her, she had no skills to offer in the work force, she washed dishes, and did what she had to do to survive and support herself and Jeb. He always had food to eat and clothes to wear. They weren't fancy, but he stayed warm in the winter and had shoes on his feet."

"I agree," Kate said. "I hope we find the man that murdered her."

"As I said, my brother is a policeman. He gave me the description of the man that murdered Jane Spencer. I may have spotted the man, at least he fit the description. I was on the way home last night and saw the man going into the Seashore Saloon. Do you know where it's located?"

"Nope, this is our fist time to Seattle, and we've only been here a few days."

He pointed. "Go on this street until it dead ends, turn right, and go about eight to ten blocks. The Seashore is on the right, corner building. You can't miss it. It was almost dark when I saw the man. I could be wrong as a lot of men fit that description. I intend to tell my brother today."

"Let us handle it," Kate said. "Jeb can go with us and stakeout the saloon. He's the only person that can identify the man that killed his mother."

"I hope it's him and you get him," the gunsmith said.

"We fully intend to do that," she said. "Maybe with your help, we can put him away."

"Save the tax payers the expense of room and board in a jail. Put him in the ground where he belongs."

"Kate took the sack to one of the mules and rode to a mercantile store for clothing for Jeb. She had to guess on sizes, but felt they would fit close enough. She got two full sets, a warm coat, fur lined gloves, and a felt hat. As she was walking out, she saw a boot store across the street and went in. Again, she had to guess on his size. She bought riding boots and spurs.

She stopped at another store and bought a few more supplies. Now that Jeb was eating like a growing boy, she was cooking twice the amount she normally cooked for

156

her and Man.

Man and Jeb saw her coming and walked out to meet her. Without being told, Jeb began unloading the mules. He eyed the sack with the weapons, but didn't attempt to open it.

Man took Redbird and the mules to graze with Arabian and Jeb's horse. When he got back, Jeb was dressed in his new clothing. He was smiling from ear to ear. They were too large, but so much better than what he had been wearing, he was elated. Besides, he was still a growing boy.

The boots fit perfectly and he walked around listening to the spurs jingle with a huge smile on his face. "This is the first time I ever wore boots," he said.

Kate opened the sack and tossed him the pistol and holster. He caught it in the air and quickly pulled the weapon and inspected it. "It's loaded," she said. "As somebody once said, an empty pistol is no better than a stick of firewood in a fight."

Man took the rifle from the sack, looked at it, and then worked the leaver. "Smooth," he said.

"Almost like new," she said.

Man handed it to Jeb. He looked at the Henry and another huge smile crossed his face. "I know this rifle. I helped clean it when it was brought in by the widow lady."

"Have you fired a rifle?" Kate asked.

"No, well, a few times helping adjust the sights, but no, not really shoot one outside. I could never afford a rifle or ammunition."

"Now is as good a time as any," Kate said as she tossed him a box of ammunition.

Man stood beside Jeb and gave him pointers. He knew the basics and was a quick learner. On the second magazine of bullets, he was hitting the target with every shot. Having experience with the pistol helped, and he was blessed with good hand to eye coordination. After watching Jeb fire more rounds, he turned to Kate. "He's a natural."

157

She nodded agreement and in her mind's eye, she hoped to be the mother of a young man like Jeb. Seeing Man and the boy stirred the mother instinct deep inside her being.

Kate took the saddle scabbards from the bag and tossed the scabbard she bought for Jeb to him. Then she began putting the extra on her saddle. Man saw her and reached for his that Kate put on his saddle. She pulled her extra Winchester Model 1873 from the bedroll. Jeb saw it and almost ran to her. "Wow," he exclaimed. "You have two of them, a twin pair of the most remarkable weapon ever made."

"We live in a violent land," Man said. "The best weapons available are necessary to survive. That's why we both carry two Walker Colts and each has two Winchester Model 1873 rifles."

Kate led Man and Jeb to rocks beside the fire to sit before speaking. The wind was cold and Jeb welcomed the new coat. "The gunsmith told me his brother is a policeman and gave him the description of the man we're hunting. He said on the way home last night he saw a man that fit the description. The man was going into the Seashore Saloon. Gunsmith gave me directions if we want to do a stakeout tonight and see if the man you saw shows. I know it's a long shot, as there are a lot of men that fit the description."

"If it's him, I would recognize him," Jeb said. "I got a good look at him, and his face. I'll never forget, and could pick him out of a crowd."

"The gunsmith said it was almost dark when he went into the saloon. But we need to set up a place earlier and watch."

"I know where the Seashore Saloon is located," Jeb said. "A lot of fishermen go there. From what I heard, it's a rough place."

"If I recall correctly," he said, "there's a store across the street with a false front. If we could get up there, we would have a good view of the entrance to the Seashore

158

Saloon."

Kate stood and went for her cooking pan. "I brought more food, it's on the packsaddle. Jeb, would you bring it to me. We need to eat before going. We may be there a long while waiting."

Jeb led the way and they found the store across the street closed. Man folded his hands together as a step for Jeb and helped him scramble up on the porch. He then offered them to Kate and Jeb reached down and helped her up. Man jumped and caught the edge of the porch and pulled himself up.

They found a place to sit and Man reached for his binoculars and handed them to Jeb. He showed the young man how to adjust them to his eyes, and they sat back to wait and watch.

Jeb was ready with each new arrival, and time after time shook his head.

They watched for three hours before Man stood. "It's getting late and I doubt he'll come now. We'll try again tomorrow night unless something else turns up."

He jumped down, and was ready to help Kate. Jeb jumped off like Man and they went to where their horses were tied. "I'm sorry," Jeb said.

"Don't apologize," Kate said. "It was our decision to watch the saloon tonight. Besides, it's the only option we have now. Unless he goes back to Logan's house, which is doubtful, it beats doing nothing."

The moon offered adequate light for them to go back to the camp. As they rode, Kate glanced at Jeb. His eyes were alert, and he was in deep thought.

"What are you thinking about?" she asked.

"Something that was said earlier, when this is over, what will I do. I have no place to go or live, and no money."

"That put Kate's mind in gear as she began to think. She was hesitant to take Jeb with them they couldn't just turn him out. They would be after Bull, and that would surely end with a bloody gunfight. Bull would never go

159

down easily as a hanging would be waiting.

To change the subject, she asked, "Have you thought of a name for the horse?"

Jeb turned to face her. "What about Socks?" he said. "He has four white stocking legs."

"That's a good name and fits his description," Man put in. "I expect Redbird was named because of his color, and I named my horse Arabian for his heritage."

They rode in silence for a few minutes before Jeb spoke. "I never knew there were nice people like you. Usually, I was put down because of where we lived, and the clothes I wore. It was no secrete what mom did, I mean, well, besides Logan. Chief Winkle, then Mr. and Mrs. Curtis, he took me in and gave me Socks, but more especially you two. Helping me and outfitting me with clothes and weapons. I'll never be able to thank you enough for your kindness."

"We enjoy helping you," Man said. "As I said before, return the favor to somebody in the future."

The following night they went back to the saloon. They sat on the front of the store again and watched for three hours with the same results, nothing.

It was on the third night a man came down the street. Jeb instantly sat up and focused on the image in the binoculars. "That's him," he said with excitement reflected in his voice.

"Are you sure?" Kate asked as she strained her eyes looking at the man in the darkness. "He fits the description of the suspect."

"Yea, it's him. There's no doubt in my mind. I got a good look at him. He killed my mom and tossed her body in the river. I'm positive, that's the man that murdered my mom."

"I'm going inside the Saloon," Man said. He pulled his badge from his shirt and put it in his pocket. "You two wait outside." He looked at Jeb with a meaningful stare. "We need him alive to answer questions and have proof of Logan's involvement. Don't let your emotions override

160

your good sense. With him dead, there would be no way to prove Logan paid him to kill your mother."

"I won't kill him unless he forces me to shoot, I promise."

"Don't let him get you. He may come out shooting, if so, take him down with a leg shot if possible. What I'm saying is, shoot to kill, but only if that's the only option to save yourself."

"I'll be with Jeb," Kate said. "What are you going to do inside?"

"I'll make contact and hopefully get him outside where we can make the arrest, and turn him over to Chief Winkle."

He was wearing his town clothes, and would blend in with the saloon crowd. Man waited and watched Kate and Jeb take positions on each side of the saloon before shoving the bat-wing doors open, and boldly walk inside. He let his eyes adjust to the light and spotted the suspect at the bar talking with another man about the same age. Neither man glanced at Man as he maneuvered to the bar a few feet away.

Man ordered a beer, and stood listening to the men talk. They were discussing women and laughing. He waited, hoping they would talk about something more useful than bragging about their conquest.

The man with the suspect asked, "Any jobs in the horizon? I'm almost broke."

"One possible, I'll know in a couple of days."

"What is it?" the other man asked.

"Logan wants a major critic shut up, permanently, and I have a contract on the son of the woman I whacked. That was an easy five hundred. It's a shame the boy wasn't around to earn the other five. But, I'll find him. Logan said the police have him hidden somewhere, but so far doesn't know the location. I suspect Logan has ears in the police station and will get the information for me in a few days."

"Are you going to share the job with me?" the other

man asked, hopefully.

"Hell no, not to take out a kid, it'll be like shooting fish in a barrel. Why should I share with you for doing nothing? All I have to do is find him and one shot and I collect another five hundred."

"Novak, I thought we were friends. I let you join me on a couple of jobs. I need the money, let me take the boy for half."

"Only because you needed me on those jobs," Novak said. "I'm not into charity Tony. If I need you to side me, then I'll cut you in for half, but on a simple job like killing a kid, no way. Maybe on the other job Logan has lined up I'll need you. But, I don't have the details as yet. The critic works for the newspaper and has been writing nasty things about Logan."

"I read the paper," Tony said. "I know the critic that's bad-mouthing Logan. From what I hear, Logan is pumped up and high strutting like a peacock. I also heard he imagines himself as a future president."

Man had heard enough. He left over half of the beer and turned away from the pair of killers and angled to the door. He turned to the side toward Kate and motioned for Jeb to join them.

He quickly told them what he overheard. "Jeb, get your horse and go after Chief Winkle. Tell him we have two men to take into custody, and to bring backups. Both are armed, and I expect a fight. I doubt Winkle is at the police station this late. Do you know where he lives?"

"Yes sir. It's not far from here."

"Go to his house first and tell Winkle we'll keep the Seashore under surveillance until he and his men get here. There are three doors. Front, back, and one on the side that opens into a storage room. We need to cover all three in case they try to break out. But hopefully, we can take them by surprise when they come out and avoid any shooting."

Jeb mounted Socks and spurred him into a lope.

"Which door do I watch?" she asked.

"I expect if they attempt to leave, it'll be through the front door since they have no idea anybody is on to them. But, to be safe, take the rear. Surely, they won't use the side door as that is used for deliveries, and to get to it, they would have to go through the storeroom."

She moved quickly toward the rear of the saloon. Man took a position behind a water barrel at the corner. As he was moving into position, two men came down the street laughing until they spotted Man. One of them grabbed his pistol and shot much too quickly. His shot went well over Man's head. "That's the deputy marshal," he shouted.

The inside of the Seashore Saloon erupted as if a swarm of bees invaded the room. Men stormed out in a rush, more through the rear door than the front where the gunfight raged.

Man scrambled down behind the water barrel as four bullets plowed into it. Water poured from the holes. Both men were shooting at him.

Man had both pistols in his hand, but waited for an opening to show his head. He knew they would be waiting for a target.

Kate came around the corner of the building with her pistols blazing. She had the advantage, and could see both men clearly. Her shots were well placed and both men went down with blood gushing from two wounds each in their chest.

Man leaped from his hiding place and hurried toward the two men. He kicked their pistols away and bent to examine the faces. Kate joined him, replacing the bullets in her pistols.

"Do we know them?" she asked.

"I don't think so," he replied. "But they knew me on sight."

"I heard one of them saying you were the deputy marshal and the shooting started," she said.

Chief Winkle and four policemen raced down the street, and they dismounted beside Man and Kate. "I see

163

you got them before we got here."

"Nope," Man said. "The one with the beard recognized me as a marshal and opened fire. We were waiting for you. The other joined him shooting at me. I don't know either of them."

"If both opened fire on you, they must have been lousy shots for you to be standing without a scratch."

"The bearded one saw me and shot too fast and his bullet went over my head. I was close to that water barrel and took cover." He gestured toward it with his hand. Water was still trickling from the bullet holes.

"Kate was covering the rear door and came around the corner. She had a clear view of both and put them down. I never got off a shot. Damn, it's great having a partner to have my back."

Chief Winkle bent to examine the faces. The policeman made a circle around the bodies to keep the spectators away. The Chief struck a match to offer more light. "I've never seen them before, but when we get the bodies to the station, maybe somebody will recognize them."

He turned to one of the policeman. "Go tell Hank to bring the meat wagon."

Jeb was standing well back in the crowd watching holding the reins to Socks. Kate saw him and motioned him to join her. Together, they walked to where Redbird and Arabian were tied. "Let's get out of here," she said. "Man will need to go to the station with the Chief. I don't want you to be out here exposed since Logan wants you dead. There may be others looking for you."

Man hurried to them when he saw Kate mount Redbird. He took the reins of Arabian from her. "I'll meet you at the camp as soon as I can."

She nodded and turned Redbird into the night. Jeb followed close behind her, but occasionally, looking back.

Kate dismounted at their camp and waited for Jeb. She began to unsaddle Redbird and Jeb did the same with Socks. "Stake them out and come to camp. I'll put something on to cook. It's been five hours since we had anything, and I'm hungry. I know you must be starved," she said.

Jeb came back to camp a few minutes later and sat on a rock to watch Kate. "I heard what happened," he said. "So the man that killed mom got away?"

"I'm sorry," she said. "When the shooting started everybody rushed outside. I went to help Man. I didn't see him leave."

"I understand," he said. "You did the right thing. Can I ask a question?" he said.

"Of course, but I may or not reply, it depends on the question."

"What does it feel like to kill a man?" he asked

Kate stood and faced the young man. "I hope you never have to experience it," she said. "But if killing is for the right reason, you can live with it, and accept it."

"What is the right reason?" he asked.

"If the man is attempting to murder you, or someone else, like those two were, it doesn't bother me at all. It was two against one with Man. They had the advantage, and he was pinned down behind the barrel. One of them would surely have killed him. I killed to save my husband. That is one of the right reasons. I would kill to save you as well."

Jeb was listening to her, intently.

She continued, "I certainly recall the first man I killed. It was a situation where Man was about to be shot in cold blood. I didn't hesitate one second, and there were no regrets, or remorse. I didn't lose any sleep over it."

"I think I would kill the man that murdered mom without regrets or remorse," he said. "But, I would take him to Chief Winkle if I had the choice, and let the courts decide his fate, but would be standing on the front row when they hung him."

Kate nodded she understood. She could see this boy turning into a fine man. He could become another Man is a few years. He needed more maturity, but his head was

165

screwed on right, and he had the right set of values. The gunsmith said he was honest.

**

Man joined them and Kate filled a tin plate for him. She and Jeb sat and sipped hot coffee until he was ready to talk.

"A policeman at the station recognized one of them. Not the one with the beard that shot at me first. The one he knew was a local outlaw. Nothing serious, but he had been arrested several times for minor offenses, each time, the crime was larger than the one before. He was working up to be a real problem. But Kate put an end to his career in crime. Good shooting Kate, both were hit twice in the center of their chest. I was so happy to see you charge around the building with both Walkers blazing. They had me pinned down where if I stuck my head out, it would have been blown away."

"Chief Winkle will investigate and try to identify the bearded one. I have a theory from his dress and beard. He could have been one of the men with Bull. If I'm right, they know us, and what we look like. We have to play this from now on as if they know we're here, and behind them. They could pull out immediately, and we have a case to solve first."

"I'm sorry," Jeb said. "I'm keeping you away from catching Bull and his gang."

"Keeping you safe and putting Novak behind bars, or under the ground, is more important now," Kate said. "If Bull becomes a rabbit, we'll pick him up again. We have before."

"Chief Winkle is looking into the names Novak and Tony," Man put in. "So far nothing, they're assuming Novak is a last name and Tony a first, but so far, nothing more."

"But, worse, Logan will know we know about his hit man. That kind of information will get back to him. Novak said he has ears in the police station. We know he has friends in the courthouse. I expect one of two things to happen, Novak will be found dead or disappear."

"What do we do now?" Kate asked.

"Get some sleep, there's nothing we can do tonight," Man said with a yawn.

Chapter 11

Man led the way the next morning and the three rode into town. It was unlikely anybody would we waiting in downtown Seattle gunning for Jeb, but Kate and Man watched both sides of the street for any unusual attention given them. The streets were crowded, but nobody paid any attention to the trio. They were dressed in town clothes.

They tied their horses at the hitching rail and went into the police station. A policeman at a desk saw them and motioned with his hand. "Chief Winkle is in his office and hoped you would drop by."

Man led the way and tapped on Winkle's partly open door. "Come in," the Chief said. "I have news for you."

He stood and gestured toward chairs and waited until they were seated before speaking. "First, we identified the shooter with the beard. His name is Theo Geyser and there were several wants out on him. We haven't nailed it as yet, but there's evidence he may have been riding with Bull."

Man and Kate moaned. "I suspected as much," Man said. "His clothing and beard fit the men riding with Bull. He knew me on sight and that worries me. He also called me deputy marshal."

"What about Novak?" Kate asked.

"We have information on his as well," Chief Winkle said. "Novak is a gun for hire out of Vancouver. It appears he would gun anybody down for a fee. My theory is that Logan hired him to murder Jane and Jeb, five hundred each. He got half and is waiting for a chance to finish the boy."

They all glanced at Jeb. He was seated with his back straight and there was no evidence of fear on his face. "I have a reliable pistol and rifle now, and I'm pretty good with them," Jeb said. "If he come for me, I hope I have a chance to prove it."

"We have to be careful," Kate said. "I read Novak as a back shooter."

"Did you learn anything about the man with him at the Seashore Saloon, Tony?" Kate asked.

"We have three men with the first name of Tony," he said. "All three generally match the description you gave us. Any of the three fit the bill as a gun for hire like Novak. Our men are checking the last known address of all three this morning. Maybe we can find the right one and get a lead on where Novak is staying."

"Chief Winkle," Man said. "I'm considering going to Logan for a face to face chat. You know him, what are your thoughts on that?"

"Logan is sharp, and I doubt you'll get a thing out of him. He's a smooth talking politician, and will say anything with a smile on his face. He's a well-trained lawyer, and can lie with the best of them. Before he turned politician, I have seen him tell bald faced lies to the jury in such a fashion, you would think he was reading from the good book."

"I wish the lawyers had to put their hand on the bible and swear to tell the whole truth and nothing but the truth, like the witnesses. But I guess that since a majority of the lawmakers in congress are lawyers, that'll never be put into law. They protect each other. Even Judges overlook them lying to the jury. They appear to fight each other in court, but that's only for show. I've seen them after a fierce court battle toasting a few, and laughing together about their performance in the courtroom."

Since neither Man nor Kate were experienced in that phase of the law, they just nodded. Jeb was taking it all in, listening intently."

"So you think I would be wasting my time going to talk to Logan?" Man asked.

"In my opinion, I expect he would learn more from you being there than you would learn from him. I think he would play dumb and ask why and what you were there for, and he would be outraged at such an allegation. He could, and I expect, he would contact his friends and supporters to contact Joe Meek and put pressure on Joe to order you to back off."

"What if Man plays dumb as well and inadvertently give him the location of Jeb. We would set up a trap for whoever he sends to kill Jeb and likely us."

Chief Winkle rubbed his chin in thought. "That could work, but you would have to be careful. I could loan you a few men to back you. Do you have any idea where?"

"Where we're camped," Jeb said. "There's only one good way to approach with the ocean and the terrain. I could be on top of the hill with the binoculars. I would have a clear view of any approaching riders. There are plenty of places to hide, and let them ride into a trap."

Everybody was looking at the boy, but Kate was the first to speak. "That seems to be our best option at the moment. We need to get this case finished, so we can get back on the trail of Bull."

"How many men do you want and when?" Chief Winkle asked.

"Since we don't have any idea how many men Logan will send, if any, what can you spare for a few days?"

"I can let you have three to a shift. I'll pick men that I know will keep their mouth shut. As I said, Logan is sharp, he might smell a trap and do the unexpected. If word is leaked to him what we're planning, the scheme would be dead in the water before it ever starts."

"I have another thought on that matter," Chief Winkle said. "From what you overheard, I have a stooge working for me. I've been thinking about who, and have it narrowed down to one suspect. I may be able to work it so I'll be sure. What about me leaking that information to him and see if he goes to Logan? If he does, I can rid myself of a bad cop, and Logan could buy it better coming from his source here. In my opinion, he would see right through your plan if you went to him. Like I said, he's plenty smart and has a devious mind. There's no doubt of that."

"I agree to your suggestion," Man said. Kate was nodding.

They left the police station and Man led the way to the telegraph office where he sent as wire to Joe Meek. He gave his report on the developments, and outlined his plans.

A one-word reply came within minutes. Proceed.

Before he left the telegraph office he said, "One word to anybody, and you could be charged with abetting a criminal."

"I've been at this job for over twenty years," the operator said. "I can keep my mouth shut, and have suspected Logan was a crook for a long time. Since there's only one telegraph line out of Seattle, I read every message sent and received."

Man filed that bit of information away for future use if needed. Did Logan contact Novak by telegraph?

***

They dismounted and Man took the reins of Redbird when they got to the campsite. Jeb dismounted and he and Man led the horses to a fresh place to graze. Kate went to the camp.

Kate was waiting at the fire, making coffee when they came back.

"It'll take time for Chief Winkle to set it up. He'll have to arrange a way for the word to leak to his suspected spy, and for him to get word to Logan. Then Logan would have to get word to Novak."

"At the earliest, it'll be dark before we have visitors, but I really expect it will be tomorrow. That is, if the scheme works at all. First, Winkle has to be right on the informer. Second, the word has to get to Logan and he believes it. Third, he gets word to Novak and I doubt Novak will try this alone when he learns we are with Jeb. He may recruit Tony and possibility others to help."

"But we need to eat, and then get into position, just in case Novak comes visiting tonight. It could be a long

171

night as we have to be ready. He might show up at dawn hoping we are all asleep."

Kate filled the plates and they sat on rocks to eat. As soon as they finished, Man went for the binoculars and handed them to Jeb. "Wear your new coat and take a couple of blankets. With the wind, it'll be cold up there. Once you're in place, we can decide how to communicate. They might hear you if you shout down at us."

They noticed he was wearing his pistol and had the rifle under his arm.

"Put an extra bullet in the pistol and jack a shell into the firing chamber," Man said. "Don't do it after they get here, as they could hear. Be ready, and stay alert," Kate said. "But don't shoot unless a fight starts. As we discussed, we want Novak alive so he can talk. As we discussed, I think Novak will bring a few more to help. So be careful, and don't give them a target. Find good cover and stay behind it if shooting starts."

"I'll be careful," he said.

The agile young man scrambled up the slope of the hill until he was at the top. He stood on a rock shelf and looked down. "From here I can see anybody approaching for at least a half mile. How do I let you know?"

"Your voice could carry much too well from up there. Toss a rock down on the top of the bolder at the foot of the hill. We need to see if we can hear it from where we'll be hiding in the trees. Wait until we're in position to toss one to make sure."

Jeb waited until Man and Kate were hidden in the trees and Man shouted, "Okay, try it."

He dropped a rock the size of an apple and the sound echoed loud enough for them to hear.

"Perfect," Kate said. "After you see them approaching, take cover, and don't show yourself. On top of the hill, they would have a good shot after the moon is up. Wait patiently and keep watch, but more important, don't shoot until it's necessary. I know I keep mentioning that, but this is your first time under fire, and

172

your emotions will be at an all time high."

"Yes mom," he teased. "I see three riders coming. It's the policeman Chief Winkle is sending."

The policeman dismounted where the other horses were staked and Man and Kate joined them. "Jeb is on top of the hill with binoculars and can see any approaching riders," Man said. "We intend to let them ride into camp, and close the trap behind them. We want them alive to do some talking, that is, if they throw down their arms."

"Find a good place to wait several yards back down the trail and let them pass, and then close in behind them."

"I hope they show up soon," one of the policeman said. "It'll be cold sitting here in the wind off the ocean tonight."

"I hope you brought blankets. If not, we can spare one each for you."

"We have our bedrolls, this is not our first stakeout," the older policeman said. "I hope the plan works and Logan sends the man that murdered Jane Spencer. A killer for hire is about as low as a man can get in my opinion, especially, a man that will take a job to murder a woman and a kid."

"Only men that steal women for sale is lower in my opinion," Kate injected.

Both policemen looked at Kate, surprised by her comment. The spokesman tapped his forehead in thought. "You two are the couple that took down Truman Vincent and Bedford Leach. We heard about that. Yea, I agree, they were worse than a hired murderer. Their victims suffered a long time before they died. I saw some of the Indian women sold to loggers a few years back. It was awful the way they were treated. Maybe it isn't as bad as Indians treat captured white women, but it was still bad."

"It's getting dark," Kate said. "We need to find our positions before dark. Jeb will drop a rock from the top if he sees riders approaching."

173

Kate took one side and Man the other so they would have an open shooting lane should the invaders attempt to fight instead of surrendering.

"Jeb, do you hear me?" Kate asked just above a normal speaking tone.

"Yes," he replied.

"You must stay awake, we're depending on you to give us warning. If you doze off, they could be inside the camp before we knew they were close, which could cost us our lives if they surprise us."

"I'll be awake and alert," he said. "You can depend on me."

Darkness settled over the camp and only the night sounds could be heard. The ocean was calm, but they could hear the faint sound of waves splashing on rocks.

Midnight passed and the moon was moving toward the western horizon. It would soon be so dark seeing anything would prove to be difficult. Yet they waited as the time passed slowly. Nobody moved from their position until the sun peeked over the mountains to the east.

Man walked out and threw wood on the fire. Kate saw him and crawled from her bedroll and joined him. "Jeb, pack it in," he said. "They aren't coming."

The three policemen came walking in from their hiding place with their bedrolls over their shoulder. "Damn," one of them said. "It was a long night with nothing to show for it."

"It's not the first time and won't be the last," the older policeman said. "That goes with the job."

Kate had a pot of coffee making. "I didn't hear your names," she said.

"I'm Wilson," the older man said. "My partners are Suter and Thomas." They held their hand up as they were introduced. "Chief Winkle told us your names. Hello Kate, nice to meet you."

"You to, Wilson," she replied. "The coffee is about ready, and I can put some breakfast on to cook."

174

"Just coffee for us," Wilson said. "We need to report back to the Chief. I know he'll ask, what are your plans now?"

"Get some sleep and wait for night, but we'll keep a sentry," Man said. "I doubt they'll try during daylight, but you never know. I don't want to wake up looking at the business end of a pistol pointed at my nose."

"If they got that close," Wilson said. "I doubt you would ever wake up. You would be dead. Those kinds of men play for keeps."

Kate passed out cups for the coffee, and walked around filling them from the big pot."

Man and Jeb went to move the horses and mules to a new place to graze, and brought the three mounts back to the policeman. "Will you be back tonight?" he asked.

"It'll depend on the Chief," Wilson said. "But, I expect we'll be here. The Chief is taking this matter seriously. Us three have been with Winkle for years and he knows he can depend on us to do our job and keep our mouth shut. He warned us there's a leak among us."

"We're taking this very seriously. Jeb's life may depend on it." Kate put in. She put her arm around Jeb. "Jeb is a special young man, and we're going to do our best to keep him safe."

***

It was late in the afternoon when Kate built up the fire. They had each taken a two-hour shift on lookout. "Maybe Logan didn't get the word, or he had trouble finding Novak on such short notice yesterday," she said. "Or Chief Winkle was wrong about the identity of the informer. But, if they don't come tonight, we'd better come up with plan B."

"What would be plan B?" Man asked.

"I have a couple of thoughts on that matter, but we need to give this one more night before going in another direction."

Jeb sat listening without speaking. He stood and faced them. "What if it's not Logan?" he said.

His comment surprised both Man and Kate.

"It has to be from what I overheard in the Seashore Saloon," Man said.

"I know, but from what mom said, Logan loved her. Not as in giving up everything for her, but she was special to him, or he wouldn't have kept her for so long. I'm almost seventeen, and she was with him for a year or so before I was born."

"What are you driving at?" Kate said.

"Mrs. Logan knew about mom and hated her guts. She has more ambition than Logan, and she was pushing him to run for the Washington congress. If she found out her husband was paying mom such a large sum of money, and she wanted to make sure we never caused any scandal for Logan, she may be the one that paid Novak. When you overheard the conversation between Novak and Tony, was anything said that pointed to Mitchell Logan exclusively?"

Man sat scratching his chin in deep thought. "Novak only used the name Logan, he never said Mitchell or Senator Logan. And his wording on taking out the critic was generic. Jeb, you may be on to something. If Logan didn't tell his wife about us, and where we are camped, she couldn't have sent anybody."

"Do we wait unto tomorrow morning?" Kate asked. "If we don't have visitors tonight, then Mrs. Logan can be plan B. Even if she's not the guilty party, it could push Logan into doing something. She would tell him."

"The thought I had for plan B would become plan C."

"What is plan C?" Jeb asked.

"We were told that Logan has ears in the police station, and in the courthouse. What if we leaked the rumor to a reporter we had proof that Logan hired a killer to kill Jane and Jeb Spencer to keep it quiet that Logan is the father of Jeb. That rumor would get to Senator Logan or Mrs. Logan. That should cause a mild earthquake."

"You have a scheming mind, Mrs. Manchester," Man

176

said. "But I like your suggestion. Chief Winkle will know how and where to drop that rumor so it will get to the critic at the newspaper. I expect the reporter will make sure it gets to both Logan and his wife."

The sound of horses approaching caused them to scatter and take cover. Wilson, Suter, and Thomas rode into camp and dismounted. "Chief Winkle sent us back for another wonderful night of stakeout," Wilson said with a moan as he rubbed his back.

They repeated the actions of the previous night with the same results, nothing.

At breakfast, after the policemen left, Kate stood and faced Jeb and Man. "Plan B or C?" she asked.

"B," Man said. Jeb nodded agreement. "Me too, I vote for B," Kate said.

"Have you ever heard Mrs. Logan's name?" Kate asked, looking at Jeb.

"A long time ago, mom called her Mable. At least, I think that was what she said, but it could have been Myrtle. I wasn't really paying attention at the time. I could care less. But, now that I'm thinking back, it's Mable Dean. I heard mom complaining about the way Mable Dean treated Mitchell."

"Regardless of her first name, I think we should move on it," Man said. "I want to go through town and send a report to Jo Meek and give him an update on what we're doing. There may be a wire waiting on the whereabouts of Bull, or other information we need."

"Jeb, can you take us by the Logan's home?" Kate asked.

"Sure, it's easy to find. I didn't until after I followed Novak there and Chief Winkle told me the house belongs to the Logans. They live in a mansion on the side of a hill overlooking the ocean. It's her family money that got Mitchell Logan where he is today. Mom said she inhered the home and substantial property."

"Can I go in with you and confront her? It would be interesting to see her reaction if she knew I was the bastard

177

son of her husband. If she's the one that paid Novak to kill mom and me, it could cause her to lose control."

Kate and Man exchanged glances, considering that possibility. This young man had a mind that is constantly working. They both knew if he survives, someday he would be a man worthy of building the new territory into something wonderful. And they intended to keep him alive if at all possible.

Kate gave Man a slight lifting of her eyebrow as approval. He knew her so well, they often didn't have to exchange words to communicate.

"Saddle up and lets go," Man said.

"They stopped at the telegraph office and Man send a report to Meek. There was no wires waiting for him.

Jeb led them to a majestic three-story home with huge white pillars on the porch. "Novak went to a door in the rear. I hid in the trees and watched until he came out. He wasn't there more than fifteen minutes."

They tied the horses and Man motioned for Kate and Jeb to stay behind the pillars out of sight, as he went to the door. "When I'm inside, Jeb take the back door. Kate take the door leading out toward the stables." Jeb pointed them out when they rode in.

A black man dressed as a butler opened the door. "United States Marshal Manchester to see Mrs. Logan," he said.

The butler stepped back out of sight and Man gestured for Jeb and Kate to get into position. He entered a parlor and the butler asked him to wait.

A woman dressed in a floor length print dress buttoned at the collar entered. Her almost silver hair was shoulder length.

"What do you want?" she demanded in a gruff voice.

"I came here on official business," Man said in a similar gruff tone. "Somebody paid a man named Novak to murder Jane and Jeb Spencer. He was successful on Jane, murdered her, and threw her body in the river. We have an eyewitness. Novak was overheard telling a friend,

Tony, that Logan hired him to kill both. We have reason to believe it was you that hired them."

Her face went ashen and she screamed, "Winston, help."

The butler came through the door with a pistol drawn. "Do I kill him, Ma'am?"

"Yes, but not here. The blood would stain the Persian rug. Take him to the stables and wait until dark to dispose of the body. Dump it in the river."

She turned to leave by the same door Winston used.

Man let the butler usher him from the parlor and toward the door.

Man didn't see Kate when he stepped outside, but quickened his pace to give room between himself and Kate to allow a clear line of fire if it erupted. The butler gestured toward the stable and kept his pistol aimed at Man with the hammer cocked, ready to fire in an instant.

Man saw movement behind a bush and walked where they would pass close to the bush. The moment Winston was passed her position, she stepped out and brought the butt of her Walker down on the butlers head with enough force to put him on the ground. Man scooped up the pistol from where it fell, eased the hammer down, and put it in his pocket. "Thanks," he said as he cuffed Winston to the trunk of the bush.

"What now?" she asked.

"We arrest Mrs. Logan. If nothing else develops, we have attempted murder as a charge."

She nodded and followed him back into the house. "What about Jeb?" she asked.

"Leave him where he is for now. Who knows what a cornered woman will do. She may have a weapon hidden in the folds of her dress."

Systemically, they silently searched the rooms downstairs, nobody was in any of the rooms. Kate gestured toward the steps with her pistol. Man nodded and led the way to the stairs.

They went up side by side, their weapons aimed at the

top in case she or somebody was waiting.

At the first landing, they went in separate directions, searching each room. They met back at the stairs and went up to the third floor. A bedroom door was open, and they walked softly to the door. Mrs. Logan was seated in front of a mirror. The moment their images appeared, she turned and fired without warning. The shot went between them. "I'll take her alive," Kate said as the Walker in her right hand fired. Her bullet went between Mable's elbow and wrist. The slug jarred the pistol from Mable's hand and it sailed to the floor.

Mable screamed in pain and grabbed her arm in an attempt to stop the blood and pain. Man hurried to her and gripped the wound. Kate brought a towel she found on the vanity and wrapped it tightly around the bleeding wound.

Kate pulled her up and quickly searched the dress for another weapon, but found nothing. "Take her to the stable and harness a team to the buggy. I'll get Jeb."

She raced to the back door and saw Jeb standing with his pistol drawn. "Come with me," she shouted.

They found Mable Logan seated in the buggy holding the wounded arm with her other hand. Jeb helped Man harness the team, and then and they dragged the butler to the rear of the buggy by his arms. Kate met them and helped toss the unconscious man in the back.

Mable saw Jeb and screamed, "You little bastard. It's all your fault. You and that whore mother of yours."

Kate wanted to slap Mrs. Logan, but held back.

"It's fine," Jeb said. "The word doesn't offend me anymore. I've been called that all my life."

"I'll drive the buggy," Man said. "Get your horses and Arabian, and then follow me. The police station first."

Two policemen saw them approaching and one came to meet the buggy and the other rushed inside. Chief Winkle came to the door and watched Man escort Mable Logan toward the station door. The policeman and Jeb with Kate's help was pulling Winston from the buggy.

Winkle waited until they were inside before speaking. "What's going on?" he asked.

"I went to Logan's home and Mrs. Logan ordered her butler, Winston, to kill me and throw my body in the river. As you can see, that didn't happen thanks to Kate. Mable shot at us, and Kate put one in her arm." Man handed the chief the pistol from his pocket. "She used this."

"This is the weapon Winston had," Kate added as she handed the pistol to Winkle.

He took the weapons and put them on a desk.

"Hello Mable," Chief Winkle said.

"You'll regret this," she shouted. "When Mitchell gets here, your job is history. These two invaded my home and took Winston by force and shot me. I've never seen that pistol before."

"We have a suspicion it was Mable that hired Novak to kill Jane and Jeb Spencer, not Mitchell" Kate said. "From her actions, she's certainly capable."

"Get a doctor," Chief Winkle said to one of the policeman. "Put Winston in a cell until we get this sorted out. Come with me to my office, the doctor can treat your wound there."

He placed Mable in the chair in front of his desk and went behind it and sat. "Mable, you and Mitchell are in serious trouble. Murder is involved. A man named Novak was hired to murder Jane and Jeb Spencer. He was successful on Jane and threw her body in the river."

Mable ignored Chief Winkle. "These two invaded my home and knocked poor Winston unconscious and shot me," she shouted. "If somebody killed that wretched woman, I'm glad. She had poor Mitchell in agony. She even claimed that boy is his son. Pure nonsense, she was only a money-grabbing whore, and saw a way to extort money from us."

Mable pointed her finger at Jeb as if she wanted to shoot him. "There's no way you could have come from the loins of Mitchell, and I hope that whoever killed that whore you call mom is successful with you. Seattle doesn't need scum like you."

"That's enough Mable," Chief Winkle shouted with his fist doubled up and his face was flaming red with anger.

"When Mitchell gets here," she shouted, "he'll see that all of you are punished severely. He's a State Senator, and is going to Washington as a congressman. He'll become president of the United States, and I'll be the First Lady. His opponents will use this to try to defeat his election. It would be better for you if you finish the job on that bastard kid. Kill this horrid mess now, and Mitchell will reward you handsomely when he gets to Washington. I'll have Mitchell demand those two are fired. She aimed her finger at Kate and Man."

Kate pulled her pistol and walked to Jeb. "I have a better idea," Kate said. "How much will you pay me to put a bullet in his head right now?" she demanded. "End this here and now." She gestured toward Chief Winkle. "He will keep his mouth shut if he knows what's good for him. I'm sure your husband will offer him a lush job in Washington."

"I paid Novak five hundred each for that bastard and his whore mother," Mable shouted. "But if you'll end it here, and stop this potential scandal now, a thousand. Mitchell will pay you when he gets here. Do it now, kill him."

They heard a noise at the door and saw Mitchell Logan standing there. He heard his wife's confession. "Mable, don't say another word," he screamed as he rushed to his wife.

She saw him and held up her arm. "That woman shot me and knocked poor Winston unconscious. Do something. They brought me to the station in handcuffs, and people saw me. I'm Mable Logan, don't these imbeciles know who we are? They can't do this to us. Tell them I'm going to be the First Lady."

Logan shouted again, "Shut up, Mable."

Man motioned to Kate and Jeb to go out the door.

He followed and saw several policemen and two reporters standing outside the door listening, they heard it all.

Chief Winkle followed them to the door. "Mable is crazy. I'll take it from here. You need to report to Joe Meek and find Novak. With him in custody and talking, that leaves the Logan's with no wiggle room even if he does have influential supporters. But, they'll evaporate when the news of this spreads, and it will." He gestured at the reporters.

"However, I want each of you to write a full detailed report before you leave." He turned to one of the policeman. "Take them to another office and provide each with paper. Bring their reports to me when they finish."

Jeb went with them, and also wrote a report on what he knew and saw.

They finished and each made a copy of the report for Meek. They would send a telegram and follow it up with the detailed reports. The trio left the police station through a side door at the suggestion of the policeman. "The front is packed with spectators, and I spotted a lot more newspaper reporters' frantically writing. It didn't take long for the story to spread through town."

Nobody paid any attention to them as they led their horses away from the station. As they were leaving, they saw Chief Winkle come out of the station, and was holding a news conference. "I read Chief Winkle as an honest cop, he'll do what's right," Kate said.

"That's the word on the street," Jeb added. "That's why I went with him after I saw Novak take mom's body to the river. How'll we find Novak? We have no idea where to look."

"Me neither," Man said. "We need a lucky break."

They stopped at the telegraph office and Man went inside and sent a wire to Joe. Again, there wasn't anything for them from Meek. He came back, mounted Arabian, led the way to the post office, and mailed the lengthily reports he, Kate, and Jeb had written. "Where are we going?" Kate asked.

"Back to camp, that is, unless anybody has any better suggestions on what we should do." Nobody had any, so they went to camp and Kate made a pot of coffee.

"We know Novak is looking for me," Jeb said. "Let me go into town and be seen, use me as bait. Maybe I can draw him out for you."

"Only as a last resort," Man said.

"We know he's a back shooter, and could take you out with a rifle from hiding. We would be helpless to help you,"

They sat drinking coffee and Jeb turned to look at Man. "You said that Novak mentioned taking out one of Logan's critics. I think we would have heard if he has carried out that job. If not, if we knew who, we could put surveillance on him."

"How would we get that intelligence?" Kate asked.

"Chief Winkle or possibly, Joe Meek," Man said. "Tomorrow morning, we can do some investigating on that aspect."

"I expect Novak will hear about Mable Logan being arrested," Kate said. "He could leave Seattle immediately. How would he expect to be paid with her in jail?"

Man and Jeb groaned, she was right, of course. Why should he hang around where it might be impossible to be paid. He would also know the law had his name and were searching for him.

***

The next morning, Man, Kate and Jeb used the side door at the police station. One of the policeman they knew saw them and gestured for them to come in.

"What happened after we left yesterday?" Kate asked.

"It was chaos for a while. This place was overrun with politicians, newspaper people, and spectators. But Mable Logan was admitted to a sanatorium for observation, as they phrased it. That woman is as nutty as a squirrels nest. She was in a rage and making all kinds of threats to everybody that they couldn't do this to the First Lady."

"Have you seen the morning paper?" he added. "The episode of yesterday filled the first two pages. Logan's chances of being elected now is at zero."

His gaze focused on Jeb. "Somebody leaked the entire story about you and your mom. Everybody that can read knows you're Logan's son and those that can't, have heard several versions."

"Damn," Kate said.

"It's fine," Jeb said. "When this mess ends, I intend to go somewhere else, maybe change my name, and start over. That was my hidden intent from the start of this mess. I can't stay here any longer."

"I'll tell the Chief you're here," the policeman said. "Wait here, he was huddled with a group of aides of congressmen from the Capital Building earlier. I expect congressmen were afraid to be seen, and sent their flunkies. "I'll see if Chief Winkle is free now. So many came and went that I lost count."

He left them and hurried down the hallway to Winkle's office. He tapped on the door and upon hearing the Chief's approval, he opened the door. The policeman was out of sight for only a few seconds, and came out and motioned for them to join him.

Chief Winkle met them at the door. "Come in," he said. "I'm glad you dropped by. A lot of water has gone down the river since you left yesterday."

"Like what?" Kate asked. They wanted to hear it from him, as well as what the policeman told them.

"I have the name of the reporter that's the chief critic of Logan. He could be the target of Novak. I also learned there's another Congressman going to run for the Washington job."

"They are both thorns in the side of Logan on his election chances." Logan would like for both to be silenced. There's nothing as dirty and vicious as politics. Most think anything goes to get elected, or to get reelected."

"We were told by one of your men that it was all over the newspaper this morning and Logan's chances of being elected had gone to zero. Is he still running?"

"Logan is sharp, he thinks he can weather the storm, turn this into a positive, use sympathy about his poor wife. Unfortunately, voters have a very short memory. By the day of election, only what happened the week before has relevance. And, unfortunately, too many voters only have one thing in mind when they go to the polls, what's in it for me."

He handed Man a sheet of paper. He looked at it and nodded.

"This is the home address, and office location if you want to check them out. Listed are the people that Logan would like to have out of his hair. If you want surveillance, I can spare you people."

"Thanks Chief," Man said. "We'll pay them a visit and see what we can learn. Are they aware their name may be on the hit list from Logan."

"They do now," Winkle said. "The reporter was here and I told him personally. The aide of the congressman is aware as well. He was here earlier, and I filled him in on the situation. The reporter understood the significance and was about to wet his pants. He took off like the devil was hanging on his coattail. The aide said he would get word to his boss immediately."

"Kate had a thought," Man said. "She said Novak would run as soon as he learned Mable was arrested. Who'll pay him with her gone, or was it also Mitchell Logan himself involved. She may have handled the hiring and actual payment to Novak, but did he know, and used her to keep possible suspicion away from himself?"

"Only time will tell, I hope," Winkle said.

Their first stop was the office of Congressman Robert Aldridge. Man showed his badge to the clerk outside, and they were ushered to his office. He stood and examined the badge of Man and his identification.

"Who's your boss?" Robert asked.

"I work for Joseph Meek, United States marshal," Man replied. "My wife and partner, Kate, and this is Jeb Spencer."

"I know about you two, but I wanted to be positive," Congressman Albright said. "Chief Winkle told me. Of course, I know about Jeb as well. You're a brave lad from the reports."

"Thank you, sir," Jeb said. "But it appears I have no choice in the matter. When I saw Novak take mom's body to the river, my choices were limited. Policemen came to my home and Chief Winkle took me to stay with Max Curtis and his wife. Then these two took over and I've been with them since."

Congressman Albright turned to Man. "What are you doing? I mean, to stop this before Novak kills me."

"We're doing our best to locate him. So far, we've been unsuccessful. Seattle is a big town, and he has no address. He may be with friends, or in a hotel using an alias name. We don't know where to look. There are so many men that fit the general description of Novak."

"About all we know, he may be from Vancouver, and he has a friend here named Tony. They've worked together. Winkle has three leads on men with the first name of Tony that fit, but so far, none of them have been found, at least, not that we know about."

"What do you propose?" Congressman Albright asked.

"We have to get him out in the open somehow. Jeb has volunteered to be used as bait, but Novak is a back shooter, and we're afraid he would shoot from hiding. There would be no way to keep Jeb from being killed, or severely wounded."

"I'm not that brave," Albright said.

"I recommend you change your habits," Man said. "Don't leave by the same door at the same time each day. Eat lunch here, post extra guards, and put heavy drapes over the windows. Vary your habits on going home, hire

187

somebody to guard your home. Your wife and family may be in danger, he might abduct them to get to you. Tell them to stay inside until this is resolved. Maybe send them to visit her family or stay with friends."

The Congressman gulped and sweat popped out on his forehead.

"However, you may be in no danger. Kate thinks as soon as Novak found out that Maude Logan was in custody he took off. Her reasoning was that with Maude in the sanatorium, who would pay him? Hired killers don't work for free."

Man stood, "Unless you have more questions, we're going to see the other man on the list that Chief Winkle gave me. He's a reporter. We'll give him the same advice we gave you."

"I know the man you're talking about," Albright said. "He's one of my supporters in the campaign against Logan. Unofficially, of course, due to his job at the paper he has to work behind the scenes."

They left the congressman's office and went to the newspaper. A security guard questioned them and looked at Man's identification before he allowed them inside the offices. Man, with Kate and Jeb walking behind him, stopped at the first desk. "We need to visit with Andrew Kent," Man said.

They were led to an office. An overweight man of fifty met them at the door. "I'm Andy Kent," he said. "I know why you're here. Chief Winkle filled me in on the situation with Logan. Take Logan into custody and beat it out of him. He has to know where Novak is living."

"They can't do that," Man said. "And you reporters are always howling about protecting the civil rights of citizens from harassment by the government and policeman. Do I detect the double standard at work here?"

"This is different," he whined. "It's me facing possible harm."

"I was told you're a proponent of gun control, and I

see you have one on your hip."

"We need to get back to the situation at hand," Kent said. "It's your duty as a United States marshal as to protect me. I'm a newspaper reporter and entitled to protection."

"This is going nowhere," Man said. "We need to be out looking for Novak. We can't do that sitting here guarding you. My advice, be careful, and use your head. Don't give him a shot at you, and you might consider moving your families to stay with friends or family. Alter your routine and hire a bodyguard."

Kent was frowning, but nodding agreement.

"We gave that same advice to Congressman Albright a short while ago."

***

"What next?" Jeb asked as they rode toward camp.

"I don't know," Man said. "Do either of you have any suggestions besides using Jeb as bait? It was easy to see that neither the congressman nor reporter was willing to do that. That reporter was a sad case if you ask me. He's hanging on to Albright hoping for a handout job after the election. He's using the newspaper to farther his greedy agenda."

Again, nobody had a suggestion what they should do next. They were waiting on coffee to make when a rider raced toward their camp. They grabbed their weapons and took cover. It was a policeman they had met at the police station.

He pulled his horse to a sliding stop and shouted, out of breath. "Come quick. Somebody shot at Congressmen Albright."

They were in the saddle quickly and racing back toward town. "Where did it happen?" Man shouted above the clatter of the horses hooves.

"In Albrights' office, they shot through the window. From the initial report, Albright wasn't hit, the bullet intended for him hit the wall behind his head. Congressman Gene Whitmore was hit and is the worst.

Congressman Yost, took a round through the shoulder. From the number of shots fired, Chief Winkle suspects two or more shooters."

They found the area around the office building used by the Congressmen surrounded by policemen. Spectators were being held back by men on horseback. Chief Winkle met them, and led them out of hearing range.

"The whole delegation of Congressmen are demanding immediate action and protection. Logan has disappeared along with his wife Mable. The shooters got away, we know they were two of them. We found the location on a hill about a hundred yards from the office building."

"We have one witness that said he saw two men racing north immediately after the shooting."

"That's the direction where Logan lives," Jeb said.

"That's where we'll start," Man said. He turned his horse and led the way through the hoard of onlookers.

As soon as they were in the open, Man spurred Arabian into a run. Redbird was close at his side, but Socks wasn't able to keep the fast pace.

Man stopped and they looked at the mansion. Jeb pulled his horse to a stop beside them. Man gestured toward the rear of the house. "Take the same doors as before and be on the alert."

Kate and Jeb turned their horses toward to the right and circled the house. Man tied Arabian and pulled his Walker as a precaution, and went to the front door.

The door was open, and he peeked in and saw a body on the floor. He pulled his other Walker, stepped in, and away from the doorway to prevent having light at his back if somebody was waiting, watching, they would have a good target if he was framed in the open doorway.

He listened for any sound and heard nothing, and then silently went to the body. It was the butler, Winston. He intended to ask how he got out of jail so fast, but suspected bail was posted by Logan. A bullet hole was between his eyes. A pistol was in his hand.

190

Man made his way through the house, looking in every room until he got to the back door. It was also open. He stepped out where they could see him, and motioned for Kate and Jeb to join him.

"Winston was shot," he whispered. "I haven't been upstairs."

They followed him through the house looking in every room. They met at the steps and Man took the point with Kate and Jeb walking behind, but at either side of him. They all had their weapons ready. They stopped at the first landing and listened. Not a sound.

Man went in one direction and Kate the other. Jeb stood at the top of the stairs looking in both directions until they returned, and they continued up the steps to the third floor.

A noise alerted Man and he stopped to listen. Sounds were coming from the bedroom of Mable. They spread out and Kate motioned Jeb to stay back. She and Man went to the door and peeked in. Novak was standing in front of Logan, and he was tied to a chair. Mable was on the floor. He wondered why she wasn't in the sanatorium. That was where Winkle said they took her. He suspected he knew, Logan got both Winston and his wife released.

He heard Novak demanding money. "Where is it? I know you have money here. I was told you have your election slush fund stashed here. Tell me or I'm going to beat it out of you." He hit Logan in the nose with his fist and the blood splattered.

Logan only moaned. He had already been beaten so bad his eyes and lips were a mess.

Man leaned forward to see inside. He expected the other shooter was Tony and he would be here. There was nobody else was in the bedroom. He stepped inside with both pistols aimed at Novak.

"Drop the pistol and put your hands up," Man said softly. "You're under arrest."

Novak reacted like a snake striking and got off a shot before Man had time to react. The sound of a pistol firing at his side was almost simultaneous. A bloody spot appeared on Novak's left shirt pocket as Kate's bullet went through his heart. Man felt a burning sensation on his side, but ignored it.

Jeb yelled from the stairs. A man just ran from another room and went down the steps. He had a sack over his shoulder. I think he was robbing them."

Man turned and raced after the fleeing intruder. Kate went to the window and was waiting when she saw Tony run toward the trees where horses were tied. She took her time and aimed the Walker Colt in her right hand. She didn't want a kill shot, but a takedown. Her bullet entered the thigh of the sprinting man, and he tumbled head over heels in the grass. Before he had time to recover, Man was standing over him, and kicked the gun out of his hand.

Kate watched until Man had cuffs on Tony, and then went to Logan. He was unconscious from the severe beating. Mable was on the floor. She knelt and rolled her on her back. A bloody bullet hole was between her breast. She was dead.

Jeb walked into the room and was watching Kate. "Is she dead?" he asked.

Kate stood and walked back to the young man and put her arms around him. "She's dead. Logan is in bad shape, and we need to get him to a hospital."

"I'll go get a buggy from the stable," he said.

"Tell Man to do that, and you go tell Chief Winkle. Tell him to bring enough policemen to secure the area."

She saw Man marching Tony back to the house. A bandage was tied around the wound, and the bleeding had almost stopped. He had only a flesh wound. For the first time, she saw Man's bloody shirt. She raced down the steps and met them in the kitchen. Jeb was beside her.

"Jeb, point your pistol at Tony," she said. "And if he makes one move toward any of us, shoot him."

"Yes Ma'am," he said. "It would be my pleasure."

"I'm bleeding to death," Tony complained.

"Go ahead," Man said. "We won't stop you."

192

Tony began to curse. Man stepped to him and thumped him on the head with the pistol barrel. "Not in front of the lady and boy," he said.

Kate opened Man's shirt and saw a bloody scratch on his side. "It's no more than a rope burn," she said "I'll bandage it for you as soon as we have time."

"We'll take it from here," Kate said. "Go get Chief Winkle. Tell him what happened and to bring plenty of policemen."

Jeb went for Socks, and spurred the horse into a run toward town. Man and Kate went upstairs. Man knelt to examine Logan. "He's dead," he said as he felt for a pulse in Logan's neck. "I wonder way Novak beat him to death? A dead man can't talk.

"As we heard him say, for money, and he got carried away. He was hoping Logan had a stash here at the house."

He examined the pockets of Novak and found less than ten dollars. "Maybe Logan refused to pay him for shooting the Congressmen. Unless Tony talks, we may never know."

Chief Winkle arrived with two policeman and hurried up the steps with Jeb leading the way. He smiled when he saw Novak on the floor and Tony with cuffs on his wrist. He walked to Mitchell Logan and lifted his head up.

"Novak beat him to death wanting money," Man said. "We heard part of that when we got here. They shot Mable and Winston."

"I have a dozen more men on the way to secure the house. I came on with Jeb and Delmar is bringing the others. This winds up this case except for the reports," Chief Winkle said.

He saw the bloody shirt on Man. "Are you wounded?" he asked.

"Just as scrape," Man said. "Novak shot me when I came through the door."

"Do we need to take you to the hospital?"

"No, Kate will bandage it, and it'll be fine. She has

doctored me for much worse wounds."

"I have a question," Man said. "For my report, how did Winston and Mable get out. Winston was in a cell and Mable was taken to a sanatorium?"

"A lawyer brought a court order to me. Logan got a Judge to issue it, one of his courthouse buddies."

"What are your plans now?" Winkle asked.

"Contact Joe Meek, make another report, and go back on the trail after Bull unless he has something else more urgent."

"If you would, go back to the station and use an office to write your reports. Leave them with the clerk."

"We will, and make a copy for Meek."

They stood to leave. "It was good working with you, Chief Winkle. Good luck on the next election, we need honest cops like you."

"Thank you, Deputy Marshal Homer Manchester," Winkle said.

Chapter 12

They went to the police station and all three wrote out a report and made a copy for Meek. They stopped at the telegraph office and Man send a brief report on the Logan case. He would mail the long versions.

When he finished the operator handed him an envelope. "This came in for you today."

He walked outside where Kate and Jeb waited and opened the telegram.

"Unverified report, Bull, and gang were seen at a cabin owned by a man named Charles Evans. No address or directions available."

Jeb was listening. "I think I know where the cabin is located. If I'm right, it's a couple of miles south of town. If I recall correctly, Evans was sent to prison a few months ago for armed robbery."

"We need to go to camp first and change into our skins and get our supplies," Man said. "If he's there, it's possible we'll be on the trail again. We could ask for assistance, but since it is out of Seattle, the city police have no jurisdiction. Besides, it may be a false alarm. I suggest we check it out first. I know Chief Winkle has his hands full at the moment with the shooting of the Congressmen, and the Logan situation."

They rode to their camp. Kate and Man changed into their working clothes while Jeb was putting the packsaddles on the mules. When they walked out, Jeb was watching. "I wish I had skins to wear like you," he said.

"I think there are a few Indian women around The Fort that will make them for you," Kate said. "If you're still with us when we go back, I'm sure they'll make them for you. Ours are getting worn in places, and it's time to replace them as well."

"I hope to be with you," Jeb said.

Man took the point as they rode toward town. He reined up at a store, and they replenished their supplies. It could be they would again be on the trail where supplies weren't available.

Jeb took the lead when they left town. Man was next with Kate behind leading the pack mules. "There are several canyons out here," Jeb said. "The cabin that belonged to Evans is in one of them. We may have to search a few before I locate it. I only saw it once and these canyons all look alike. I came out this way soon after Evans was sent to prison, curiosity. I was on a young horse that needed to be ridden."

They rode to the end of two canyons without seeing any sign of a cabin. However, on the third, Man saw tracks on the winding trail. He moved up beside Jeb. "Go back and take the mules from Kate. There has been several horses come this way since the last rain."

Jeb started to protest, but Kate rode close and cut off his objections with a hand gesture. She handed him the rope to the mules. "Do as Man said, we're experienced at this, and we don't want to be worried about you. Follow orders if you want to stay with us."

He lowered his head and nodded agreement.

"Stay well back of us. If you hear shooting, take cover. Hold Socks and the mules. If the gang tries to escape on this trail, you could be killed if you're standing in the open when they come racing toward you."

Jeb nodded again at her reasoning. He didn't like it, but wanted to stay with Kate and Man.

Man rode forward, keeping a close watch on both sides of the canyon. If Bull was here, there would be sentries.

"I have that feeling," Kate said.

"Me too," Man agreed. They stepped down and tied the horses well back from the trail in a tangle of bushes where they couldn't be seen.

Man went forward, with Kate following behind, watchful. She saw Man suddenly drop to his knees behind a fallen log. She crouched behind a bolder. Man aimed his rifle upward toward a rock shelf on the side of the hill.

196

She looked where he pointed and didn't see anything. She crawled to where he waited. "I saw movement for only a second," he said.

"How do we handle it?" she whispered.

"There's no way to get by him. The canyon is too narrow and there's not enough cover. I don't see a way to climb up from this side. The hill is much too steep. I wonder what's on the other end. Could we pull the same trick and come in from the other side as we did before, and with the slave traders?"

"It's worth a try," she said. "If the sentry saw you trying to get past him, you would be caught with no place to go. We don't know how many men Bull has with him now. But I expect several. They would come charging toward us, and you would be caught in the middle."

"Find a good place beside the trail and wait for me," he said. "I'm going back and talk to Jeb, and asks if he knows what's at the other end of the canyon. But, then, he may have never been past the cabin. That is, if there is one here, and if the movement I saw was a man. It could have been an animal."

"As I said, I have that feeling. It's them," she said.

He crawled back the way they came and soon disappeared. Kate moved deeper into the brush beside the trail until she found a bolder that had fallen from the rock shelf sometime in the distant past. She climbed to the top and sat behind a bush. She was high enough to see the trail, and had a good line of fire should it become necessary. She checked her rifle and added an extra bullet after jacking one in the firing chamber. She added another round to each of her Walker Colts and sat back to wait.

Man crawled far enough away he could stand and walk safely back to where he tied Arabian and led him back to where they left Jeb. He found him perched in a tree watching the trail. The boy jumped down and met Man. "I spotted what might be a sentry," Man said. "If I'm right, he has the trail blocked. Kate is watching, and I'm going around to the opposite side. Is there a way I can come this way from the other end of this canyon?"

"I'm sorry. I've never been past the cabin. I only rode to the point I could see it. I never actually went to the cabin itself."

"Find a better place to wait and watch," Man said. "I saw you in the tree, and so would they if they come out this way. You would be a sitting duck if they started firing at you up in the tree. Find a place you would be protected from bullets, like behind a rock or a heavy log."

"I will," he said. "Thanks, I'll remember that."

He mounted Arabian, and circled around, hoping to find the other end of the canyon above the cabin. It took a while, but he found what he hoped was the right canyon and proceed slowly. He saw Arabian raise his head and test the air. He caught the scent of something, hopefully, other horses.

Man dismounted and crept forward, his rifle ready for action. He kept hidden as much as possible as he moved forward. Cautiously, he was looking in every direction as he moved from tree to tree. He smelled smoke before he saw the cabin. A corral was off to one side, and he counted eleven horses. There was no way he could get to them without being seen, and the odds of eleven to one was too much. He started to retreat back to where he left Arabian. The sensible thing to do is go after reinforcements.

Suddenly, a bullet tore bark from a tree only inches from his head. He scrambled for cover before the shooter could fire again. Rolling to the side, he found a place offering protection behind a log. He saw men running toward the corral firing his way. He had to keep his head down as bullets were gouging wood from the log he was behind.

He shifted his position where he could see, and aimed his Winchester '73 and squeezed the trigger when he had the sights lined up on a man with a full beard.

The bullet took the man in the breastbone and he fell at the hooves of the milling horses. The gunfire was causing them to jerk the men around that were attempting to put saddles on their backs.

Man found another target of a man in the saddle. He fell to the ground at the force of the bullet striking him in the side. The gunfire toward him became more intense, and he had to move.

When he found a suitable place, he saw the men were mounted and one was opening the gate. He quickly aimed and put the man at the gate down with a bullet through his chest. Another took his place and Man got off another round. The Winchester's aim was perfect and the hot slug of lead took the top of the man's head away. That was the only target he had as the men used their horses as cover.

Somebody shouted. "Give me covering fire and I'll get the gate open."

A steady volley of shots caused Man to keep his head down. He heard the sound of horses running and looked again. He aimed and the last rider in the procession took a round in his left arm, but he stayed on the horse, and disappeared from sight.

Man ran to where he tied Arabian and raced after Bull and his men. Shots from in front of him sounded and he recognized Kate's Winchester booming. A few seconds later, the sound of Jeb's Henry reached him. He found another body beside the trail and knew she dropped another of the outlaw gang. He saw Kate running toward him. They joined and she jumped on Arabian with Man and held on as the horse ran forward to where Jeb was stationed. They found him standing beside the trail looking down at the body of a man on the ground.

Kate went to him, put her arm around his shoulder, and gave him a hug.

"Good shooting," Man said.

Jeb looked up and met Man's gaze. "I killed him," he said.

"I know. But he was shooting at you. He was a killer and would have killed you if he could."

"I may have got another," Jeb said. "But he didn't

fall from the saddle."

"How many escaped?" Man asked.

"Five including the one I may have wounded, and another with a bloody arm," Jeb said. "A big man with a full beard was leading them."

"I expect that was Bull himself," Kate said.

They went back to the corral and walked through the bodies and Man pulled two pistols belts from men. He tossed them to Jeb. This will upgrade your pistol. Keep the other and yours in your saddlebags."

Kate shouted, "Come here."

Man and Jeb hurried to where she stood.

She was standing beside a body. "I think this is Don Watson," she said. Man knelt and looked into the face for a moment, then did a search of his pockets. He found an I D card from the mine where he worked.

"You're right, it's Watson," he said and put the card back in the pocket for identification later.

We're going after them," Man ordered. "Jeb, follow us with the mules."

Redbird and Arabian took off at a hard run. Jeb couldn't keep up leading the mules. He hoped he could follow their tracks as the faster horses left him behind.

Man and Kate reloaded as they rode.

Kate saw something on the trail and pulled Redbird back. Man saw her and slowed to wait for her to ride beside him. "What did you see?" he asked.

"I'm not sure, but we don't want to ride into an ambush. Something moved in those bushes in front of us, on the right."

They both sat and looked, but saw nothing. He pulled the binoculars and scanned the trail in front. "I don't see anything now," he said.

They walked the horses forward, slowly, their rifles aimed toward the trail in front of them. When they neared the bushes where Kate saw movement, they saw a bloody shirt blowing in the breeze.

"Damn them," Man said. "They left that to slow us

down, and that old trick worked."

Jeb came from behind and smiled when he saw Man and Kate in front of him. He thought he had been left behind.

They waited for the young man to stop beside them. Man pointed toward the shirt. "An old trick you need to be aware of. They put the shirt on a limb to blow in the breeze. We saw movement, and slowed down and stopped. Then we moved in cautiously to see what we saw moving. That trick gave them another ten minutes or more lead. Riding into an ambush is always foremost when chasing anybody, and you must always be careful. Remember that."

"I will," Jeb said.

They rode to the shirt and saw the blood and bullet hole on the sleeve. "This came from the one I shot," Man said. "I saw my slug tear into his left arm."

"What do we do now?" Jeb asked.

"Follow them, of course," Kate said. "This case won't be finished until Bull is put down, or in custody. That was our original assignment."

"They're headed south," Man said. "What town is south of here?"

"Tacoma," Jeb said. "But, that's a long way from here. There's a lot of towns and communities along Puget Sound. They could be headed to any of a dozen within a day's ride."

"Maybe they're just running with no destination in mind," Kate added.

"We need to find a telegraph office and notify Joe," Man said. "We also need to ask Chief Winkle to go to the cabin for the bodies, identify them, and do a search."

Man again took the point, but held Arabian to a ground-eating pace. The killers had too much of a lead to race after them now. It would be too easy to lose the trail, and be forced to backtrack. That would consume more time than staying on the trail.

Kate dropped back and rode beside Jeb. She wanted

to talk to him.

"How do you feel after killing a man?" she asked.

He met her gaze, "Pretty darn good. I have no regret and hope to have another opportunity to help you and Man. He was an outlaw and killer and it was the right thing to do under the circumstances."

"Good," Kate said. "It's never easy, but we must do what we have to do."

"We discussed this some before," she said. "I hate to bring up a depressing subject, but do you have plans. You're almost on your own now. I wasn't much older than you when my father was killed. Mom had passed away the year before. It's an awful and lonesome feeling to be alone."

"I'm not alone, I have you and Man."

"That's true for now, but when this case is finished, we'll be going on. Should Man continue as a deputy marshal, I'm sorry, but you can't go with us."

She wanted him to know now, and prevent embarrassment, or awkwardness in the future.

Jeb rode in silence for a time. "How can I become a deputy marshal?" he asked.

"I expect you must be at least twenty-one and having experience in law enforcement would help. Contact Joseph Meek at the United States Marshals Service. That would be the place to start. But that's a few years away for you."

A plan was forming in her mind, but it would have to wait until later to go any farther.

Man pulled Arabian to a halt and waited for Kate and Jeb to ride to him. "I see building in front of us," he said. "Bull's tracks lead toward them. Spread out and Jeb, stay back with the mules, but be ready like before.

They noticed he had both of the pistols Man gave him on his hips. He frowned again at being ordered to stay behind, but didn't argue and waited for them to move on forward. The trail they were on intersected a road and the tracks of Bull and his men were quickly lost in the multitude of horse and wagon tracks.

Man gestured to telegraph poles. They followed them to a building and Man dismounted and handed his reins to Kate. She and Jeb waited while he went inside to send wires to Meek and Winkle.

He came back and mounted his horse. "This town can't contain more than a couple of hundred people," he said. "I expect the telegraph line runs through here on the way to Tacoma, otherwise they wouldn't have one."

They were turning away when the telegraph man came out waving a yellow sheet of paper. "A wire for you, Marshal," he said. Man leaned down to take it.

The telegraph man waited for Man to read it, and then asked, "Do you want to send a reply?"

"Nope, but thanks for asking," he said and turned the head of Arabian toward the south. Kate's curiosity got the better of her. "What did it say?" she asked. Jeb had moved Socks closer to hear as well."

"It was from Joe. He said Gus is on the way to meet us. We're to continue after Bull and report in as often as possible so Gus can find us."

"Who is Gus," Jeb asked.

"Augustus Schweitzer, another marshal," Man replied. "He was with us until Joe pulled him off the Bull Blevins case, and sent him to investigate a threat by a man named Harry Orchard. Orchard threatened to kill the Idaho Governor, Frank Steunenberg."

Jeb whistled in amazement.

The trio continued on the road hoping to pick up the trail of Bull again. He could have veered in any direction and they wouldn't be able to locate his tracks leaving the small town.

"We need luck on our side," Man said as he rode, studying the ground. They were at least a mile from town when he spotted a familiar track. He had looked at the tracks made by the horses they were following for so long, he picked them out of the others.

"They're still in front of us," he said. "Jeb stay in the

middle of the road, and we'll be on either side. If they left the road, hopefully, we can spot their tracks."

They rode until dusk and made camp under a cluster of trees a half mile from the road in case Bull send somebody back to see if he had a tail. There was a small creek for water for them and the horses and good grass for the horses and mules.

Kate knew better than make a fire. They ate a cold supper and Kate took her and Man's bedroll behind a thick clump of bushes. Jeb placed his close to where the horses were staked.

Man picked up his rifle and walked to a small knoll. He took a blanket with him.

Jeb watched, then asked. "What's he doing?"

"When tracking somebody," Kate said, "it's always wise to keep out a sentry. I'll relieve him about midnight."

"Wake me and I'll relieve you," Jeb said.

"I'll do that," she said and went to her bedroll.

At about four in the morning, she touched his shoulder. Jeb rolled out and pulled his boots on. "Wear your coat, take your rifle and a blanket," she said. "The night wind is cold. If you hear sounds, come for us. Don't shoot unless you're positive it's them. We don't want to kill an early morning farmer or fisherman."

"I won't shoot without knowing," he said.

Kate was up at the first hint of pink in the east and walked to where Jeb sat looking toward the road. "I heard the sound of two wagons on the road earlier, but that was all," he said.

"Then there is nothing to worry about, Bull and his men are horseback. I'll have breakfast ready when you get back to camp. Go move the horses to a fresh place to graze."

He nodded and slid down from the hill and walked toward the horses with his rifle over one shoulder and the blanket over the other. She looked at his back and how straight he walked. He was going to make a handsome man someday.

Man had a small fire burning and the coffee pot was on a flat rock inside the flame. "If they were scouting behind, it would have been seen last night," he said. "But, in daylight, the fire can't be seen from the road."

"Kate put water in a pot, and started breakfast cooking. Hot shaved jerky and rice would beat parmesan and hard jerky on a cool crisp morning.

They spent the day in the saddle following Bull. They seemed to be on the move to a destination unknown. The tracks circled the small towns, but they always came back to the road headed south.

"Tacoma," Man said. "I wonder what Bull has in mind, or is just hoping to hide out in a larger town."

Man stopped at the next settlement when he spotted telegraph poles. He sent a wire to Joe that it appeared Bull was headed for Tacoma. An immediate wire came in for him.

As before, he took it outside to Kate and Jeb before reading it. It was short and to the point. "Gus will meet you at the Tacoma Saloon tomorrow."

When they were on the outskirts of town, Man rode to the side of the street where three old-timers were sitting on a bench under a shade tree. "Where can I find the Tacoma Saloon?"

One of the pioneers spat tobacco juice and with a toothless grin, he asked, "Need to wet your whistle young feller?"

"Yea, and meet a friend there."

"Just follow your nose on down the street you are on for another half mile or so, you'll see it on your right."

He gestured at Kate and her two Walkers, then at Jeb, also wearing a pair of pistols. "You sure are packing heavy?"

Man pushed his coat to the side so his badge would be displayed. "We're tracking a band of killers and need all the firepower we can lay our hands on."

"Are they in Tacoma?" the old man asked.

"Yea, or we think so, they had a day on us and we

lost their trail, but they were headed this way."

"Good luck, Marshal," he said.

"Thanks," Man said.

"Are your wife and boy on the trail of killers with you, Marshal?"

"Yep, both are crack shots and as I said, I need all the firepower I can muster."

Not yet finished with the conversation, the early day settler again eyed Kate and Jeb. "You're boy appears to be almost grown. You two must have started a family when your woman was just a little girl."

"Yep, she was about six or so."

"You're pulling my leg, Marshal."

"Yep, sure am," Man said with a chuckle and touched spurs to Arabian. "Thanks for the directions."

He pulled Arabian to a stop and turned back. "Should you see five riders, dressed mountain, beards, one with an arm wound, get word to the police."

"Be happy to, Marshal, but there ain't been none like that that passed this way. And we're here most every day it ain't raining or too cold."

They found the Tacoma Saloon with no problem. Jeb and Kate waited with the horses and Man went inside. They were early, and only a few men were drinking beer for breakfast. Man looked around and saw Gus wasn't among them, and walked to the bartender. "I'm to meet a man here today. Is there a hotel nearby? I have my wife and a young lad with me."

The barkeep saw the badge on Man's shirt. "Deputy Marshal, try the Tacoma Hotel. It's located on A Street between 9th and 10th. For a family, it's the best."

"Are you meeting another marshal?" the bartender asked. "If so, there was one that rolled in late last night."

"Did he leave a name?" Man asked.

"He said his name was Gus. That's all the information he left."

"Did he say where he would be staying?"

"Nope, but he said he could be back today. Like you,

206

he was expecting to meet somebody."

Please tell Gus that Man is at the Tacoma Hotel."

"Just Man?" the bartender asked.

"He'll know it's me." Man left the saloon and went out to where Kate and Jeb waited. "Gus is in town, and I left word we would be at the Tacoma Hotel. He got here late last night, and I expect he rode hard. It may be much later in the day before we see him. I for one would like a good bath and a change of clothes."

He and Kate were still wearing their working skins.

***

It was late afternoon when Gus knocked on Kate and Man's door. Kate opened the door and stepped back for Gus to limp in.

"Hello Gus," she said politely.

He gave her a smile and replied with a greeting as he removed his hat.

"The barkeep told me I could find you here," he said. "Ol' Joseph said you two are doing a damn good job. You solved a murder case and put down several of Bull's gang. I want to hear the details. But, could we talk over supper. I haven't had a bite since an early breakfast."

Man and Kate were dressed in their town clothes. "We're hungry as well," Man said. "Kate, if you'll go next door and get Jeb, we can go eat. We had a sandwich at noon and the café in the hotel is okay."

"Who is Jeb? Gus asked.

"Jeb's mother was murdered," Kate explained. "That was the case we were working on. Jeb saw the murderer putting his mom's body in a buggy and dump it in a river. Jeb's father was a fancy lawyer and State Senator in Seattle. His name was named Mitchell Logan. As it turned out, the congressman's wife hired a man named Novak to murder both the mother and son. Joe and Chief Winkle asked us to investigate. Since Jeb had no place to go or live, he's been riding with us. He's a damn good kid and killed one and wounded another of Bull's gang. That's it in a nutshell and it's better we told you the facts here than talking about it in front of Jeb at supper."

"I think I got it, Jeb is the son of Logan, and his wife didn't take to that kindly."

"Yep," Kate said. "Logan was running for congress and his wife, Mable had her sights on being the First Lady and Jane and Jeb Spencer was a bump in the road in his campaign."

"How old is Jeb?" Gus asked.

"Sixteen, almost seventeen," Kate replied.

"I see, almost grown," Gus said. "What do you plan on doing with him? I mean long term."

"I have a couple of thoughts on that," Kate replied. "But we need to finish the Bull Blevins case first."

Man gave Kate an inquisitive glance. She caught it and reached for his hand. "We'll discuss our options about Jeb at the right time."

He nodded.

They walked to Jeb's door and Man knocked. Jeb opened the door and stepped back.

"Gus is here," Kate said. Gus stepped inside the room and extended his hand to shake with Jeb. Jeb took it and returned the manly shake. He learned how to shake properly from Man.

"I'm Augustus Schweitzer, United States marshal," Gus said. "But if you call me that I won't answer. "It's Gus to my friends and enemies."

"It's nice to meet you Mr. Gus, sir."

Gus laughed. "You can dispense with the Mr. and the sir. We're going to the café for supper, and I never saw a boy your age that wasn't hungry."

He turned and led the way. Man walked beside Gus and Kate and Jeb followed behind them. They found a table at the rear and Man and Gus took the chairs with their backs to the wall as by habit.

"They always chose the chairs as neither want their backs exposed," Kate said.

"I understand, in their occupation. I expect they have enemies, I'll remember that."

The waitress came to the table and Gus took the lead. "I want a big steak and all the fixings. Bring a pitcher of beer to the table and four mugs."

The waitress was about the same age as Jeb and focused her eyes on him. She had watched him walk in with the marshals, but only Kate noticed.

"The same for me," Kate and Man replied at the same time.

Her doe eyes went to Jeb, and she waited. He gulped a couple of times before he was able to respond. "A steak for me as well," he managed to say.

Kate wanted to chuckle, but kept it in check. Man and Gus didn't notice the contact between the two youngsters. They were busy talking.

The waitress came back with a pitcher of beer and Gus was ready to take it from her since it was heavy, and she had four beer mugs in the other hand.

She nodded her appreciation with a smile.

"This young man is named Jeb Spencer," Kate said, wanting to help the poor girl.

"Alice Kitchens," she replied as she offered her hand toward Jeb.

"Shake her hand," Kate said to Jeb.

"He reached for her hand. She took it and gave him another smile. "It's nice to meet you Jeb. I haven't seen you here before. But then I work in the café only at night, and at times in the back."

"I'm riding with these marshals," he said. "We're after a killer and his gang. We tailed them here from Seattle."

"That's so exciting," she said. "Working here is boring. My mom and dad own the café. That's dad at the front. Mom is in the back cooking and supervising. I do what needs to be done, from waitress, to cooking, washing dishes, and cleaning up after we close."

Gus and Man had stopped talking to listen to the conversation between the youngsters. Kate gave Man a concealed wink and grin.

Alice was called to another table and hurried away.

"She's a very pretty girl," Kate said.

Jeb grunted and kept his eyes on the mug in front of him.

As soon as Alice could manage to get back to their table, she went to Jeb's side. "I would like to hear about the chase. Did you actually see them up close?"

"Not only did he see them up close," Man said, "Jeb took one down and wounded another as they were racing by where he was stationed. They were shooting at him as well."

"Oh my," she exclaimed. "I would have been terrified. You shot and killed an outlaw?" she asked.

"That was why I was where I was," he said, looking up at her face. "I was beside the trail. We were outnumbered eleven to three. Five escaped, and that's why we're here. But we lost their tracks when we got close to town. Too many other tracks they were mingled with."

A man in the kitchen said, "Alice, an order is ready."

She went back to the serving window and brought their food. Two platters were balanced on each arm.

"How do you do that?" Jeb asked. "I would dump a couple on the floor if I tried to balance the plates on my arm and walk."

"It's easy for me, but then I've been doing this for so long."

He reached for one of the plates on her arm and Kate took the other.

"Thanks," she said. "Putting them down is the hard part."

She hurried back to the window and brought a basket of biscuits and a jug of honey.

"Can we talk more," Jeb asked.

"Maybe," she said. The man at the window was calling her again.

They ate in almost silence, but Kate noticed that Jeb's eyes followed her. Alice was giving him glances as she worked.

When they were finished with the food, she came back to their table. "We have pie for desert." She looked at Jeb as she said, "I made the chocolate."

"I'll have a slice," he said immediately.

The men nodded, but Kate shook her head. "I'm too full," she said.

Alice brought three slices and they noticed the one she put in front of Jeb was almost double the size she gave Man and Gus. Gus noticed and grinned, but kept his mouth shut. He didn't want to embarrass Jeb. Kate smothered a chuckle. Man was busy eating and didn't notice.

"Anybody for coffee?" she asked. The beer pitcher and mugs were empty.

Everybody nodded. She took the pitcher and mugs, and hurried for the coffee pot and cups.

As she put the cup in front of Jeb, she whispered. "I get off in twenty minutes. I'll leave by the back door that opens in the alley. I asked off tonight with the cleaning. Mom said it was okay."

Jeb nodded.

As they stood to leave, Kate slipped Jeb a half-dollar. He looked at her in surprise. "Put it beside your plate," she whispered.

"Why?" he asked.

"A tip for good service," she whispered. She knew eating in a café was foreign to him.

They walked outside and stood on the boardwalk enjoying the evening.

Kate motioned for Jeb to follow her away from the men. "Are you going to meet Alice?" she asked.

"I want to, but should I. I've never done this before."

"If you want to talk to her, then meet her, but let me say something first."

He waited as Kate gathered her thought on how to word what she wanted to tell him.

"I'll be blunt and say this. We know nothing about

211

Alice. Keep your pistol in your holster, you aren't shooting blanks."

"What are you talking about?" he asked, confused.

"Then let me go another direction. About seventeen years ago, your mom met Logan. She was young, about your age, and probably very naïve. She got pregnant. Alice may be naïve, and what I'm saying, don't get involved with her."

He still had a questioning look on his face. "Keep your pants buttoned up," she said.

Jeb gulped when it dawned on him what she was talking about.

"Think with your brain, not your emotions and desires," she said. "A boy your age is aware of the special attraction you have for Alice. That's only natural. She has the same feelings. Remember this, you have no money, no home, nothing to offer now. Should, well, it happen, you would have two choices, stay and try to get a job and find a place to live and marry her, or leave. Look what that did to your mom. We'll be leaving Tacoma tomorrow or the next day. I expect you'll want to go with us. I know I'm talking to you like, well, a mom. But I wanted you to think. I know you're inexperienced with girls, and I'm trying to help. Don't get evolved and carried away is what I'm saying."

"I understand," he said and walked away.

Man and Gus heard most of the exchange. "Good sound advice for the boy," Gus said.

The next morning, they knocked on Jeb's door, but there was no answer. They found him at the same table at the café drinking coffee. Neither Man nor Kate made a comment as Alice brought their cups of coffee without asking. Gus hadn't made an appearance.

"Eggs and ham," Man said.

"Eggs and bacon," Kate added as she glanced at Jeb.

"I've already eaten," he said.

Alice was even more attentive than the night before. There were only two other tables occupied, and they were

212

already eating. When the food was delivered, Alice sat in the empty chair beside Jeb.

"Jeb told me the advice you gave him," she said. "It wasn't necessary, but thanks you for caring. I've worked here so long, I know all the lines, and this is the truth, Jeb is the only boy I ever asked to meet me."

"I believe you," Kate said. "I suspect he went into detail why he's with us."

"Yes he did, we talked for over an hour sitting on a bench. Mom and dad stayed to get ready for today, and dad did the bookwork. I usually go home after I clean, but stayed until they left last night."

More customers came in and Alice went to the front to take them to a table. Gus came in behind the new arrivals and walked to the table.

"We've already ordered," Man said. "I ate at another place before this one opened," he said. "I checked the telegraph office. There was nothing from Meek. I went by the local police station and checked in with them. They hadn't heard Bull was in town. They'll have men looking and asking informants. There's nothing for us to do but wait for a lead."

Jeb sat grinning and when he got a chance, he hurried to where Alice stood behind the counter. They talked until she was called away.

Jeb came back to the table with a huge smile on his face and he seems to be glowing in excitement. Kate patted his arm. "Slow down, take a deep breath," she whispered. "But, don't hyperventilate."

They finished eating and noticed Jeb still had coffee in his cup. He was only taking small sips to make it last. "I'm not finished, you two go on, I'll go back to the hotel when I finish."

Man started to object, but Kate understood and stopped him from speaking with a hand gesture. "We'll meet you here at noon."

Before they went back to the hotel, Man and Kate walked the streets, enjoying the sights and window-shopping. Kate bought a couple of things in a women's store and they went back to the hotel.

"What's going on between Jeb and Alice?" Man asked.

"Very simple," Kate said. "A case of boy meets girl. Girl looks back and instant puppy love."

Man laughed. "Alice seems to have hit Jeb squarely between the eyes the way he's acting."

***

They walked to the café at noontime and saw Jeb in the kitchen. He saw them and waved. Alice came to their table with a grin on her face. Jeb volunteered to help today. One of our workers didn't come in, and we're shorthanded. Jeb said he would help."

"An older woman brought their food to the table and sat beside Kate. "I'm Alice's mother. My name is Winnie Kitchens.

"I'm Kate and this is Homer Manchester, my husband," Kate said.

"Please tell me about Jeb," Winnie asked. "It seems those two only have eyes for the other. Alice has never acted like this before. She has messed up orders, and dropped a plate of food. I know it's because of Jeb." She offered a knowing smile. "I was young once."

"What has Alice told you about us and Jeb? That'll give me a starting place."

She said he's an orphan and he's traveling with you. She said that your husband and that other man are marshals and are in pursuit of a gang of killers."

"That's true, and we'll leave as soon as they're located. We lost their trail when they came into Tacoma."

"Maybe that will be best. Alice is only sixteen. Even though, I think it'll break her heart when Jeb leaves. I've never seen such immediate attraction between a boy and girl."

"That's sure easy to spot with him as well," Kate said. "I gave him some motherly advice; he has no job, no money, and no place to live. I hope that soaked in, but looking at them, they could care less."

"I know," Winnie replied. "We had a long talk last night. Those two sat on our front porch until Hank had to go out and make her come inside."

"Hank is her father?" Kate asked.

"Yes, that's him at the front. He's worried about her, as well as me. We ran off, and married at sixteen. It was rough for several years, but we managed. We both worked here, and when the man that owned the café retired, we bought it. The man had no family and helped us by letting us pay a little each week until we got it paid for."

"But we want more for Alice. We want her to go on to school, maybe become a teacher or something. Working in the back room of a café seven days a week is hard, very hard."

"I understand that," Kate said. "But as I said, we'll be leaving at anytime. It could be today, tomorrow or the next day. We just don't know now. Jeb says he'll go with us."

"I don't know if I want you to leave quickly, or stay a few days. Look at those two."

Kate glanced back toward the kitchen. Alice had her arms around Jeb kissing him.

"I had better go break that up," Winnie said. "I've had to do that a dozen times already, but every time she has an opportunity, she's back there with her arms around his neck."

The distraught woman hurried toward the kitchen. Alice saw her coming, and hurried out to the tables with a sheepish grin on her face. Jeb got busy washing dishes with a red tent on his cheeks.

Jeb was still in the kitchen when Man and Kate came in for supper. They hadn't seen Gus all day, but then, he knew where to find them when they got word on Bull's whereabouts.

Winnie and Hank both came to their table and Winnie made the introductions. Hank was polite, but it was obvious, he was concerned about his daughter.

"Jeb is a good boy," Kate said. "As I told your wife, we'll be leaving soon, and it'll be over between them."

"I hope so," Hank said. "She's too young."

A customer was leaving, and Hank hurried to the front to take his money.

The café was filling fast and everybody was busy, including Alice and Jeb. He was frantically trying to keep clean dishes ready for the cooks.

Kate and Man finished and left. Hank took their money without further comment.

The next morning, Jeb wasn't in his room, but they found him back at the café. Alice came to their table with a grin on her face.

"Ham and eggs for you and bacon and eggs for Kate," she said.

"And a pot of hot coffee," Kate added. "Is your new dishwasher making a hand?"

Alice laughed. "The best ever, he can turn out more than any two dishwashers we've ever had. I think I'll keep him, I hate that job."

Gus came in the door and hurried to their table. "I have a wire from Joseph. We need to go."

Jeb saw Gus and hurried to the table for the news. He had a frown on his face, expecting they would be leaving.

"We're moving out as soon as we finish eating," Man said. "You may want to talk to Alice, tell her goodbye, and we're leaving."

He hurried to where she was standing behind the counter. Kate was watching as tears filled Alice's eyes as she listened to what Jeb was saying. She pulled him toward the kitchen and they were hidden for a time. When they came out, Jeb and Alice brought the food to the table.

Gus and Man were taking in the situation. As soon as Alice went back to the kitchen, Gus reached over and put his hand on Jeb's shoulder. "That goes with the job. Are you sure you want to be a United States marshal? I've left so many women behind, I lost count. We never stay in one place long enough to put down any roots."

Gus's eyes went to Man and Kate. They knew his comment was meant for them, as well as Jeb.

Alice brought the coffee pot and filled the cups and then stood behind Jeb with her hand on his shoulder. Tears were trickling from her eyes and her nose was runny.

Alice walked with Jeb to the door, doing her best to keep from crying as she clutched his hand. As soon as they were outside, he opened his arms for her, and she met his lips for one last kiss.

Winnie and Hank stood at the door watching. Neither spoke, but Alice's mother came out and put her arm around her daughter as Jeb walked away. He was wondering if he would ever see her again. He looked back several times. He gave her a final wave before they turned the corner on the way to the stable.

Gus waited until they were mounted, and on the way from town. "Joe got a wire that a family was murdered. The facts are sketchy, but he wants us to check it out to see if it could be Bull and his men. It happened a couple of miles out of town. The bodies were found by a neighbor."

They found the cabin without difficulty, the directions supplied Gus were accurate. A man dressed as a farmer was waiting at the gate. Gus dismounted and walked to the man.

"I found the bodies, and my wife went into town to report it," the farmer said. "She came back and told me somebody was on the way. I never suspected United States Marshals. I thought the local police would investigate."

"We're tracking a gang of killers, and they've done this before. We were sent out to check."

Gus stuck out his hand to shake," I'm Gus." He gestured toward Man. "This is Homer Manchester, a deputy marshal, and his wife Kate. The young lad traveling with us is named Jeb."

"Hunter Whitley," the farmer replied as they shook

hands. "Nothing has been touched since we got here. I expect you want to go look. It's awful. It really shook my wife up. She went back home after going to report the murders. She and Mayme were friends."

"What are their names?" Kate asked.

"Mayme and Caleb Browne," he replied. "Our farms join, and we often help the other. Caleb was to meet me this morning to haul hay. When he didn't show up, I came here to check on why. Caleb was shot in the head. Mayme, well, come see."

They saw the body of Caleb on the ground in front of the porch. A dark hole was between his eyes, and dried blood was on his face.

"Jeb, stay outside," Kate said. "You don't need to see this."

She felt he didn't need to see inside, as she expected to see the same as with Rachel Knox after Bull and his gang finished with her.

They found Mayme on the bed. Her hands were tied to the bedpost. Her throat had been cut.

"The same as we found when we were on the way to Portland," Kate said. "However, it was the son that was shot."

"Did Caleb and Mayme have children?" she asked.

"No, and they wanted kids, but it didn't happen," Whitley said.

Man walked outside and started looking for tracks. "Help me look," he said toward where Jeb stood under a tree at the edge of the yard holding the horses and mules.

"I've already found where the horses were tied. If I'm reading them right, there were five. And I think I recognize them, but come look." He gestured toward the other side of the tree.

Man hurried to him and they walked to where the outlaws' horses were tied. Man made a circle and found the tracks leading away toward the south. He knelt and examined the prints in the dirt. He stood and saw Gus and Kate standing beside Jeb. "It's them," he said. "They

218

went that way." He was pointing with his finger.

Whitley followed them to their horses. "What do I need to do?" he asked.

"The local deputy is on the way," Gus said. "When he finishes with his report, do what he says, but I expect you can start the funeral process."

"I'll go home after the deputy gets here and get my wife and go notify the parson. I hope you catch them marshals, after what they done."

"We will," Kate said. "We're close now. They managed to lose us several times by hiding their tracks in towns, but hopefully we're no more than about three hours behind them. From the condition of the bodies, it can't be more than that."

Gus took the point and rode hard. Kate and Man were behind him and as usual, Jeb brought up the rear leading the pack mules.

It was mid afternoon when Gus slowed his horse from the ground-eating trot. He urged his horse forward in a slow walk with his pistol in his hand. Kate and Man joined him and the three rode abreast to where Gus spotted the remains of a campfire.

Man dismounted and felt the coals with his hand. "Still warm," he said.

"Spread out," Gus ordered. "Stay alert."

Kate dropped back and stopped beside Jeb. "Keep a good two hundred yards behind us. If shooting starts, take cover, and cover our back."

"I want to be in on the fight," he said.

"They may set up a trap with us caught between them in a crossfire. We need you to stay far enough back to see if that's the case. If so, shoot straight and keep behind cover."

"I will," Jeb said proudly after she explained the important role he would play. "I'll have your back."

Kate went to the left of Gus as Man was on the right. They kept twenty yards between them, ever watchful for any movement in front of them.

Gus pulled up and sat his saddle, eyeing a rock outcropping in front of them. Man pulled his binoculars and scanned the jagged rocks and boulders. "Nothing moving," he said.

They moved forward in a slow walk. Each had his pistol aimed ahead for any sign of an ambush.

A sudden shot from high above echoed down through the canyon. Gus was knocked backward from the saddle. Man and Kate dove to the side at the sound, and evaded bullets aimed in their direction.

Kate rolled to a rock, stretched out behind it, and peeked around for a target. Man made it to a fallen tree and knelt behind it. Nothing moved in front of them.

Kate glanced back, but couldn't see Jeb, or his horse and mules. He was where she told him to be. They waited for what seemed ages, when in reality, only a minute passed. The roar of a rifle behind them caused Kate and Man to turn to look. A second shot followed a few seconds later.

"I got two that were closing in on your back," Jeb shouted.

"Keep down, there are at least three in front of us, or somewhere," Man yelled.

He turned back to the front and pulled his binoculars to scan the ridge. Movement caught his eye and he moved to a better position and aimed his Winchester at the place he saw something.

Kate was watching, and was ready in case a target appeared.

She was the first to see the top of a hat behind a rock. She pointed her rifle and waited for a face to appear. First the hat brim, and then one eye peeked around. She sighted, but waited. That was a very small target at a hundred yards.

Sweat dripped from her nose and her body felt clammy waiting for the shooter to appear. A moment later, the barrel of a rifle appeared and she took a deep breath, held it for a second, and let it out slowly, aiming at where she hoped the ambusher's head would appear.

Man fired much farther to the right of the shooter Kate was tracking with her sights. Her shooter must have seen Man and moved from behind the rock, and aimed at Man.

Kate squeezed the trigger of her Winchester 1873 and the satisfying jolt hit her shoulder. The shooter stood a second looking down at the bloody spot spreading on his chest. His rifle fell to the ground and a second later, he toppled forward and slid down the side of the hill on his belly.

Kate didn't watch his progress; instead, she shifted her aim to where Man had fired. "I think I nicked him," Man said. "But it wasn't a kill shot. How did you do?"

"I got one of them. Unless they recruited more, it's down to two."

The sound of horses running reached them. "It sounds like they took off," Man said. "But be careful, it may be a trick to pull us out in the open if one of them led the horses away leaving one to kill us."

"What's going on," Jeb yelled.

"Stay down," Kate shouted. "We got one, but there are still at least two."

"But, I heard horses leaving," Jeb said.

"It could be a trick," Kate replied, "to lure us out for a shot. Stay where you are out of sight until we know for sure."

"Okay, I never thought about that," he said.

Man counted to a hundred ten times before gesturing for Kate to work her way forward. He did the same moving to where he saw the shooter.

Kate climbed upward until she located the body of the ambusher she shot. There was no doubt, he was dead. "Clear here," she said.

Man was behind the rock where he nicked the bushwhacker and found where their horses were tied. He followed the tracks a few yards until he was sure they were gone. "Clear here," he said.

"Come on in Jeb," Kate yelled. "They've hightailed it." They walked back to the foot of the hill and met Jeb riding Socks and leading Arabian, Redbird and the mules.

For the first time, he saw Gus on the ground. "Oh my God," he said. "They killed Gus."

Kate went to him and put her arm around his shoulder. "They shot without warning, from high above. Gus had no chance. Man and I were lucky. They shot Gus first and it gave us time to get away. Two shots came our way, but we were already on the ground scrambling for cover."

They went to Gus's body. The bullet entered his left breast just a half inch under his badge. The shooter was good as the bullet pierced the heart.

"Damn," Man said. "What a way to die, an ambush from trash like Bull Blevins. But, it was fast, and there was no pain. We need to bury him here, it's too far back to Tacoma, and Bull is getting farther away." He took Gus's wallet, weapons, and badge. Jeb and Kate helped roll his body in a blanket.

Without being told, Jeb went for the shovel on one of the mules. "Where?" he asked.

Kate had walked to a large Pine Tree and pointed toward the ground. Jeb and Man worked together, and quickly had the grave deep enough. They gently lifted the blanket with the body and lowered it into the hole. Jeb covered it with dirt.

"I wish we had some kind of marker," Kate said.

Man cut two green limbs from a tree and tied them together with a leather cord he had in his saddlebags for repairing their bridles and saddles.

"It will only last a year or so, but I expect Joe Meek will send somebody to move the body to a more suitable resting place."

Kate walked to the foot of the grave and bowed her head. Jeb and Man stood on either side as Kate said a short prayer.

Kate went to her saddlebags and brought a bright

yellow ribbon and tied it to a limb above the grave. "This will make it easier to locate his grave," she said.

They walked back to their horses. "Jeb, go find Gus's horse while we search the bodies for any identification, and take their weapons," Man said.

"Why?" Jeb asked.

"We never leave weapons to rust, or to be picked up by a band of Renegade Indians," Kate said. "Man needs their identification when he sends in his report to Joe Meek. It may clear up wants that have been sent to the area police."

Jeb nodded, it made sense to him, and he was learning the ways of the west in a hurry traveling with Kate and Man.

They went back to where Jeb took down two of the bushwhackers. One had a bullet hole in his neck, under his ear, the other; the slug went in his side and was placed where it went through his heart and lungs. A sure kill shot as well as the neck shot.

He was learning fast.

Jeb rode Socks in a circle looking for Gus's horse. He spotted the gray gelding grazing in a meadow not far away. The sound of gunshots didn't excite the horse, as he had heard them so many times before.

Kate and Man rolled Gus's weapons, wallet, and badge in a blanket and tied them on the packsaddle. The weapons and everything else from the ambushers was put in an empty cloth sack from one of the stores when they bought supplies.

Man took the point with Kate at his side. She motioned for Jeb to move back as before. He led the mules and the gray horse belonging to Gus.

Man glanced back and saw he was out of hearing range and turned to Kate. "Jeb reminds me of myself when Jake and Slats took me in. I was as green as could be, but being on the Oregon Trail makes a boy grow into a man in a hurry."

"Being on the Oregon Trail makes a girl grow up fast,

as well," she said. "Then seeing the massacre and being left alone in the wilderness certainly caused me to mature in a hurry."

"I'm concerned, Jeb is maturing much too fast," she said. "And I doubt he had much of a childhood from what we've learned about him."

They rode in silence for a time, each lost in their thoughts. Man was busy concentrating on the tracks, and Kate glanced toward the west. "Man," she exclaimed, "it looks like storm clouds are moving in from the ocean."

He looked up and studied the dark blue clouds moving over a peak. "Jeb," he said as he turned to look backward. Jeb spurred his horse into a lope and rode beside Man.

"Move out to the left and look for a shelter for the night." He gestured toward the menacing clouds. A rainstorm is moving toward us. Ride out about a quarter mile, but keep the trail in sight. If you spot something we could use as a shelter, come back and we'll see you. Don't yell or fire a shot. Bull may be within hearing distance."

Kate reached for the lead rope to the mules. "I'll take them; you'll have the gray to contend with."

Without being told, she rode to the right of the trail about the same distance as Jeb on the other side. Man went out another half mile and they rode forward looking for a dry place to sleep.

The wind changed directions and a fine mist began to fall. They rode on, searching. Jeb came back toward the trail pointing back the direction he came from.

Man and Kate saw him and turned their horses to meet him. "I saw an abandoned cabin," he said.

"Show us," Kate said.

Jeb urged Socks into a lope. They saw a log cabin with its back against a sheer cliff, similar to their cabin.

A corral was beside the cabin with a shed over a portion of it that would offer some protection for the animals. Man rode to the front of the cabin, dismounted, and went to the door. It was open, and one of the leather hinges was broken.

He stepped inside and looked around. There were no windows, and it was gloomy inside. The heavy mat of dark clouds had taken away the sunrays. He struck a match and walked farther into the darkness. "Bring dry sticks and Pine needles, there's a fireplace."

Jeb and Kate hurried to gather things for a fire. Man took them, arranged them in the back of the fireplace, and struck another match. The Pine needles caught quickly and spread to the small sticks he put on top of the blaze.

Jeb had already gone back outside and they heard the sound of an ax and knew he was cutting firewood without being told. Kate was examining the inside of the cabin. It was very similar to theirs, a bed on the opposite side from the fireplace. A table, two chairs and shelves along the rear. Except for one old cast iron pot, there was nothing but the furniture.

Jeb brought in an armful of larger sticks and placed them beside the fireplace. "The mist has turned into a heavy drizzle," he said.

"I can manage in here," Kate said. "Bring the supplies from the mules and our saddles inside. There's no need for them getting wet tonight. Then care for the livestock."

Jeb and Man brought the supplies, put the bags on the table, and tossed the four saddles in the corner along with the packsaddle.

"There's ample grazing in the corral for the night," Man said. "There haven't been any animals in there in a year or more. I'm glad Jeb spotted this cabin, the drizzle has turned into a rain, and from the heaviness of the clouds, and I expect we'll have torrential rain before the night is over. Bull's tracks will be wiped out again."

"We'll pick them up again," Kate said. "That is, unless he leaves the trail. It seems we're continually saying that."

"He's done it before, but we can't help it," Man put in. "Moving on in this rain would be stupid, and accomplish nothing."

Kate put three plates on the table filled with a hot stew she made. Jeb picked up one and sat on the bed to eat. He ate every bite before Kate and Man were half finished.

Kate noticed and gestured toward the pot on the hearth. "There's plenty more, help yourself."

He stood and filled the plate again. "He must have a hollow leg as much food as he eats," she teased.

"He's just a growing boy," Man said.

Jeb ignored them and wolfed down the remainder of the stew he had on his plate. "That was good," he said. "You're a darn good cook, almost as good as my mom. But then she never cooked under such circumstances. I mean, cooking out of things from a packsaddle."

"I know you miss her," Kate said.

"I do, a lot," he said as he wiped his eyes with the sleeve on his shirt. "She was all I had."

He looked up at Man with concern and concentration etched on his face. "Can I ask a question?" he said.

"Of course," Man replied.

Jeb glanced at Kate and then back at Man. "It's kind of a man thing," he said.

"Let's take a walk out to the shed and check on the horses," Man said as he stood.

They ran to the shed and stood out of the rain and watched the horses and mules eating the belly high grass that grew in the corral. What's on your mind?" Man asked.

Jeb dug the toe of his boot into the dirt as he spoke. "How can you tell if you love a girl?" he asked. "I've never loved anybody except my mother, but that was different."

Man held back a chuckle, knowing Jeb was serious, and dealing with a foreign emotion.

"You're thinking about Alice," he said.

Jeb offered a shy grin as his head nodded up and down.

"I'll tell you how I know I love Kate," Man said. "That's the best I can do since she's the only woman I've ever loved. Well, that is, except my mom and sisters, but as you said, that was different."

"We met under unusual circumstances. I had been shot and she saved my life. The first time I saw her, I honestly thought she was an angel coming to take me to heaven."

"Anyway, she got me to my cabin and nursed me back to life and we were faced with several battles where our lives were at stake. In fact, she once again saved my life by shooting a man that was aiming a pistol at my nose."

"Then one night, we were in the cabin, and I was sleeping on the floor in front of the fireplace. She was on the bed. A very strong wind was blowing, and the temperature was well below zero. It was freezing cold in the cabin. She asked me to come to the bed to keep both of us warm."

"What happened?" Jeb asked with curiously and excitement reflected in his tone of voice.

"Kate asked me if she could be my woman."

"Golly, what did you say?"

"I said, yes, of course. I knew I loved her, but didn't know how to tell her. That's harder than you may think," Man said. "As soon as we found a preacher we married. And, that was the best thing that ever happened to me."

"That's a nice story, but you didn't tell me how you knew you loved her."

"I guess there're a couple of things I can say about that," Man said as he rubbed his chin with his hand. "I wouldn't hesitate a second giving my life to save her. And another thing I could add, Kate is the other half of my life. I would only be half a person without her. The good book says something like this, when a man and woman are joined, they are of one flesh. I found my mate for life, and will do anything in my power to protect her, and make her happy."

227

He met Jeb's eyes before speaking again. "Did that help?" he asked.

"I think so, but I need to think on it for a while," he replied.

"Alice and you are only sixteen," Man said. "My advice, give it a couple of years or more. See how you feel then. There are other girls out there, and you may never see Alice again. You may forget her in time; remember you knew her only a very short time."

"Maybe so, but I can't get her off my mind. I continually think about what we said to each other, and it keeps rolling around in my head. When we kissed, I mean, I had never felt so good in my life. It jolted me from my toes to my head. I just couldn't get enough. I wanted to make love with her so much I thought I would explode inside."

"That I understand," Man agreed. "The same with Kate and me. And the longer we're together, the better it gets. I guess that is also part of loving a woman. If it was only passion, it would soon fade away. That's one reason to take it slow."

They ran back to the cabin as the rain was coming down harder. Kate was busy at the fireplace when they came in. She glanced at Man, but knew this wasn't the time to ask what they talked about. He would tell her when they were alone.

***

Kate was up first the next morning, went to the fireplace, and started the morning fire. The cabin was cold with the rain and wind whipping around the log walls and found its way inside through cracks. Jeb was rolled up in his and Gus's bedroll, and Man was snuggled in the warm bed covered with the bearskin Kate added to the packsaddle before they left The Fort.

She felt the need for a nature break and went outside. The rain was coming down in sheets of water now. She went back inside and found the waterproof ground cloth they used under their bedroll when sleeping on frozen ground, or on wet dirt. She put it over her head and dashed to the shed, and went to the back.

As she was covering her head for the dash back to the cabin, movement in the trees caught her attention. She reached for her Walkers on her hips and was glad she remembered to buckle them around her waist. But then, she never went outside without them. A habit she got from their time at the cabin.

She saw a man creeping forward with a rifle in his hands held in front of his body. Kate waited to see what he did. She found a good place to hide by the fence out of sight of the intruder.

Her eyes darted from side to side to see if there were more. If it were Bull, there would be more. That is, unless they were coming in from another direction, but for now, the man she was watching appeared to be alone.

He crept forward, looking from side to side. The wind shifted slightly and she caught the scent of his unkempt, unwashed body. The warning Jake gave her on the wagon train rushed back. If a mountain man had a stench, he was probably trouble. This man was dressed in dirty frayed pants, and a poncho made of a tattered blanket. Bull and his men dressed in much better store bought clothing. But, they had money to spend.

She waited to see what he did before confronting him. If he was only hoping for a handout of food, she didn't want to startle him and cause him to react suddenly. He could bring his rifle into play without thinking. It was possible the rifle was only for protection if somebody started shooting from the cabin, but she had doubts that was the case. He came to kill and rob."

Kate kept one eye on the cabin door hoping man or Jeb didn't come outside. The other eye was on the man as he crept toward the cabin. The pistol in her right hand was ready and aimed at the man still creeping closer to the cabin. She saw him kneel behind a rock large enough to shield his body from gunfire from the cabin, and aimed the rife at the door.

"Hello the cabin," he yelled and sighed the rifle. It was obvious his intent was to shoot the moment the door opened and a target appeared.

Kate aimed both Walkers and shouted. "Drop the rifle."

His reaction was expected. Her turned toward her and fired in one motion, but his aim was off to the side of where Kate waited. She squeezed the triggers on the pistols, and felt the jolt in each hand as the twin bullets flew toward the shooter.

She saw two red spots appear on his chest, and the impact drove the assassin backward where he disappeared behind the rock. She knew both were kill shots, as the hot lead slugs entered the body dead center

Man opened the door and dove outside with his weapons in his hands, but there was no target to shoot at.

"I think there was only one," Kate said, as she looked for any movement. "He was aiming at the door. When I confronted him, he fired at me."

Man ignored the rain and went to the rock where Kate pointed. He ran in a zigzag pattern to prevent a possible shooter from having a clean shot at him should another killer be waiting.

Jeb was peeking out the door with his weapon in his hand.

"Cover Man," Kate shouted. "Watch for any movement in the trees."

Man made it to the rock and disappeared behind it. He came out in a couple of minutes with the gun belt and rifle of the dead man. Kate waited until Man was in the cabin and saw him aiming his pistols toward the trees to cover her, even thought the odds were small another shooter was nearby. He would have either gotten into the fight, or fled by now.

Kate put the waterproof cloth over her head and dashed to the cabin. Man closed the door as soon as she was inside. He put the weapons he brought back on the packsaddle and put a greasy bag on the table.

Jeb and Kate walked closer to see what was inside. Man opened the drawstring and dumped the contents on the table. They saw a few coins and a folded sheet of paper.

Jeb reached for it and spread it out on the table. "It's a wanted poster," he exclaimed. "Wanted dead or alive. A two hundred dollar reward," he said. "Harry, "Hackberry" Morgan," he added.

Jeb continued to read. "Wanted for armed robbery and murder."

"At least he wasn't part of the Bull gang," Kate said. "When I saw how he was dressed, and how he smelled, I didn't think he's part of the Blevins gang."

"What do you mean, smelled?" Jeb asked. "What difference would that make?"

Kate and Man explained the significance of the smell and dress of a mountain man that has no personal pride is the kind of man that had rather kill and rob than work for a living.

"What do we do now?" Jeb asked.

"I'm going to sit on the porch," Man said. "I want to watch to make sure the shots didn't draw attention from Bull and his men. Would you lead the livestock out of the corral and stake them out in a better place to graze? But first, take them to the creek to drink and find the horse belonging to Hackberry. Put him with the others. Keep a sharp eye out for riders approaching even though I doubt the sound of the shots would carry very far in the rain. The shots coupled with the thunder would be hard to distinguish from a distance."

"I'll have a hot breakfast ready for you when you get back," Kate said.

Jeb ignored the rain and went out with his hat pulled down on his head. Man took one of the chairs out on the porch, sat with his Winchester across his lap, and watched Jeb work.

Kate had breakfast ready and took a tin plate to Man. Jeb sat at the table at Kate's insistence, and she perched on the bed to eat as Man had the other chair.

"Did you and Man have a good talk yesterday?" she casually asked.

He glanced at her as he chewed. "I guess so, but I still don't know," he said after he swallowed.

"Alice?" she asked.

"I asked Man how I would know if I love her."

"That was a tough question," she replied.

"It didn't appear to be for Man, he told me how he knew he loved you."

"Really," she said. Hopefully, not to appear anxious to hear what Man said. She waited, eager for him to go on without her asking.

He took another bite before speaking again. "You want to know what he said. I can see it in your eyes." He went back to eating his breakfast.

She waited as long as she could stand it before asking. "What did he say?"

"Man said he wouldn't hesitate a second giving his life to save you. He said you're the other half of his life, and he would be half a person without you. He also said the good book says something like this, when a man and woman are joined, they are of one flesh. He said he found his mate for life, and will do anything within his power to protect you and make you happy."

Kate was glowing inside at Jeb's words. She felt the same about Man.

Jeb went back to eating.

"How do you feel about Alice?" she asked.

"I like her, I like her a lot. But, I know I don't feel as strongly about her as Man does for you. Man said for me to give it a couple more years and there are other girls out there. I think what he said makes good sense. As was pointed out to me, what could I offer her? I don't have any money, no job, and no place for us to live. A real man will provide those things for his wife."

He remembered what she mentioned earlier.

"Smart thinking," Kate said.

***

The rain cleared out during the night and morning brought a bright sun to beam down on the freshly washed earth. The grass and leaves glistened with droplets of sparkling water. The horses were well rested and full of rich grass.

The horse Hackberry was riding was older, and there were signs of abuse. "Turn him loose," Man said. "He'll find a wild bunch to run with, and there is ample grazing for him. Besides, having one more horse to deal with would slow us down if fast riding is needed, he couldn't do it."

Jeb took the hackamore from his head, slapped him on the rump, the horse trotted away a few yards. He stopped to look back at the other horses. "Go find new friends," Jeb said, and made a sudden lunge toward the horse. He turned and trotted into the trees and disappeared from sight in a few seconds.

"We'll leave the saddle inside the cabin, somebody may need it someday. It's so worn and old it would be worthless to anybody, except for somebody in dire need." Man took the saddle and used a leather cord to tie if from the roof of the cabin. "This may help keep varmints from chewing it up," he said.

Jeb opened the saddlebags and peeked inside. "Dirty clothes in this side," he said. He opened the other side. "A few bullets for the rifle and pistol," he said.

"Put them with his weapons on our packsaddle," Kate said.

They rode back to the trail and continued after Bull. Jeb was looking down mocking Man's actions. "Not a sign of any tracks," he said.

"Nope, as expected, the hard rain washed them away. All we can do now is go on, and hope to pick them up again, or get another sighting from Joe Meek."

The next morning, they found where somebody had camped under an overhang of rock on the side of a cliff. Man and Jeb dismounted and went to the ashes. Man felt of them. "Cold, I expect if it was Bull, they moved out yesterday morning like us. They're a full day in front of us, but now we have tracks to follow, hopefully."

Man rode, bending down carefully looking at the tracks. "Several horses. I can't be sure, but think four or five, maybe more. They are walking single file. Hopefully, they will scatter and I can get an accurate count."

"They took horses with them," Kate said. "I know, but I can't tell how many has riders."

They rode until dusk and moved away from the trail a quarter mile to make camp. "No fire tonight," Kate said.

"We'll post sentries," Man added. "Jeb, take the first watch. Don't fall asleep and use your ears and eyes. If you hear or see anything suspicious, come get us immediately."

"Yes sir," he said.

Kate handed him pemmican and jerky. "I'll relieve you about midnight; don't shoot me when I approach you in the darkness."

"Maybe you should whistle a happy tune," he teased.

She was softly whistling when she found him awake with a blanket around his shoulders. "Your bedroll is ready. Get some sleep."

Man came to Kate sometime during the early morning hours, sat beside her, pulled the blanket around his shoulders, and she snuggled against him.

"Jeb told me what you said about me and us," she whispered.

"What?" he said, but knowing what she meant.

"About how you feel about me," she said with a happy sigh.

"Oh, that," he said.

"I feel the same about you," she said, and kissed his cheek.

"I meant every word," he said as he pulled her around and kissed her ready lips. As the kiss continued, their passions began to rise, the moment was right for both of them.

"Here on the ground with only a blanket," she giggled

as she helped him with his clothing.

"Jeb has been with us, and we haven't had any private time in too long," he said as he settled in her cradle of love."

"I know," she sighed in contentment. "Someday, I want a son, and if he's anything like Jeb, it would make me happy. He's a fine young man."

***

They were on the trail at dawn and rode hard, hoping to close the gap between them and Bull. That is, if it was Bull and his gang they were tracking. Man wasn't able to identify the tracks in the muddy ground.

Man was riding point with Kate off to his left, and Jeb was several yards behind leading the mules and Socks. He had been riding Gus's gray gelding at Man's suggestion. "The gray is of better quality than Socks, if we must run, I had rather you be on Gus's horse so you can keep up with Redbird and Arabian."

It was late afternoon when Man suddenly pulled Arabian to a halt and held up his hand with the palm toward Kate and then at Jeb. He pulled back on the reins and Arabian began to back up. As soon as he was below the rim of the ridge, he turned and rode back to Jeb. Kate joined him to hear his report.

"We found them," he said. "Three riders, leading two horses. I don't think they saw me. At least, there was no reaction from them."

"Is it Bull?" Kate asked.

"It was too far to be positive, but I think so. Get off the trail and make camp. I'm going to scout ahead, and be positive before dark," he said.

Man circled and rode hard to get ahead of the men on the trail. When he was sure he was in front of them, he worked Arabian high on a hill and pulled his binoculars and scanned the trail below. There was nothing in either direction. He uttered a few choice words under his breath. Either he was in front of them, or they hadn't come this far. It was possible they had already passed this way, but he had no way of knowing. At this distance, he couldn't distinguish any tracks. Another thought flashed in his mind. They left the trail, which had happened all too often.

He had three options, wait and see if they appeared, go back to meet Kate and Jeb, or make another circle hoping to get in front of them.

He decided to go back and meet Kate and Jeb. If he was careful, he could go down to the trail, and look for tracks. Why hadn't he thought of that first? Then he would know which way to go. Ashamed of himself for being so slow, he mounted Arabian and worked his way down the hill weaving between the trees. Before riding into the open, he stopped and listened, as he scanned the trail in both directions. Only the natural sounds of birds chirping reached his ears. Arabian was busy munching on grass. He gave no indication any other horse was close.

He urged the horse into a trot, went to the trail, and dismounted. A multitude to tracks greeted him going back toward Kate and Jeb, but what scared him most, they were unshod. All of the horses Bull and his men rode had steel shoes. It had to be a band of Indians. He hoped they weren't renegades looking for scalps and loot. If they saw Kate, he knew they would be after her like a bird after a grasshopper.

He mounted quickly, moved away from the trail a few yards, and urged Arabian in to a lope. He rode no more than a half mile when the horse lifted his head and Man knew he caught the scent or heard another horse.

Not wanting to ride into a group of Indians, he pulled back and eased Arabian into a ground-eating walk. The horse kept lifting his head and shifting it from side to side catching the smell of something. Man slowed the horse and picked his way through the trees, standing in the stirrups trying to see the riders ahead.

As if Arabian understood, he stopped and turned his head toward the right. Man dismounted and crept in that direction. He soon heard the sound of men talking and stopped to listen. The words were garbled due to the distance, and rustling of leaves. He dropped to his knees and crawled forward keeping brush between himself and the sound.

An opening between two bushes offered him a place to see. Dropping on his belly, he snaked forward until he saw people. His heart went cold at the sight. Bull and his three men were talking with a dozen Indians. From their dress, he knew them to be renegades, and could cause serious trouble.

Bull seemed to have the ability to communicate in their language, which Man didn't recognize. It soon became obvious that Bull was negotiating a deal. The Indians were examining the spare horses and Bull was pointing back down the trail toward where Kate and Jeb were approaching.

He eased backward until he was hidden, and ran to his horse as fast as his legs would carry him. Kate and Jeb were about to ride into an ambush.

Man urged the powerful horse into a run as soon as he was out of hearing distance and went back to the trail. Me met Kate and Jeb and felt relief they were safe. They saw the urgency in Man the way he was racing toward them, and waited side by side on their horses for the news.

"Bull is recruiting help from a dozen Renegade Indians. I saw him offering the spare horses to them, and pointing this way. That could mean only one thing, trouble for us. We need to find a place to defend, should Bull and his men join the Indians, it will mean thirteen to three."

"We spotted a place about a quarter mile back," Kate said. She turned Redbird, and raced back down the trail and rode into a horseshoe shaped concave made of fallen rocks. An overhang of rock covered part of it, and would help prevent shooters from above them.

"How were they armed?" she asked.

"As best as I could see from my vantage point, they had rifles, but I was too far away to distinguish the type. I expect Bull has extra weapons with him as we do. Jeb, take the horses under the overhang and tie them out of harm's way. I saw some rocks and trees that'll help prevent them from being hit by stray bullets. Bring all the spare weapons and ammunition from the pack mules."

Man grabbed the ax from a mule as Jeb was leading them by, hurried to a tree, and began chopping frantically. The tree fell across the opening. He ran to the other side and began working on another. It fell across the opening and without stopping for a breath, his ax slashed at the trunk of another tree. By the time it fell, Jeb was back.

Kate began arranging the weapons at three strategic locations that would offer a firing lane at approaching riders.

Jeb helped Man move the two trees that he felled on top of the first and Man hurried to another. Jeb ran and grabbed the ax, he saw Man need a breather from working so fast and hard.

Kate was ready and the three tossed the forth tree on top of the other three. "One more," Man said. "And it should offer a barrier high enough to prevent riders from getting inside our makeshift fort."

He and Kate watched the last tree fall and helped toss it on top of the others.

Man and Kate hurried to their station and began getting the weapons ready for the pending fight. They jacked a bullet into the Winchesters, and added one to the magazine. Jeb saw what they were doing and copied their actions.

Kate walked to Jeb. "Aim and fire, but only when a target presents itself. Don't stand up or give them an open shot at you. When the rifle is empty, grab the other, and be ready. Only reload in a lull, they may make one rush, and then fall back to regroup giving us a chance. If you see one of us go down. Stay at your post firing. If they get inside, it will be the end for all of us. If you go down, we'll help as soon as we can. If you're able, stop the flow of blood yourself by tying something around the wound."

He gulped as that thought soaked in, they were going to be in a battle that would end in one of two ways. They, are the enemy would be dead. This was a battle for survival.

The sound of horses approaching caused Kate to run back to her post. Man was standing behind a rock with his extra rifle leaning against the barricade they built. It was within easy reach when the other was empty. Kate took her place and sighted toward the trail. Jeb was at his station with his Henry in his hands. He forced his mind to concentrate and forget about the impending danger. Sweat dripped from his nose and he wiped his face with the sleeve of his shirt.

Kate saw his actions and knew the young boy was nervous. "It'll be okay," she said. "Relax and aim and fire as I know you can. We'll get out of this. Just do your job and cover the area in front of you."

"You can count on me," he said. "I'll uphold my end."

"Here they come," Man shouted.

Bull was riding in front. His men were at his side with the Indians behind them. Bull saw the fortress and turned toward the Indians. They couldn't understand what he said, but from his gestures, they knew he was giving orders.

The Indians moved forward and formed a scrimmage line, and raised their rifles in the air as a signal they were ready. Bull pointed toward the barricade and shouted something, as he lowered his arm, as a signal to charge.

The line of Indian horseman came at a run. "Hold your fire until they're within range," Man yelled. "And then give them hell. We must stop the first charge, and empty as many horses as possible. Jeb, aim before you shoot, if there isn't a target, take down a horse, and do what you have to do to stop the charge. The Indians will be riding low offering as small a target as possible."

"Bull and his men are hanging back, letting the Indians be cannon fodder," Kate said. "If you get a chance later on, take out Bull and his men. With them down, the Indians may pull back and be happy with the Bull's horses and weapons."

The riders were shooting as they came storming forward in a straight line. When they were near enough for a good shot, Man yelled, "Fire."

Three bullets winged toward the Indians. Three riders fell from their horses. Man, Kate and Jeb were shooting as fast as they could lever a bullet into the firing chamber, and select a target. As Man had predicted, the Indians were now riding on the side of their horse, and only a foot and head could be seen. They were skilled in the art of shooting from a running horse. Bullets were ricocheting from the rocks in front of Man, Kate and Jeb.

Man saw one of Bulls riders veering to his right. He saw the reason, trees would offer protection, and he was attempting to flank them. Kate was closer to that position. "To your right, Kate," he yelled above the roar of the rifles."

She turned and saw the man working his way forward, now on foot in a thick grove of trees. He kept the trees between them, and she only got a glimpse of him as he darted from tree to tree.

The Indians were circulating in front of their stronghold, and Jeb and Man were keeping the remaining riders from storming their stronghold. Having extra weapons to put into use prevented a lull in the shooting. This surprised the Indians, as they expected to make a charge when the rifles were empty.

Kate ran to a better location to be in position when the shooter presented a target.

He was within a hundred yards now, and coming closer, still darting between trees preventing an open shot at him. She waited, and when he stopped, and propped his rifle on a limb, she squeezed the trigger of her Winchester '73. A split second later, she saw a puff of dust from his shirt and he was thrown backward.

She ran back to her post in time to see five Indians

turn tail and retreat. Bull and two of his men were waiting.

It was obvious Bull was furious. He'd been watching the fight through his binoculars, and knew the three people on his trail were not injured.

The Renegade Indian leader was listing without speaking. Bull finally stopped his tirade, and the Indian turned and gave orders to his men.

They rode back toward the fortification slowly, with Bull and the remaining two men in the line.

Man shouted, "Reload and be ready for another assault. I expect them to use another approach; riding in front of us wasn't effective."

Four riders veered to the left and four to the right, but they were outside rifle range.

"What are they going to do?" Jeb asked.

"I don't know," Man said. "Maybe try to approach us from two directions, or one group will try to circle behind, while the other keeps us busy. The rock overhang will offer some protection for us, but I'm not sure how much since we didn't have time to scout it before the attack. They could sneak up to the edge and shoot down on us. Kate, that will be your duty. Keep track of the two groups and should one disappear, be ready for whatever they try especially if they get above us."

Kate followed the men that circled to the right with her eyes. The two white men were with two of the Indians. Bull was with the other group. The men Kate watched separated, with an Indian and one of the white men kept going on around the hill behind where they defended. The other two seemed to be waiting for something, probably a signal.

"They appear to be preparing for a three or four prong attack," Kate yelled.

"They split into two groups here," Man replied. "Two are going on to the left. Expect an attack from all four sides. There are only three of us; one of the points of attack will be left unprotected."

"What do I do?" Jeb asked.

"Your area of responsibility will be the left flank. Kate, the rear, I'll do my best to keep the two men in front, and the two to my right in check until we whittle down the numbers. If either of you should drop the two in front of you, come help me."

Man kept the movement of the two men in front and to the right in sight by darting his eyes from group to group.

"Attack," Bull yelled, and all four groups began rapid fire into the stronghold. Jeb and Man were returning fire as fast as they could lever a bullet into the firing chamber and locate a target. Bull and his men kept cover in front and on the right side of Man. Their heads came up, and they fired, ducked down again, and moved to another place for the next shot.

Kate couldn't find a target as the shooters were well hidden, but apparently, they were shooting blind, as they couldn't see anybody.

Jeb was firing as fast as he could at the two men approaching from the left side. They would both shoot and then hurry to a closer place while Jeb had his head down.

His first rifle clicked, and he grabbed the spare. "The kid is out of bullets, charge before he can reload," Bull yelled in English even though the Indians probably couldn't understand, but they understood and charged toward Jeb shooting as they ran.

Jeb was ready, aimed, and fired. The first bullet took an Indian in the stomach. He doubled over with a scream. The second slid to a stop when he realized Jeb had another weapon. He tried to turn and run back for cover, but didn't make it. A bullet from Jeb took him between his shoulder blades and he plowed headfirst into the dirt.

Jeb grabbed his empty rifle and raced to Man's side. "I got my two," he said.

Kate was frantically searching for a target, but as yet, hadn't spotted them.

"Take the two on the right," Man said. "I'll have the

front. Keep an eye above, those two are maneuvering around, looking for a place to shoot down on us."

Bull kept firing, but the Indian hadn't fired in several minutes. "I think the shooter with Bull is trying to sneak in," Man said in a soft voice where Bull wouldn't hear. "Watch for any movement in the bushes."

"I will," Jeb said. "And I've only drawn fire from one position. Maybe one of them is doing the same."

Kate kept looking up, and when the firing from above stopped, she hurried to another location, hoping to be in a better position to find a target.

"A volley from two rifles opened up from above, but at different places than before. Kate saw movement, sighted the rifle, and waited for the shooter to offer a target.

A head appeared around a small rock close to the edge of the overhang. He was trying to get to a location to see Man and Jeb below his position. She waited until the man stood and aimed his rifle. Kate was faster and her bullet entered the chest of the Indian, and he dropped from sight. His shot went into the air as his dying spasms pulled the trigger.

The other shooter was unaware his partner was down. He yelled, "Bull, did we get one? I can't see."

"No, the woman got the Indian, get back down here."

Man heard the order, and shifted to watch the side of the hill where the shooter could appear. He spotted the man moving cautiously down the side of the steep slope, and drew a bead on where he hoped the man would appear. His guess was good, and a bullet belly ripped through the startled man. His body slid on down the hill and stopped when it hit a tree with a loud thud. If the shot didn't kill him, the collision with the tree would.

Kate came running from the rear, and took the left side of the enclosure. "I think there's only three left," Man said.

As to reinforce his statement, three horses ran from

the trees in front of them. Bull was in the lead, and shielded by the two Indians. Kate and Man were ready, their Winchesters spoke in unison, and both Indians fell from their saddles.

Jeb joined them, and for the first time, they saw blood matted on his shirt. "How bad are you hit?" she asked.

"I don't know, it hurts awful, but I knew I had to keep on fighting as you said."

She pulled her knife and slit the shirt. It would hurt too much for her to take it off his arms. A slice across his rib cage was bleeding profusely. Man ran to the horses and brought Kate's saddlebags. She reached for it and ordered, "I need moss and the cooking pot."

Man understood, went to the mules for the pot, and then started a fire with small limbs on the ground. He filled the pot with water from the canteen, and hurried to look for the moss.

Kate took Jeb to the shade of a tree and told him to lie on his left side so she could work. She cleaned the wound with water, and then packed the gash with yellow sulphur powder, and wrapped a white bandage around the bleeding wound. She tied it as tight as possible to staunch the flow of blood.

Man soon had the pot boiling and dropped a wad of moss into the bubbling liquid. On Kate's orders, he removed it with two sticks and brought it to her. She waited for it to cool sufficiently, and then removed the bandage carefully. She placed the wad of moss evenly over the four-inch gash.

Jeb turned his head and frowned at the sight of the awful looking mess she was putting on his wound, but said nothing.

She saw his expression. "It works," she said. "It'll draw out any infection that may set in."

"I thought the same thing when she put moss on me the first time we met," Man said. "I had a similar wound and it worked. Except for a scar, I'm fine. Kate's a darn good doctor on bullet wounds."

Man stood and went for Arabian and led him back to Kate and Jeb. "I'm going to scout around, and see what I can find. I doubt Bull will be back, but keep a watchful eye."

Kate helped him move the trees away from the opening to allow a narrow opening to lead Arabian outside. He rode away following the tracks of Bull.

Kate went to the gray gelding Jeb was riding, brought his bedroll, and made a place for him to lay. As soon as she had him comfortable, she went to the fire Man built and started cooking a hot meal. Jeb would need nourishment to heal faster.

Man came back in less than an hour leading two horses with several weapons tied on the empty saddles. Jeb saw him, moved back with a groan, and leaned against the tree so he could see.

"I cut the other horses loose," he said. The Indian ponies weren't worth keeping. But, I brought in the weapons that were useful. Most of the rifles the Indians were using I would be afraid to shoot for fear they would explode in my face. I'm amazed they were so accurate with those antiques."

"What about Bull?" Kate asked.

"I followed his tracks for about a mile and he was headed south in a heck of a hurry."

"At least he's alone now," Kate added.

"For now," he said. "But his kind can always find followers with the promise of easy money. As the old saying goes, birds of feather flock together, and there are enough outlaws out here to make a heck of a flock. Bull is a natural leader and can always recruit more followers."

"I know, I think it was Jake that told me that a lot of the mountain men came west to escape a rope party, or running from the law. Bull will have plenty to choose from."

Jeb was listening and continued to learn from Man and Kate. As Slats once said about Man, if he survives,

245

he'll someday be a man to be reckoned with. Jeb was the same as Man had been, he listened, watched, and was a fast learner. He'll someday be a man fitting to shape the Oregon Territory for future generations.

After supper, Kate examined Jeb's wound, and decided he needed a couple of days rest. This would give the wound time to begin the healing process. Man agreed with her assessment. Taking care of Jeb came first over chasing after Bull. They would pick up his trail again.

She dressed the wound twice a day, and was happy there were no redness or swelling around the slice in his side. The moss and sulphur drug again prevented infection. On the second day, she removed the moss and left the wound open so a scab would form over the wound.

On the third morning, Jeb was up and moving without much pain. "I can ride today," he said as he sat and sipped hot coffee. "We need to be on the trail after Bull. I caused us to be two days behind."

"We'll catch up with him again," Kate said. "There are too many eyes out there looking, and every law enforcement person is on alert for him. Killing a United States marshal got the attention of everybody."

This time, Kate led the extra horses and pack mules due to the pain in Jeb's side. Man rode point, following the trail, hoping Bull didn't veer off somewhere along the way.

On the third morning, as they were eating breakfast, Man sat in deep thought. He stood and made a slow circle around the fire, sipping coffee. "I have a gut feeling Bull is going back to Portland. Why, I can't say, but I suggest we go there. I haven't been able to identify his tracks since yesterday. A shower may have washed them away, or he left the trail somewhere along the way. Anyway, we'll have access to a telegraph and our supplies are getting low."

Kate and Jeb were both nodding agreement. "A soft bed in a hotel would be nice," Kate said. "That cold hard ground doesn't help much for a deep restful sleep. I know

Jeb will appreciate it with his wound."

***

Their first stop was at the police station. The desk clerk recognized Kate the instant she stepped through the door. "Welcome back to Portland," he said as he stood.

"I'll tell Chief Forest Kline that you're here.

Kline came out of his office and welcomed Man with a shake and he gave a welcome smile at Kate. She returned it, and turned to Jeb with a hand gesture. "This is Jebediah Spencer, but called Jeb of course."

Chief Kline eyed young man for a couple of seconds. "May I ask why he's traveling with you on the trail of Bull?"

"It's a long story, but the very short version, his mother was murdered, and he had no place to live, so we invited him to come with us."

"He's been valuable to us," Man put in. "He downed several of Bull's men. He's a damn good shot, and very mature for his age."

Kline eyed Jeb with doubt in his expression, but didn't comment. Instead, he invited the three into his office, and Man and Kate gave him a complete report.

So you think Bull came back here?" he asked.

"We lost the trail after the battle with the remainder of his gang and the Renegade Indians he recruited. The last time I saw his tracks, he was headed this way, but that was a few days ago. He could be anywhere, but we came here on a hunch, the need to replenish our supplies, and make a report to you and Joe Meek."

"And a soft bed to sleep on," Kate added with a chuckle.

"What are your immediate plans?" Kline asked.

"Go to the telegraph office, report to Meek, go to the hotel, and take a bath. Then, we'll sit at a table for a hot meal," Man replied.

Chapter 13

Kate tapped on Jeb's door the next morning. "We're going down and find a café. Do you want to go eat with us?"

The door opened immediately, and he stepped out smiling. "I'm starved," he said.

"So what else is new," she teased. "Does that hollow leg you have need filling again. I was sure you ate enough last night to fill it."

"I'm just a growing boy as I've been told so often."

Man was listening with a grin on his face, and led the way to the stairs.

They sat at the table and a waitress came to the table with three cups and a pot of coffee. "I expect you want coffee this early in the morning."

"That we do," Man said.

Jeb was looking at the waitress with an expression of uncertainty.

Kate noticed, but didn't comment.

"Eggs, ham, biscuits, and gravy for me," Man said. Kate and Jeb nodded agreement.

The waitress turned and went back to the window at the kitchen to turn in their order.

"Does she remind you of someone?" Kate asked facing Jeb.

"Of course she does, Alice. But she isn't near as pretty as Alice. Besides being beautiful, Alice was extraordinary special. A great personality and well... unique."

The waitress was very attentive, but Jeb managed to keep his eyes averted and only answered her direct questions, usually with a simple yes or no.

They finished and Man went to the front and paid with a voucher.

Kate and Jeb followed him, and as they approached the front door, a city policeman met them. He handed

Man a telegram. "I was asked to deliver this to you," he said. "I tried the hotel first and the desk clerk said he saw you go out. I expected you would be here."

Man took it as he said, "Thanks."

He stepped outside and tore the envelope open with the others watching. "It's from Joe Meek," he said.

"The body of a woman was found outside Portland about ten miles north. Investigate. This crime fits the other rape and murder committed by Bull Blevins."

"I'll report this incident to Chief Kline," the policeman said.

"Tell him we'll be going to the location as soon as we change into our working clothes, and get the horses. I expect he needs to arrange for somebody to go out and take charge. If it was Bull, we'll be on his trail again."

"While you change, I'll saddle up and get the mules and our supplies loaded," Jeb said. "If you would bring my things from my room. All I have is my saddlebags and rifle there."

"Will do," Kate said.

Jeb had the horses saddled and the mules loaded when Kate and Man hurried out the front door of the hotel. People stopped to look at the pair wearing deerskin clothing with two pistols on their hips. Man and Kate ignored the gawkers as they saw this every time they were in a town.

It was easy to find the cabin as the road was filled with spectators and friends of the family. Man, Kate, and Jeb were allowed to enter the yard by a men at the gate keeping everybody away from the cabin. He stepped back seeing the marshal's badge on Man's shirt. Kate motioned for Jeb to wait on the porch. There was no need for the young man to view what they expected to find. If Bull was the murderer, the woman would be naked, tied to the bedpost, with her throat cut.

They found the local constable inside. Man showed his badge and approached the blood stained bed. "What did you find here?" he asked.

249

The constable took out a notebook from his pocket and reported. "Edna Black, age thirty-two. She was nude and had her hands tied to the bedpost. Her throat was cut. We later found Jake Black, and their two children dead. They were in two separate places. Jake was in the field below the house, and the two kids, a boy about five or six and a girl about four were behind the cabin. They were both stabbed in the throat."

"How was Jake killed?" Man asked.

"The same as the kids, knife, but to the chest. It appeared Jake was plowing. We expect the killer approached as a friend or lost traveler and stabbed Jake suddenly. His body was beside the plow. Then we think the murderer went to the cabin, and killed the children before going inside the cabin. But that is only speculation from where we found the bodies of the children."

"Who found them," Kate asked.

"A neighbor saw Jake lying beside the plow and went to investigate. He then went to the cabin and found Edna and the kids. He didn't touch anything and came to town to report it. He's at the gate. I asked him to keep everybody out until you got here. But I never expected a United States deputy marshal."

"We were in Portland and got a wire for us to investigate. This fits the method Bull Blevins has used several times before. We were on his trail, but lost it after the heavy rain. Did you find his tracks?"

"Yes, we followed tracks across the field to where we found Jake, then to a place behind the cabin where horses were tied."

"How many sets of tracks?" Man quizzed.

"Three," the constable replied.

"Darn," Man mumbled under his voice.

The lawman heard and asked, "What does that mean?"

"We've been tracking Bull for a long while. We had a fight with him a few days ago, and Bull was the only survivor. He was left alone and headed this way. As I said, I lost his trail due to a rain-washing out his tracks. We went on to Portland where we got a telegram from Chief United States Marshal Joe Meek about this crime. He ordered me to investigate to see if it was Bull again."

"Will you or one of your men show me where their horses were tethered? We need to be back on their trail."

"Of course," he replied.

"I'll show you, in fact, I'm the man that found the tracks."

He led the three through the crowd standing outside the yard. One of the women spectators made a comment as they walked by. "Look at her, wearing deerskin clothing and two pistols on her hips."

Another woman followed up with a comment about Man. "I would hate to have him after me. Did you see the look in his eyes and the expression on his face. Whoever did this, will regret it. Just mark my words."

"I wonder about the boy with them," another woman said. "He can't be more than sixteen or seventeen. He can't belong to them, she's only four or five years older than him."

The constable led them to a clump of trees not far from the house. He gestured toward the tracks.

Man knelt, examined them, and walked in a circle looking for where the tracks left the cabin. It was easy to find them, as the earth was soft after the rain.

"Somebody from Portland will be out soon. Tell them to send a wire to Joe Meek we're back on Bull's trail."

He mounted and took the point. Kate was following behind and Jeb was riding Gus's gray and leading Socks, and the pack mules. His wound was healed to the point it was no longer painful. They left the other horses at the stable. They knew they might need to move fast, and the extra livestock would slow them down.

However, the tracks led south toward Portland. Man was shaking his head. The tracks would soon be lost in the multitude of other tracks. He was right, the three sets of tracks merged in with others on a well-traveled road.

He pulled Arabian to a stop under a tree and waited for Kate and Jeb to stop beside him.

Kate knew the situation as she had been watching the trail. "What do we do now?" she asked.

"Darn if I know. Bull is lost in the city again. He could be anywhere. I hoped after the murders, he would bypass Portland and keep going. When we finally meet, I was hoping it would be away from a town."

Since they came back to Portland, Man stopped at the police station and gave his report to Chief Kline.

"I notified the sheriff and he sent two deputies out to the Black's farm. We don't have any official authority out of Portland."

"A local constable was at the scene and waiting for somebody," Man said.

"They rode on to the telegraph office to send a report to Joe. In Man's report, he stated a similar report would be forthcoming, as he wasn't aware the trail would lead back to Portland."

It had been a long morning in the saddle, so they went to the hotel where Man and Jeb took the horses to the stable. Kate went to their room and changed out of her working skins.

A few minutes later, Man came in and saw she was wearing her city clothes and offered a wolf-whistle. He knew she wanted to go out, so he changed into his store-bought duds, as he sometimes joked.

"I'll tell Jeb we're going out," she said. She tapped on his door and said, "We're going out shopping and sightseeing, if you want to go with us, change into clean clothes."

"I'll be ready if a minute," he said.

"Meet us in the lobby," she replied and went back to their room for Man.

Jeb was seated in a chair watching the people walk down the boardwalk when Kate and Man came down the steps. "See any pretty girls?" she teased.

"Yep, a few, but none that would come close to Alice," he offered with a sheepish grin.

He followed Man and Kate out on the boardwalk and waited for Kate to decide which way to go. "What are we doing, or looking for?" Man asked.

"Nothing in particular, I want to look in more of the stores and shops. A woman thing, I suppose. I want to see the new fashions, the pretty dresses, and fancy shoes. But, when we see a men's clothing store, I want to replace the shirt I cut off Jeb. Besides, he needs more clothing. He only has the working things and the two sets we bought."

Man dropped back and Jeb fell in beside Kate. "Do you think I'll ever see Alice again?" he asked out of the blue.

"Probably, since she's on your mind a lot. I expect you'll find a way someday to get back to Tacoma."

"Why do men get such a funny butterfly feeling in their gut when a pretty girl walks by?" Jeb continued with his never-ending questions.

"I expect Man could better explain it, but the same happens to us. Mother Nature has to have a hand in it. If men and women didn't have that attraction, the human race would cease to exist. It's that way with all species of animals, birds, fish, and even insects. The male and female mate, and the next generation is started."

"Do you think you'll have kids someday?" Jeb asked, straightforwardly.

Kate glanced back at Man for his expression if he was listening. He was smiling and gave a quick nod.

"Yes," she said. "We'll have children when the time is right. But, now we have a job to finish."

Their route took them closer to the river and Man and Jeb followed Kate as she looked into windows, or went inside the store. Usually, they waited outside as the women things didn't interest them, but they stopped at the saddle shops and gun stores to gaze at the merchandise.

Kate bought a few things and a new red flannel shirt

for Jeb as well as another pair of pants and shirt that would be more suited in town than out in the wilderness.

They were leaving the shopping area and entering the saloon and dancehall area. "It's time to turn back," Kate said.

"Just as it was getting interesting," Man teased. "The sun is about down and the fun is just getting started."

He gave her a teasing grin, which she returned.

They went to the street corner to cross to the other side so Kate could do more window shopping on that side, on the walk back to the café.'

Man grabbed Kate's arm and stopped her as a Chestnut with a blaze face came toward them. A mountain man with a beard was on his back, and two similar dressed men were riding at his side. The smell almost made Kate gag.

"Is that Bull Blevins?" Man whispered. Both Kate and Jeb went instantly on alert as they watched the trio ride past.

They let the three killers ride by without making a move. Now wasn't the time for a showdown. There were too many people on the streets with the possibility of innocent people being hurt or killed in a gunfight. They knew Bull wouldn't surrender.

"Kate, go to the hotel and bring our horses and rifles. Jeb, go to the police station and get word to Chief Kline that we have Bull located. I'll follow them until they alight somewhere, and meet you at this street corner."

Jeb took off at a run, and Kate walked as fast as she could carrying the packages. Man stayed on the boardwalk, and followed the riders, doing his best to be only another person going home after a long day at work. At times, he had to rush to keep pace as the horses were walking faster than he could.

The three men rode for another four blocks and stopped in front of a salon named the, Red Garter. They tied their horses to the rail in front and went through the swinging doors. Man watched until they were inside, then went to the window, and peeked. The three took a table near the back, and signaled for the waitress to bring a pitcher of beer.

He watched until the waitress delivered the pitcher and three mugs. She filled the mugs and picked up the money Bull put on the table.

Man felt they were settled in for a while drinking beer and hurried back to the place he was to meet Kate and Jeb with backup policemen.

It seemed like ages, but in reality, it was only a few minutes. Kate was the first to arrive with their horses. She had changed into her working skins and had both Walkers on her hips.

Man saw she had his skins tied to the saddle. He took them and ducked into a dark alley to change. Somehow, going into battle dressed as a city dude didn't feel right.

She waited and held the three horses. He was back in less than a minute, and put his town clothes in his saddlebags.

They saw Jeb with four policemen coming, and stepped out to meet them. Chief Kline was in the lead with Jeb.

"They're in the, Red Garter Saloon," Man said. "Three men, seated near the back. There's a window nearby, as well as a back door. We need to have both covered when they make a break. The Saloon is about half full, maybe thirty people."

"How do you want to handle it?" Kline asked.

"I wish we could get them isolated," he said. "They won't surrender, as a noose waits them. If nothing else, given the opportunity, they'll take hostages as human shields and walk out behind them."

Man led the way to the alley behind the Red Garter Saloon. They tied their horses to a handrail beside porch steps for a store several yards from the backdoor of the saloon. They would be out of harm's way if a gunfight started in the alley.

"Take the window and back door," Man said. He was addressing Chief Kline, and felt funny giving orders to the Chief of Police, but that was how Kline wanted it. After all, Man was a United States deputy marshal and had rank over him.

Man, Jeb and Kate went to the front where Man peeked inside the window where he had been earlier.

The three were still at the table talking and drinking beer. He backed up and gestured for Kate and Jeb to follow. He moved to the alley entrance and stopped. He motioned for Chief Kline to come to them and hear his report. "They're drinking beer. If we wait, hopefully, they'll get drunk, and will be easier to handle."

For an hour, they waited, watching, getting more impatient. Chief Kline walked to where Man was standing in the alley. "How much longer?" he asked.

"I don't know. The Saloon is packed. A gunfight could be awful if it erupted inside. I see no other way other than wait them out, and be alert. I expect them to come out the front, since their horses are tied there. If I see them going in that direction, I'll let you know and come running. Maybe we can get the innocent bystanders out of the way."

Kline nodded agreement.

"What about moving their horses to the rear with ours?" Kate asked. "That would prevent them mounting and racing away."

"Good suggestion," Man said. He and Jeb went to the three horses and led them to the alley.

"There are plenty more horses in front should they decide to run," Jeb said. "Stealing more horses to escape would be what I would do."

"I agree, but we can't move them all. As customers come outside and their horses are gone, that would alert Bull that something is going on."

Kate heard their comments. "Not if we were waiting and told them where they were located, and to get out of here as quickly as possible," Kate suggested. "We could move the horses located directly in front of the Saloon, and that would give us more opportunity to take them down, if they couldn't jump on a horse and run."

Man agreed and went for four horses tied to a rail. Jeb did the same to another hitching rail. Kate waited in front of the Saloon in case customers came out looking for their horse. Two men came out and glanced at the empty hitching rail. Kate hurried to them before they caused an uproar. "There are outlaws inside. You're horses are in the alley. Get out of here as fast as possible. We expect bullets will be flying in a few minutes."

One of the cowboys wanted to protest. Beer made him arrogant, but Man came up and the marshal's badge did the trick. The two men hurried to their horses and rode away.

A total of six men came out, and were moved on their way without incident. Man was peeking in the front window when he saw Bull putting money on the table, and the three men were taking to the bargirl.

"Get Kline," he said toward Jeb. "Make it fast. Tell them to take this side of the door; we'll be on the other side. It looks like they're about to come out the front."

"What about me?" he asked. "Where do you want me?"

"Out of the line of fire," Kate ordered. "You've already been wounded and there are plenty of us for the three. However, keep your rifle ready, and should one of them escape, use caution and take him down. Watch for spectators in the line of fire or behind them in case you miss."

Man pointed across the street. "Go over there across the street and take cover. You'll have a great view of the front door."

Jeb ran in that direction.

Kline and his men took positions beside the door. Kate and Man were on the other side.

Two drunken cowboys came out first, and stood in the doorway. They saw the policeman and shouted,

"Cops." They grabbed for their weapons. The policeman had no choice, as the cowboys were intent on a shootout. It was obvious they were on the run from the law.

The policemen fired first, and the two drunken outlaws went to the floor without getting off a shot.

Bull and his men ran for the rear door leaving their horses behind, they thought.

Kate and Man ran to the corner, and slid to a stop as Bull and his men were trying to get into the saddles.

Bull saw them and fired fast since he had his pistol in his hand. His bullet went beside Man and lodged in the wood on the Saloon wall.

Kate fired her rifle, and one of Bull's men went to the ground with a bullet in his chest. The other man was scrambling to mount when Man's rifle roared. The slug took him in his side piercing his heart, and he died before he hit the ground.

Bull dived for cover behind a rain barrel. Kate and Man opened up with their Winchesters 1873 rifles and the wood barrel began to explode as the heavy bullets smashed into it. Rainwater flooded out of the many holes.

Man and Kate continued to shoot and the bullets were now penetrating through the wood. Bull stood and tried to aim, but two more bullets took him dead center in his chest and we went backward.

The four policemen were coming at a run. Kline stopped beside Man and Kate and looked at the three dead outlaws. "Thanks to you two, it's over now. Not only did you get the Bull Blevins gang, but we cleared up two other wants. The two we got on the porch of the Saloon were wanted for cattle rustling, and a stage robbery. I recognized them and have their wanted posters at the station."

"If you'll take charge of the bodies, we're going to the telegraph office and notify Joe Meek," Man said "If it's okay with you, we'll take the Chestnut horse Bull was riding. He belongs to Melvin Knox. His wife and son were murdered by Bull and his gang.

"Take the horse, Chief Kline said. "I'll take care of the bodies and paper work. Thanks for your help."

Man stopped and sent a telegram to United States Marshal Joseph Meek. It was short and to the point, but it included the necessities to end the case. The telegraph operator read the sheet of paper Man handed him. "Bull Blevins and all of his gang members are dead."

The next morning, Jeb, Kate and Man were eating breakfast when a policeman came into the café and walked to Man. "This telegram was delivered to our office for you. Chief Kline asked me to find you. It's marked urgent."

"Not another case, I hope," Kate moaned.

Man tore the envelope open and read for the benefit of Kate and Jeb, as well as the policeman. "Wait for me in Portland." It was from Meek.

Chapter 14

Meek knocked on their door the next afternoon. Man met him and invited him inside. Joe looked around the tiny room and said, "Let's go down to the bar and sit at a table. It was a long ride, and I need to wet my whistle, and cut some of the trail dust out of my throat."

Man and Kate were wearing their town clothes and felt comfortable in public. Joe was dressed in riding clothes, but that was acceptable. Besides, the United States marshal's badge and the big pistol on his hip demanded respect regardless, of what he wore.

He led them to a table against a wall where there were no other customers close by. He took the seat with his back toward the wall and Man selected the one where he could see the front. Kate grinned, knowing why."

Joe ordered a pitcher of beer and waited for it and mugs to be delivered to the table before speaking to them.

He took a long drag on the beer and turned to Man. "Good job for your rookie outing. I'm removing temporary from your title, Deputy Marshal Manchester."

Kate moaned under her breath.

Joe sensed her plight, or concern.

"After losing Gus, I need a replacement. You were born for this work." Joe was facing Man, searching his face for his reaction to the offer.

"Kate and I have plans to settle down in our mountain cabin, start raising crops and kids," Man replied and saw a hint of a smile followed by a frown on Kate's face.

Joe caught it as well. "You two talk it over. I'll be here a couple of days. But I want an answer no later than noon two days from now."

"Yes sir," Man said.

"What about the boy traveling with you?" he asked.

"Jebediah Spencer," Man said.

"He has visions of being a marshal," Kate said.

"Not at sixteen," Joe said, emphatically. "Maybe when he's twenty-one or so, with some law enforcement experience, I'll talk to him."

"I told him that, "Kate said. "He's too young to know what he wants to do with his life. He also has his eye on a pretty young girl named Alice Kitchens he met in Tacoma."

"Should Man say, yes, on the job offer," Kate said. "Do you have any immediate plans, or an assignment looming?"

"There are always cases pending," Joe replied. "Why are you asking?"

"I may have a place for Jeb to live. First, a settler named Melvin Knox. His wife and son were murdered by Bull. He's alone in his cabin now, and the thought crossed my mind that he might welcome Jeb."

Another place," Kate added, quickly. "George and Maude Bowman own the trading post at The Fort. They have no kids, and are getting older and are talking about retiring. George is also a fur and grain buyer. He ships the products he buys here, and returns with merchandise for the store."

Joe was nodding. He knew about Knox and Bowman due to the robbery of George, and the murder of Knox's wife and son.

"We retrieved Melvin Knox's horse from Bull and would like to take it back to him," Kate said. "We want to introduce him to Jeb and see how it goes. If they don't mesh, we'll go on to The Fort, and visit George and Maude Bowman."

"I expect you think your husband will accept the job offer," he said, "Otherwise, you wouldn't be asking about taking a week or so off and finding a place for the boy."

"Could be," Man said. "We'll have an answer for you by the deadline."

"What does Jeb say about this?" Joe asked.

"We haven't discussed it with him," Kate said. "But, should we accept the job offer, I don't want him traveling with us. He was wounded, and is too young to be put in danger."

"I agree," Joe said. "That would be one of the stipulations should you accept. He can't go with you."

Man and Kate both nodded agreement. "We had already discussed and decided that before you offered the job to Man."

Joe chuckled. "Before when both of you replied, you used the word, we, will have an answer for you. I knew I was getting two marshals for the price of one."

"As before," Kate said, "Man is my husband and we're partners."

Joe changed the subject. "I was saddened when I heard about Gus. Tell me in detail what happened."

Gus was riding point, tracking Bull. He had us spread out about thirty yards apart because he knew an ambush was a possibility. A hidden shooter took him in the chest without any warning. The assassin was gone before we could locate him. The bullet went through Gus's heart and he was dead before he hit the ground. He never knew what hit him."

"At least it was quick and painless," Joe said. "I sent men to retrieve his body, and he's buried beside his wife. I was advised the yellow ribbon helped them locate where he was buried beside the trail."

"We have the gray gelding Gus was riding," Man said. "Jeb has been riding him. He has a horse, but it was nothing near the quality of the gray gelding. At times we needed to move fast, so I put him on Gus's horse."

"Keep the horse," Joe said. "The boy earned it. Besides, Gus had no family, and another horse, I don't need."

"We have Gus's weapons, badge and wallet," Man said.

"Get the badge and wallet to me and keep the weapons. Give them to the boy and tell him to respect where they came from."

"He'll certainly do that," Kate said. "He loves guns

262

and worked for a gunsmith in Seattle to earn money for bullets to an old blunderbuss pistol he had."

Meek stood. "I have work to do here. Give me an answer by noon two days from now. I'm staying at this hotel."

Joe walked away after placing money on the table. Man and Kate gazed at the other. "Decision time," she said.

"What do you want to do?" he asked.

"I want to be at your side wherever you decided to go, or what we do."

"That's not fair," he protested.

"Sure it is. I'm your wife, and will go where you go. That's how it should be. I'll be happy in a bedroll on the ground in the snow or rain, or in our bed in our cabin. You'll keep me warm and comfortable either place, and I might add, contented, wherever we are. Heck, you remember the early morning when we were on sentry duty on top of a bolder. That was fun and different," she said with a sigh.

"I still want a yes or no from you," he said.

"Yes or no," she said with a silly grin.

"Darn you," he said.

Kate then gave him her special grin. "Wanta to go play Man and Kate games while you decide?"

***

Kate lay on top of him and they talked for an hour, each giving their thoughts, and concerns about the job. Man couldn't tell if she wanted him to take the job or not. She refused to give him an answer to the several ways he veiled the question. She always had pro's and con's for ever question he proposed.

Finally, she sat up on him, and placed both hands on his cheeks. "I'm your wife, and I want to do what you want to do. I'll be at your side and happy. Should you take the job, we're young and we have a few years before settling down with a family. If you want to be a deputy United States marshal, I'll be elated having a husband with such an awesome responsibility."

"If you want to go back to the cabin this fall to trap and settle in to be a farmer or rancher. I'll be at you're side, happy and smiling. This is the last time we'll have this discussion. Day after tomorrow you give Joe our answer."

"No fair," he protested. "I want to know your preference."

"I have spoken," she said. She made a motion across her lips and clamped them tight.

He lay for a time before replying. She waited, giving him the opportunity to make the decision.

"Five years or less, it depends on how it goes," he said. "Then we settle down and start our family."

"Yes sir," she said as she lay forward to meet his lips. It was settled as she expected. And felt from the beginning she knew what his decision would be. In fact, she hoped it would go this way. The adrenalin surge during the battles was addictive. She felt so alive knowing they were doing something worthwhile for humanity.

Jeb met them for supper. "What did you do today?" Kate asked when they were seated.

"I walked around town some. I found a store that sold writing paper, and wrote Alice a long letter telling her what happened after we left Tacoma. I didn't know where to tell her to reply in case she wants to reply.

"That is one of the things we need to discuss," Kate said. "Joe offered Man a job as a deputy United States marshal. He's going to accept. However, one of his stipulations, you can't go with us."

A quick reaction of sadness crossed his face, but he didn't speak.

Kate went on, quickly. "I have a couple of suggestions to offer. I want you to consider both before replying."

"You're almost seventeen, not yet a man, but getting close. A man by the name of Melvin Knox lost his wife and son. He's a settler between here and The Fort. He's alone, and it's possible he would welcome you to live with him. He has a nice farm started. That would give you a stable home and address. There is more land adjacent should you want to farm. I expect Marvin would welcome the help."

Kate waited for a minute for Jeb to comprehend what she suggested before continuing.

"George and Martha Bowman are an older couple. They own the trading post at The Fort and George buys furs and grain to be shipped here to sell. He buys merchandise for his store and takes it back in his wagons. They have no children, and I expect they would welcome your help. They're nearing retiring age, and it's possible you would inherit the business someday. It would be an opportunity for a lifetime."

Kate sensed Jeb was interested. "You would have an address should Alice reply to your letters. She was brought up in a café, and should it go farther. Well, what I expect she would fit in nicely in the store. She has a wonderful personality to deal with the public. The Fort will grow as more settlers move here. The business could multiply over and over as more people arrive."

"Gorge has a nice display of guns at the trading post," Man added. "That's where we got the Winchesters 1873."

"Does he have more of them?" Jeb asked.

"We bought the last four he had, but I expect the next time he goes to the coast on a buying trip, he'll replenish them. I think he could be persuaded to stock a few Walkers as well."

"There's a cabinet full of weapons for sale. Some are new, some used, but he has almost anything a man could want."

Jeb's eyes lighted up as man talked.

Kate knew Jeb had made up his mind. The thought of being a farmer hadn't interested him at all. The possibility of the trading post did. With his personality, the citizens of The Fort would welcome him. Maude would take him in as the son she never had. At least, that was Kate's hope, but only time would tell. She decided they should play it slow when they got there, and not barge in and announce they brought a young man that eats everything in sight for them to feed. She smiled at that thought.

"Do you think George and Maude would take me in?" Jeb asked.

"I don't know," Kate replied. "The only way to find out is visit there."

"I don't have many options on what to do," Jeb said with his eyes down.

"Honestly, no you don't. You're too young to go out on your own. You need a place to finish growing into a man, and learn a trade to make a comfortable living for a family you'll someday have."

"Do you think I could visit Alice?" he asked.

"I don't know," Kate said. "Maybe you could talk George into letting you take the wagons to Tacoma on a marketing trip, and happen to drop in where Alice works. I know she would love that."

He was grinning at that comment.

***

At noon at the appointed time, Kate, Man, and Jeb were waiting at the café for Joseph Meek. He strode in and every eye turned to look at him. He had the appearance of a man that generated respect. His eyes were piercing, and the beard he wore was imposing. This topped off with the United States marshal badge on his vest and the big iron on his hip.

He didn't hesitate, and walked to the table where the trio waited. Man stood and offered his hand. The two shook and Joe turned toward the waitress and made a motion of drinking coffee. She brought him a cup and the coffee pot. She filled his first, and then replenished the coffee of the others. By the time she finished refilling the other three, Joe put his down for a refill. It was already empty.

The waitress filled it and left. Joe's eyes went to Man for his answer.

"Yes," he replied. "For no more than five years. Then I plan on settling down and raising crops and kids."

"Agreed, Joe said. "We need to go over to the police station and have you sign a few more papers. What happened to the days when all it took was putting your hand on the Bible, and taking an oath and pinning a badge on you. I swear the paperwork is worse than a bloody gunfight on me."

Joe then glanced at Jeb and waited for a comment by Kate or Man.

"We're going to return the horse to Knox, and then on to The Fort," Kate said. "Hopefully, George and Maude Bowman will want a young man to help them in their golden years."

"How long will that take?" Joe asked.

"At least a week, depending on how long we visit. Do you have something urgent that need our attention?"

"As I said before, there's more cases than I have deputy marshals to cover, but there's nothing that urgent at the moment that can't wait for a couple of weeks. After all you have done the past few, you deserve a break."

Joe gestured to the waitress. "Steak and bring us all of the fixings." He made a circle motion around the table with his finger.

They ate, and then walked to the police station where Man signed the necessary papers. When he handed the last to Joe, he took them and offered his hand to shake. "Welcome into the fold Deputy Marshal. Keep your head down, and your rear in gear. Sometimes running like hell is the best option."

Chief Kline and several policemen were watching. They in turn shook hands with Man.

"I place my deputy marshals in strategic locations as their home base, so to speak. Does any particular place fit your fancy? If I don't already have somebody there, you can call it home. You may even get to sleep there a few nights a month."

"This is sudden," Kate said. "I never thought about where we would live. But, is The Fort agreeable?"

"Sorry, Kate," Joe said. "No telegraph as yet. You must be at a place I can contact you instantly."

"Coeur d'Alene," she said.

"Why not Portland?" Chief Kline put in quickly, as a hopeful suggestion. "We need a marshal here, and it's a great place to live."

Joe ignored Chief Kline's suggestion. "Coeur d'Alene it is. With the unrest after the labor war, it's still tense there. It would be nice to have a deputy marshal stationed there as a warning to keep their tempers in check, and their weapons in their holsters."

As they walked to the door, Man tapped his forehead. "I almost forgot. We have horses belonging to the Bull Blevins gang at the stable. I'm sure they were all stolen, but finding the rightful owners would be almost impossible as the brands have been altered."

"Will you see to them?" Joe said, as he faced Chief Kline. "If you can't find the owners, use them for your policemen."

"Happily," Kline replied. "We're always in need of horses."

Chapter 15

Joe walked with them to the hotel. "Send me a wire when you get settled in at Coeur d'Alene and I'll need an address for your pay. Have a safe trip."

He turned to Jeb. "In about five years if you're still interested in a marshal's job, look me up. It appears I may have a vacancy about that time. That is, if it doesn't get in their blood, and they can't quit. It happens, but then there's also burnout. Kate may want to sleep in her own bed every night, and start her family."

"Thank you," Jeb said. "I'll remember and see how I feel in five years."

"Alice may have something to say about that as well," Kate teased.

Man handed Joe the sack containing Gus's belongs. He took the badge and wallet and put them in the pocket on his coat.

He pulled the weapons and stood. "Jeb," he said. "Please stand up."

Jeb stood at Joe's request.

"Jeb, it hurts in one respect, but it also gives me pleasure to present this pistol and rifle to you. These weapons have a great history and have served a good purpose. I hope you'll cherish them and wear them proudly. Use them wisely and follow the guidelines you've learned from riding with Man and Kate."

Jeb gasped in disbelief. "I can't accept them," he said. "I only knew Gus for a short time, but I certainly learned to respect him. His weapons should go to a museum or to somebody more worthy."

"Unfortunately, we don't have a museum. If I took them in, they would end up on a shelf and soon disappear. If you have them, I expect you to live up to the their heritage."

"From time to time, I expect to drop in and check on you. If I find you are misusing them, it will go doubly hard on you. Do you understand?" Joe said.

"Yes sir," Jeb managed.

***

Man took the point with Kate behind leading the pack mules and Jeb following, riding the gray Joe gave him, leading Socks, and the Chestnut belonging to Knox.

Jeb rode Gus's gray and wore the pistol that Gus had carried. Occasionally, he pulled it to examine it with admiration. "I wonder how many outlaws Gus shot with this pistol."

"I have no idea," Kate said. "I would expect several. I don't know how long Gus was a deputy marshal, but for many years. It would be interesting to know."

"When I see Joe Meek again, I intend to ask," Jeb said.

They found Melvin Knox in the field plowing. He stopped when the saw the riders approaching, and reached for rifle he had in a scabbard on the plow. The awful experience with Bull made him cautious.

The moment he recognized Man, he put the rifle back, and wiped sweat from his brow with a handkerchief he had in his back pocket.

A smile went across his face when he saw the Chestnut, and he came walked out to meet his guest. Jeb rode to the front and handed him the reins of his horse.

"I never expected to see him again," he said. "Thanks for bringing him home, and I never got to thank you for finding the other two horses in Portland."

For the first time he saw the badge on Man's shirt. "You're a deputy United States marshal?" he asked.

"Yep," Man replied. "We got Bull Blevins and all of his gang. They got what they deserved after what they did to your wife and son. They made it a habit, as well as robbing and killing innocent people."

"It won't bring Rachel and Junior back," Melvin said, "but it'll make me sleep better knowing they're in the ground."

Melvin gestured toward the cabin. "Come with me to

the cabin and rest a spell. I have cool spring water for you and the horses. There's food for supper and sweet fresh hay for your mounts."

"Thanks for the kind offer, and we accept the offer of the water for us and the horses, but we need to move on before dark. We're headed to The Fort to see George and Maude Bowman."

Knox led the way leading his Chestnut to the stable. The horses that belonged to Rachel and Junior nickered at their long time friend. Melvin unsaddled the Chestnut and turned him loose in the coral where the horses greeted the other by touching noses.

Man and Jeb took their animals to the pond of fresh spring water for a drink, and then Melvin led the way inside the cabin. They noticed a fresh apple pie on the table.

Melvin grinned. "A widow lady has been keeping me supplied with food."

"Good for you," Kate said. "Life goes on in spite of tragedies."

"So Matilda has said. She lost her husband to a fever less than a year ago. She's trying to carry on. I go over and help her out with the plowing, and the hard chores. She would be miffed if I told her you brought my horse home, and didn't eat a piece of pie."

"We wouldn't want Matilda miffed at us," Jeb put in, as he eyed the pie.

"You're older than my son was, but I know how young boys eat," Melvin said, as he cut a huge slice for Jeb. He cut smaller slices for Kate, Man and himself.

They finished and Melvin put the rest of the pie in paper, and handed it to Jeb. "I expect you'll enjoy more after supper tonight."

"Thank you Mr. Knox," he said. "I'll assure you, I'll enjoy every crumb and tell Matilda I said I appreciate the pie."

Jeb went out the door to where the horses were tied, and put his pie in the saddlebags.

"Who's the boy?" Melvin asked.

"The son of a woman that was murdered," Kate said. "He's an orphan. We hope George and Maude will take him in. He can't continue to travel with us now that Man is a deputy marshal. That was one of the stipulations by Joseph Meek. But we had already decided it wouldn't be right for the boy. He was wounded once and would be in danger riding with us."

"If that doesn't work out with Bowman, and he would like to live with me, send or bring him back. The bed that belonged to Junior would be his."

"Thanks, Mr. Knox, that's a generous offer," Man said. "Who knows, it may turn out that way."

"I expect in time Matilda will move here, or I'll live in her cabin. It's much larger than mine. They lost both of their children on the Oregon Trail. I know she would like to have a son as I would. We need an heir to take care of the farms we homesteaded."

Jeb led their horses to the cabin. "Thanks again for the pie, Mr. Knox. I can smell it, and I hope it survives until after supper, but the temptation is pretty strong to reach back for a bite."

They saw crumbs on his lips and suspected he had already sampled it.

Melvin laughed. "I expect either way, you'll enjoy it. I'll tell Matilda it was put to good use."

Man mounted Arabian, and turned him toward the southeast. Kate and Jeb waved at Melvin as he led his mules back to the field.

"He's a nice man," Jeb said.

"He said if it doesn't work out with the Bowman's you would be welcome to live with him," Kate said.

"Really," Jeb replied. "That's nice to know somebody wants me."

"Knox said that both he and Matilda would like to have an heir to carry on with the farms after they're gone. It could be a sweet setup for you."

"We would like for you to stay with us, but that's

272

impossible due to Man's job," Kate said. "And thank you for saying that. It's nice knowing people want me. For so long, only my mom wanted me."

They rode in silence for a while, then Jeb rode beside Kate and Man. "I understand how it is with you two, and I'm looking forward to meeting the Bowman's. I don't think farming is my thing, but then I know nothing about it. And living out here, never seeing anybody isn't appealing to me now. But, if it doesn't work out with the Bowman's I might give it a try."

"In fact, that may be my last option, other than striking out on my own. And, I'm not ready to do that. It's a tough world out there, I know from experience. I want to make something of myself. I intend to move out of the environment I was raised in. I have that opportunity now. Mom insisted I get an education. She said it was the only way to get out of our situation. I can see that now. Being smart is essential."

Man and Kate smiled.

***

It was mid afternoon when they rode into The Fort. A few people that Man knew shouted a welcome as they rode by. Man stopped in front of Bowman's Trading Post and dismounted. Kate and Jeb did the same. A loud shout from inside startled them. George came bursting out the door.

"Maude, come quick, it's Man and Kate."

She hurried to the door wiping her hands on a white cloth. There was flour on her nose from the kitchen.

She rushed past George to give Kate a huge welcome hug. George was waiting on the porch and gripped Man's offered hand. Jeb stood holding the reins of the horses and lead rope to the mules.

"Tie them to the hitching rail," George said. "Then come in out of the hot sun."

"Can we put them in your corral in back?" Man asked. "We plan on staying for a few days. But, we'll make camp where we did before."

"Of course," George said. "And I have to hear about what happened after you left. By the way, thanks for sending my wagons back, and for recovering my pelts. I was totally dumfounded when they were returned with the money for the furs. You must be a miracle worker to pull that off with tightwad Bernard and Hudson Bay Fur Company."

"It's a long story, but we have time, if you do," Man said.

"Of course I have time, and I'm anxious for the details. Especially about that badge on your vest. Al, the man that brought the wagons home told us you were a deputy United States marshal."

Maude reached for Kate's ring finger. "I see you found a preacher and your ring is beautiful."

"Thanks," she replied, as Maude held her hand examining the ring. "That's also a long story," Kate said.

"As George said, we have time to hear the details. Business is slow this time of year. The men can take care of the stock, and we'll have tea."

George led Man and Jeb around to the rear where the warehouse and corral was located. Maude gestured at the young boy.

"His mother was murdered and he's an orphan," Kate explained. "We couldn't leave him with no home, or place to go. Jeb's a good boy, and took down a few of Bull Blevins men in a couple of gun battles. He's very intelligent and polite."

"He looks about sixteen or seventeen," Maude said.

"Almost seventeen," Kate replied.

"Is he going to stay with you?" Maude asked.

"No, he can't. One of the requirements made by United States Marshal Joseph Meek was that Jeb couldn't go with us. He's too young. We're being stationed at Coeur d'Alene. But that will only be our headquarters. We'll go where we're ordered."

"You plan on riding with Man?" she asked, with concern in her tone.

"Of course. My place is beside my husband. Joe said he couldn't hire a woman as a marshal, but he had no objection for me helping and being Man's partner."

"Won't that be dangerous? I mean, you a married woman, what about children?"

"We told Joe five years, then we'll go back to the cabin, and start growing crops, horses, maybe both, and have children."

"Back to the boy you call Jeb. What will you do with him? You can't turn out a boy that age and expect him to survive."

"Bull Blevins murdered Rachel Knox, and her son after they left here. Melvin Knox is alone and asked Jeb to live with him. As of now that's the only option."

Maude rubbed her chin in thought, but said nothing.

Kate smiled inwardly. The seed had been planted, and now was a good time to change the conversation."

"I notice George is moving around good after his wound," Kate said.

"Thanks to you," Maude said, "your expert care, and rest, he's fully recovered. There's no telling what would have happened if you hadn't been here. I didn't know how to doctor a gunshot wound, and there's nobody at The Fort that knows anything about medicine."

"I had practice before I met you. On the wagon train, and the incidents with the slave traders, I learned a lot about doctoring. We worked with an Indian that was a darn good medicine man."

"Anyway, I'm glad you were here," Maude said, meaning it.

"Changing the subject," Kate said. "Jeb would like to have deerskin clothing like ours. They work great on the trail, tough and warm. Ours are getting thin in places and we need replacements. Is there any Indian woman living near here that would make them?"

"Not that I know about, but I'll make a few inquiries. There's a woman seamstress here that might make them for you. I saw a sheepskin coat she made that was

275

beautiful, as well as serviceable. It was for a trapper that lives high in the mountains."

The men came back and Kate stood. "It's getting late in the day. We need to make our camp, and I'll start something cooking. We ate only trail grub at noon." She gestured at Jeb. "As we joke and often say, that boy has a hollow leg. Melvin Knox gave him half of an apple pie, he ate the whole thing, and that was after wolfing down a double slice earlier. Now, he starving for supper."

"No," Maude said. "You'll eat with us. You're our guest and I have ample food we can cook, even for a boy with a hollow leg. You can make camp later. I'm sorry, we have only one bedroom, but there's a room we often put guest in the loft of the barn. It has a good bed and windows that will let in the cool breeze, and keep the cold out in the winter. There's a potbelly stove for the cold winter nights."

She turned to Jeb. "Would you like to sleep there tonight? I expect the bed would be better than the hard ground.

Jeb caught the glance by Kate, and quickly replied. "Yes Ma'am, I certainly would. For your generosity, I can care for the animals in the coral, and do anything else you need a strong back for."

Kate again wanted to chuckle. The second seed had been planted. She felt George and Martha would soon be asking Jeb to live with them.

Her plan was working to perfection.

The next morning, Kate and Man found Jeb at the gun case cleaning and inspecting the weapons George had for sale. George was kept busy answering questions about the used pistols and rifles.

Jeb proudly showed George the pistols and rifle that belonged to Gus. George listened in awe seeing the actual weapons used by the famous Augustus Schweitzer. "Chief United States Marshal Joseph Meek gave them to me personally," Jeb said.

Man put his hand on Jeb's shoulder. "It's true

George. I was there and witnessed it. He also gave Jeb a high standard to live by while he was packing those weapons."

Maude and Kate came from the back. "I have great news," Kate said. "Maude has a woman that will make new working skins. Including you, Jeb. You'll be so handsome wearing them. I think Alice would really appreciate seeing you in them."

Jeb lowered his head.

"Who is Alice," Maude asked."

"Another long story," Kate said. "Let Jeb tell you about Alice."

Epilogue

A week later, wearing their new skins, Man and Kate loaded their Conestoga with supplies. Jeb helped with the heavy things also wearing his new clothing made from soft deerskin.

Kate bought everything that George and Martha stocked that she would need in her new home in Coeur d'Alene.

The third day they were visiting The Fort, George, and Martha asked Jeb to stay with them. He happily agreed, a room of his own, a place to live with a couple that needed and wanted him. He would have a family again, but this time, a father figure as George was quickly becoming. He never had a father, other than Man for the past few weeks.

George let him examine and fire every weapon in the showcase. Martha was happy to cook enough to fill his hollow leg. She had the son she always wanted, and George could see Jeb taking over the business.

He was smart and quick to comprehend the business side. George anxiously answered every question Jeb asked. To his amazement, Jeb never asked the same question twice, and remembered all the rules and suggestions associated with managing a thriving business.

The night before Kate and Man left, Jeb asked her to come to his loft.

"Why?" she asked.

"I want to write a very serious letter to Alice. I want it to be perfect and say what I want to say. I want you to help me."

"And, what do you want to say to her?" Kate asked.

"I want to tell her I have a home now, and I have a permanent address where she can reply. I also want to tell her I'll see her soon. I talked to George and he asked me to take charge of the four wagons, and go to Portland on a buying trip. He said he would go along the first trip to show me how it's done. But, he said I could take the gray along and go to Tacoma to visit Alice for a couple of days."

"You don't need me to write that letter," Kate said. "My advice is be honest, be open, and express how you feel. Tell her you want to see her more than anything."

"If she replies, which, I fully expect, she'll share her feelings as well. Just take it slow. There's plenty of time for you two. It's not that far from Tacoma to Portland. I expect your first trip will be only the beginning."

"I'll write you when we have an address in Coeur d'Alene. Hopefully, we can meet from time to time, or you can visit us. I expect we'll be back this way as often as possible. We still have our mountain cabin we must visit occasionally, and we will want to see you.

Jeb gave Kate a big hug. "Thanks for everything, and I mean it from the bottom of my heart. I know you are much too young to be my mother, but I sort of feel that way about you. In many ways, well, how to say this? You and Man have been parents of mine this past few weeks. Don't get me wrong, I loved my mom very much, but well, being with you two has been special."

Man was listening, and offered his hand to shake. Jeb took it and returned a firm grip of a man.

"It was an honor to meet you," Man said. "Do your best to help George and Martha, they need you."

"I will, I promise. Goodbye for now, and good luck," Jeb said and wiped his eyes with his sleeve.

Kate sat on the seat of the wagon, wearing her new working skins with her Walkers on her hips. Both of her Winchester rifles were in the front of the wagon within easy reach. Redbird was tied to the back of the wagon.

Man mounted Arabian and rode out the gate to The Fort. Jeb stood between George and Maude and waved.

"That's a special couple," Maude said.

"Don't I know it," Jeb replied. "Someday, I hope to be like Man. Maybe someday, Alice can be as special as Kate."

279

CPSIA information can be obtained at www.ICGtesting.com
Printed in the USA
LVOW071937290712

292064LV00006B/11/P